CALAMUS LOVERS

Walt Whitman and Peter Doyle, 1869; drawing by H. D. Young from
a photograph taken by Rice. Reproduced as frontispiece to *Calamus:
A Series of Letters Written during the Years 1868–1880 by Walt Whitman
to a Young Friend* (1897)

CALAMUS LOVERS

Walt Whitman's
Working-Class Camerados

Edited with Introductions and Commentary by

CHARLEY SHIVELY

Gay Sunshine Press
San Francisco

First edition 1987

Cover: Walt Whitman, c. 1854, about 35 years old; Harry Stafford (left), c. 1876, aged 18; and Peter Doyle (right), c. 1869, aged about 24.
Cover design by Timothy Lewis

See Acknowledgments (p. 221) for details on sources.

ISBN 0-917342-17-8 (cloth)
ISBN 0-917342-18-6 (paperback)

Gay Sunshine Press
P.O. Box 40397
San Francisco, CA 94140
Complete catalogue of books available for $1 postpaid

Dedicated to
Winston Leyland
with gratitude and affection

CONTENTS

Walt Whitman, 1846; aged 27. Photo located in the Walt Whitman House, Camden, New Jersey.

CHAPTER ONE

Plunged Tongue Pungent

An Introduction to
Walt Whitman

AFTER WALTER WILLIAMS had told a University of Cincinnati class about Horatio Alger's pederasty, a student exclaimed, "Horatio Alger was not a homosexual. He was a great writer." Wrong in both regards, this answer exhibits one of the perplexing paradoxes of Whitman scholarship: a person cannot be both a great writer and a homosexual. In the past to call Whitman a homosexual was to defame him. Thus in November, 1855, Rufus W. Griswold (editor of *The Poets and Poetry of America*) concluded his review of *Leaves of Grass* with an apology for entering "such a mass of stupid filth," but explained that, "The records of crime show that many monsters have gone on in impunity, because the exposure of their vileness was attended with too great indelicacy. *Peccatum illud horribile, inter Christianos non nominandum*" (That horrible sin not to be named among Christians). Five years before publication of "Calamus," Griswold had already identified and condemned Whitman's gayness.

Defenders (including at times the poet himself) respond by claiming Whitman was not like Horatio Alger. In another 1855 review, Charles Dana wote, "His language is too frequently reckless and indecent, though this appears to arise from a naive unconsciousness rather than from an impure mind." Recent cleanser critics have suggested that Whitman was a masturbator rather than an invert (as though the two were in any way mutually exclusive!). The hidden premise of such analysis is that to be an active homosexual disqualifies anyone from poetry's cleansing powers.

Although clues have been disguised, the "manly, adhesive," erotic,

sexual themes in *Leaves of Grass* have never been obliterated. Gay
activists responded immediately. Oscar Wilde himself in 1882 spent
an afternoon with Whitman in Camden and wrote, "There is no one in
this great wide world of America whom I love and honor so much." In
1895, Max Nordau in his madcap *Degeneration* denounced Whitman as
"one of the deities to whom the degenerate and hysterical of both
hemispheres have for some time been raising altars." Among the degenerate, John Addington Symonds, Edward Carpenter and André
Gide hailed the divine Whitman. Eduard Bertz stated the case in
Magnus Hirschfeld's *Jahrbuch* (1905): "The erotic friendship, which is
found in the poetry and life of our wonderful prophet," can only be
explained "by his constitutional deviation from the masculine norm."
In Los Angeles, the One Institute took up from Hirschfeld, whose
Institute in Berlin was burnt by the Nazis. Against the homophobia of
the 1950s, David Russell and David McIntire [Jim Kepner], "In Paths
Untrodden, A Study of Walt Whitman," *One: The Homosexual Maga-
zine* (July, 1954), and A. E. Smith, "The Curious Controversy over
Whitman's Sexuality," *One Institute Quarterly: Homophile Studies* (Winter, 1959) continued to explore the untrodden paths. Evidently every
generation needs to rediscover Whitman's homosexuality. Thus, many
were surprised by works inspired by gay liberation such as Joseph
Cady, "Not Happy in the Capitol: Homosexuality in the *Calamus*
Poems," *American Studies* (Fall 1978), and Robert K. Martin, *The Homosexual Tradition in American Poetry* (1979).

The first question must not be whether but when and how did
Whitman begin loving men so intensely? That is, when did he come
out—at least to himself—and realize he was different. My own belief
is that he did it early and often; his life was one long continuous string
of bar, street, streetcar, back road and casual encounters with young
men. ("I go among them, I mix indiscriminately.") Some have suggested he had a lot of sex with his brothers—a not at all unlikely
beginning, particularly in pre-industrial Long Island and Brooklyn,
where physical contact was close and easy. When Henry David Thoreau
and Bronson Alcott visited the poet in 1856, they noticed he slept in
the same bed with his brother.

Born in 1819, Whitman was still a teenager when he began teaching school on Long Island in 1836. About that time, he wrote his first
sketch, "My Boys and Girls," which contains notes on his siblings and
(with a Horatio Alger strain) adds some local boys:

> Right well do I love many more of my children. H. is my "summer
> child." An affectionate fellow is he—with merits and with faults, as

all boys have—and it has come to be that should his voice no more
salute my ears, nor his face my eyes, I might not feel as happy as I
am. . . . Then there is J.H., a sober, good-natured youth, whom I
hope I shall always number among my friends. Another H. has lately
come among us—too large, perhaps, and too near manhood, to be
called one of my *children*. I know I shall love him well when we
become better acquainted—as I hope we are destined to be.

In the island schools, teachers received room and board from local
families, and the teacher often shared a bed with an older boy. In such
situations, anyone with the slightest sexual interest in the boys would
find easy opportunities. Rumors have persisted that Whitman upset
one of the farmers by becoming too fond of one boy. The *Atlantic
Monthly* (April, 1907) deleted from "Personal Recollections of Walt
Whitman" a passage about how "the grown up son of the farmer with
whom he was boarding while he was teaching school became very fond
of him, and Walt of the boy, and he said the father quite reproved him
for making such a pet of the boy" (Allen, *Solitary Singer,* 37).

Whitman's short story "The Child's Champion" suggests ways of
cruising on Long Island during the 1830s. (The story first appeared in
1841 in the *New World* but was stripped of erotic content in later
versions as "The Child and the Profligate.") There is a bar/inn where a
group of tough sailors are dancing together; a thirteen-year-old boy,
whose father is dead and who has blistered hands, looks in the window.
The toughest sailor tries to grab him and demands he take a drink.
" 'There, my lads,' said he, turning to his companions, 'There's a new
recruit for you. Not so coarse a one, either,' he added as he took a fair
view of the boy, who, though not what is called pretty, was fresh and
manly looking, and large for his age." A well-dressed twenty-year-old
from the city comes to the rescue (Whitman was about twenty when he
wrote the story)—

> Why was it that from the first moment of seeing him, the young
> man's heart had moved with a strange feeling of kindness toward the
> boy? He felt anxious to know more of him—he felt that he should
> love him. O, it is passing wondrous, how in the hurried walks of life
> and business, we meet with young beings, strangers, who seem to
> touch the fountains of our love, and draw forth their swelling waters.
> The wish to love and to be loved, which the forms of custom, and the
> engrossing anxiety for gain, so generally smother, will sometimes
> burst forth in spite of all obstacles; and, kindled by one, who, till
> the hour was unknown to us, will burn with a lovely and pure
> brightness.

Just as in today's gay bar, young Charles and the profligate move quickly from love-at-first-sight into bed.

> It was now past midnight. The young man told Charles that on the morrow he would take steps to have him liberated from his servitude; for the present night, he said, it would perhaps be best for the boy to stay and share his bed at the inn; and little persuading did the child need to do so. As they retired to sleep, very pleasant thoughts filled the mind of the young man; thoughts of a worthy action performed; of unsullied affection; thoughts, too—newly awakened ones—of walking in a steadier and wiser path than formerly. All his imaginings seemed to be interwoven with the youth who lay by his side; he folded his arms around him, and, while he slept, the boy's cheek rested on his bosom. Fair were those two creatures in their unconscious beauty—glorious, but yet how differently glorious! One of them was innocent and sinless of all wrong: the other—O to that other, what evil had not been present, either in action or to his desires!

As the couple sleep entwined in each other's arms, an angel enters the room and blesses them with kisses. Obviously some of this is fantasy; some rests on experience. The theme was important to Whitman; he addresses angelic kisses in a manuscript unpublished in his lifetime:

> Fatigued by their journey they sat down on Nature's divan whence they regarded the sky.
> Pressing one another's hands, shoulder to shoulder neither knowing why both became oppressed,
> Their mouths opened, without uttering a word they kissed one another.
> Near them the hyacinths & the violet marrying their perfume,
> On raising their heads they both saw God, who smiled at them from his azure balcony:
> Love one another said he, it is for that I have clothed your path with velvet;
> Kiss one another, I am not looking. Love one another, love one another
> & if you are happy, instead of a prayer to thank me—kiss again.

As a teenager Whitman, born in 1819, enjoyed meeting farm boys on Long Island, and when he moved to the metropolitan center of New York, his sexuality expanded. In his twenties, he worked for several New York and Brooklyn newspapers. Some of his editorials suggest he was cruising Washington Park in Brooklyn, swimming with the nude boys in the East River and enjoying the public baths in Manhattan.

Cities inevitably contain more opportunities to meet available boys simply because they are so much more numerous there. And as "The Child's Champion" story suggests there were many opportunities for a city boy to pick up country boys who were lured by stories of big town life.

The year 1848 brought not only the news and hopes of revolution from Europe but also awakened the first seeds of homoerotic poetry in Walt Whitman. In February, he left New York for New Orleans to work on the *Crescent*. Although he stayed there only a short time before returning home in May, the trip transformed him sexually and politically. Some have suggested that Whitman came out in the course of his trip west and south; certainly his sexuality unfolded both temporally and geographically as he approached his thirtieth birthday in May 1849. Expanding an east-coast provincialism, he internalized much of the inland landscape and discovered his own "manifest destiny." Passing through exotic Western and Southern scenery, Whitman combined sexual awakening with a Western movement. Southern poet and writer Sidney Lanier complained that Whitman's "argument seems to be that because a prairie is wide therefore debauchery is admirable."

Although only a few months in New Orleans, Whitman lived through springtime and the Mardi Gras, which always makes men a little more sexual, a little more available. Condemning the morals there, one doctor claimed that, "Probably no city of equal size in Christendom receives into its bosom every year a greater proportion of vicious people than New Orleans." One of the earliest Calamus poems, "Once I Passed Through a Populous City," recalls events (and may have been written) in the Crescent City: "But now of all that city I remember only the man who wandered with me, there for love of me,/ Day by day and night by night, we were together—all else has been long forgotten by me,/ I remember, I say, only one rude and ignorant man who, when I departed, long and long held me by the hand, with silent lip, sad and tremulous." Whitman initially chose the Gulf coast live-oak and moss to symbolize homosexual love. "I saw in Louisiana a live-oak growing,/ . . . And its look, rude, unbending, lusty, made me think of myself/ . . . it makes me think of manly love." Before he finished the Calamus sequence, Whitman, however, switched tokens and embraced the Long Island Calamus with its sweeter odor, pale pink color and more phallic shape.

Now in his thirties, Whitman followed a vagabond path during the 1850s; he frequented Pfaff's, a bohemian hang-out, where he could cruise drivers or rendezvous before and after plays, operas and other city entertainments. During these years, he lived with his family most of the time, and his sexual activities were confined to partners he picked up in bars, swimming holes, parks, public baths, streets, and aboard the horsecars and ferries. In the 1855 *Leaves of Grass*, he described "Picking out here one that shall be my amie,/ Choosing to go with him on brotherly terms." Like Lorca, Whitman uses the horse to symbolize his sexual energies, which were then unbridled, wild and promiscuous:

> A gigantic beauty of a stallion, fresh and responsive to my caresses,
> Head high in the forehead and wide between the ears,
> Limbs glossy and supple, tail dusting the ground,
> Eyes well apart and full of sparkling wickedness . . . . ears finely cut
>   and flexibly moving.

> His nostrils dilate . . . . my heels embrace him . . . . his well built limbs
>   tremble with pleasure . . . . we speed around and return.

> I but use you a moment and then I resign you stallion . . . . and do not
>   need your paces, and outgallop them,
> And myself as I stand or sit pass faster than you.

After the first (1855) and second (1856) editions but before the 1860 *Leaves of Grass*, Whitman's life changed when he took a lover for whom he wrote most of the celebrated Calamus sequence. That lover was Fred Vaughan, who formed a prototype for Whitman's future lovers such as Tom Sawyer (1863), Peter Doyle (1865), Harry Stafford (1876) and Bill Duckett (1884). Some of these boys have been identified here for the first time; doubtless there were others. A homosexual may have many lovers in life but they are all really only one person, played with many variations. I was once told, "You may get rid of me, but the problem will always be there." Because Whitman was occasionally unhappy with his lovers and because they often caused him grief, biographers (when they notice at all) conclude that these relationships were either not reciprocated or not consummated. Little do they understand a queen who complains about the deficiencies of a lover!

And among gay men, separating from a lover often becomes very liberating. Indeed, I think Whitman was so good a cocksucker and companion to his boys that he couldn't move from one to another as easily as he would have liked. They trapped him into an exclusivity alien to his expansive nature. Thus he had a curiously mixed attitude towards his young men getting married. Partly he felt like a parent seeing a child leave home; partly he felt relieved of a burden; partly he felt the loss of a lover. Different boys would bring different responses.

Walt Whitman, c. 1854. Courtesy of the Trent Collection, Duke University Library

Fred Vaughan got married in 1862 and Whitman left New York only a
few months later and never returned except for brief visits to Manhattan. In 1867 Benton Wilson, a soldier, complained, "I wrote to you
a year and more ago that I was married but did not receive any reply, so
I did not know but you was displeased with it. . . . I remain as ever
your Boy Friend with Love." A couple of months later, the same
veteran wrote, "I have a good Woman and I love her dearly but I seem
to lack patience or something. I think I ought to live alone, but I had
not ought to feel so." Whitman was probably glad to pass Benton on
to the world and, therefore, recommended that "the best and most
natural condition for a young man [is] to be married."

Whitman's meditation on the vicissitudes of love appear in a notebook entry entitled "Epictetus," July, 1870. He bemoans his own
perturbation over Peter Doyle, who was worried about having syphilis,
considering suicide and growing older. Too often and too eagerly,
readers have thought that Whitman was rejecting homosexual (if not
all) love when he wrote in his *Notebook,* "REMEMBER WHERE I AM
MOST WEAK, & most lacking. Yet always preserve a kind spirit &
demeanor to [Peter]. BUT PURSUE HER [HIM] NO MORE. A COOL,
GENTLE, (LESS DEMONSTRATIVE) MORE UNIFORM DEMEANOR — give
to poor — help any — be indulgent to the criminal & silly & to low
persons generally & the ignorant, but SAY little — make no explanations — *give no confidences* — never attempt puns, or plays upon words, or
utter sarcastic comments, or . . . arguments." He goes on to list the
characteristics of a "calm demeanor."

The *Notebook* entry makes more sense when compared to an early
story, "A Legend of Life and Love." Two brothers follow two paths: Life
(Worldly Wisdom) and Love (Perturbation). The brother of Life determined (like the stoic philosopher) "never to give my friendship merely
to be blown off again . . . nor interweave my course of life with those
that very likely would draw all the advantage of the connection, and
leave me no better than before." The hero of the story, the Love brother
explains to his more worldly sibling that passion may be painful but is
always worth the price: "Life has been alternately dark and fair," but
"the sunshine has been far oftener than the darkness of the clouds."
Although a roller-coaster, the joy of love always exceeds stoic with-
drawal.

Male homosexuality no less than other sexualities is never static and
means different things to different men at different times in their lives.
Whitman's homosexuality went through several stages: adolescent play
in the teens, pick-ups and romances in his twenties and more serious

love affairs after he passed thirty; his crisis with Peter Doyle occurred after he passed fifty. As no two homosexuals are exactly the same so no two homosexual poets build on the same sexual foundations. Instead of asking whether Whitman was a homosexual, we need to examine just what he did with the boys and then discuss how his desires worked through his poems. All of Whitman's sexual partners, whether casual picks-ups or intimate lovers, were younger than he and working-class; he was a boy-lover and most of his sexual activity was oral rather than anal.

In "Native Moments," Whitman's preference for rough trade is clearly stated: "I pick out some low person for my dearest friend,/ He shall be lawless, rude, illiterate . . ." Anonymously reviewing himself, Whitman wrote in the Brooklyn *Daily Times* (1856) that the poet was "a person singularly beloved and looked toward, especially by young men and the illiterate — one who has firm attachments . . . down in the bay with pilots in their pilot-boat — or off on a cruise with fishers in a fishing-smack — or riding on a Broadway omnibus, side by side with the driver — or with a band of loungers over the open grounds of the country . . .—fond of the great ferries . . ." Literary types like Richard Henry Stoddard "always wondered why he was interested in the class of men whom he visited" (1893). But more perceptive observers like Edward Carpenter in *Days with Walt Whitman* (1908) explained that "the unconscious, uncultured, natural types pleased him best, and he would make an effort to approach them. The others he allowed to approach him."

Whitman's preference for rough trade goes with his egalitarianism and his common-people poetry: the sex, politics and art form one united whole — a combination repugnant to many scholars. The sexual and class bias of university professors shows up in their disproportionate study of members of Whitman's family and of his middle-class friends. His mother, sister and two brothers as well as Anne Gilchrist have one or more volumes devoted to them. Concentration on heterosexual family members rubs off on Whitman and makes his life appear more heterosexual. Among Whitman friends, there are two recent biographies of William Douglas O'Connor: Jerome Loving, *Walt Whitman's Champion* (1978), and Florence Bernstein Freedman, *Walt Whitman's Chosen Knight* (1985). Artem Lozynsky wrote *Richard Maurice Bucke, Medical Mystic* (1977); Clara Barrus, *Whitman and Burroughs, Comrades* (1931); and David Karsner, *Horace Traubel, His Life and Work* (1919). None of these men would otherwise have found a biographer had they not been friends of Whitman. Other friends, famous in their own right such as Ralph Waldo Emerson, Henry David Thoreau, Bronson Alcott, John Addington Symonds and Edward Carpenter, have each found scholars who have contibuted to our understanding of their literary/intellectual relationship to Whitman. All this research, however, provides a lopsided view of Whitman's life and associates. Among Whitman's working-class friends, only Peter Doyle has received book-length attention, and that by Dr. Bucke, who snatched up Whitman's letters to Doyle and published them; virtually none of Doyle's letters have survived.

Many university people try to obliterate Whitman's own working-class background and consciousness; thus they invent intellectual genealogies on the most dubious evidence in order to offset Whitman's not being a university graduate. They silently try to answer Henry Wadsworth Longfellow's extraordinary charge that Whitman "might have done something if he had only had a decent training and education." How the snobs wish their Whitman could have been a Harvard professor and lived in a Brattle Street mansion. They share Emerson's discomfort in getting too close to the poet. In 1877, the Concord sage recalled, "I saw him in New York, and asked him to dine at my hotel. He shouted for a 'tin mug' for his beer. Then he had a noisy fire-engine society. And he took me there, and was like a boy over it, as if there had never been such a thing before!" (Edward Carpenter, *Days with Walt Whitman*).

Class prejudice against the common people shows up everywhere among academics, but among Whitman scholars such narrowness is criminal because Whitman preached so eloquently and so consistently the importance of the common people. Whitman admired the common people because he was one. He sought his sexual partners among the workers. And out of this experience and love he created his poems.

Now that Whitman's homosexuality cannot be denied, nor his poetry brushed aside, some have tried to belittle the objects of his love. Whitman's homosexual lovers are insignificant to some critics because his beloved rough trade were "illiterate," "uncultured" or "uneducated." Such snobbery totally annihilates the central message of Whitman's *Democratic Vistas*, not to mention *Leaves of Grass*. In discussing Whitman's famous "Passage to India," Tufts English department chair David Cavitch sums up the case in his *My Soul and I: The Inner Life of Walt Whitman* (1985): "This rapturous description of journeying to a symbolic India renowned in history and literature was not inspired by sickly Doyle's small promise of ecstasy. This glamour was always O'Connor's." (O'Connor was a middle-class, married, educated admirer of Whitman's.)

Whitman's boy-loving has been even less popular among the learned
than his homosexuality. He acted as both mother and father to his
lovers, most of whom were orphans, poor and lost in the great world.
His early short stories primarily concerned teenage boys; one was even
titled "Boy Lover"! With sympathy and understanding, Edgar Frieden-
berg explains man/boy love in his *Vanishing Adolescent* (1973): "Such
men love boys as a way of loving the boy in themselves and themselves
in the boy. . . . His intense identification with them may lead to an
almost uncanny empathy."

Whitman's affair with Bill Duckett is well documented (see Chapter 9). And his *Daybooks,* particularly those from the 1880s, are filled
with boy-love entries:

Hugh Harrop   boy 17 fresh Irish   wool sorter
Wm Clayton boy 13 or 14 on the cars nights — (gets out at Stevens &
    2d) April '81
young Irishman, on the boat   Matthew Kelly   works at night on the
    Phil: freight wharf
Thos: Woolston, young (19) cashier at Ridgeway House
Robt Wolf, boy of 10 or 12 rough   at the ferry   lives cor 4th & Market
Percy Ives, Mrs Legget's grandson, age 16, a student   intends to be
    an artist — lives bachelor's hall fashion in Philadelphia — reads
    Emerson, Carlyle, &c

Sammy Cox   boy, 17 or 18 — Dick Davis's nephew — butter & cheese
    business in market stand — ice cream — Apr' 81
Tasker Lay, boy 15 or 16, with Mr Lee

little black-eyed Post boy at ferry, Paddy Connelly

in the car paid no fare   756 Mt Vernon St: Walter Dean lad 14 or 15
    (in Wanamakers.) Dec 12 met him again, March 21 — he is a fine
    boy

Harry Caufield, 19, printer, "the Sentinel" — father dead, 8yr's, has
    mother & two sisters — is from Harrisburgh
Clement — — boy Stevens st cars — night

Whitman loved to horse around with his boys; a form of play that
upset John Burroughs, one of his middle-class admirers. In a manuscript version of section 29 of "Song of Myself," Whitman wrestles
with a lover: "Fierce Wrestler! do you keep the hardest grip for the
last?/ Will you sting me even at parting?/ Will you struggle even at
the threshold with gigantic spasms more delicious than all before?/
Even as you face and withdraw does it make you ache so to leave
me?/ . . . Pass as you will; take drops of my life if that is what you are

after/ Only pass to some one else, for I can contain you no longer"
(*Notebooks,* 77). Harry Stafford, a teenager, in a letter to Whitman
(November 27, 1877) compares their wrestling to his driving horses:
"They wanted to show off, you know how it is your self when you feel
like *licking* me; but I held them down as I do you, when you feel that
way." Stafford was a teenager when he met the poet, who was nearly
sixty years old.

Part of the joy and center of Whitman's poetry will always be his
eternal boyishness, his wonderful adolescence. Among his greatest
poems are certainly "Out of the Cradle Endlessly Rocking" and "A
Child Went Forth." The former contains the autobiographical line, "A
man, yet by these tears a little boy again." And describing himself in
1855, Whitman declared, "He drops disguise and ceremony, and walks
forth with the confidence and gayety of a child." Among his lovers,
separation came most often when the boy got married and Whitman
went off in search of another lover. Many psycho-critics such as Edwin
Haviland Miller, *Walt Whitman's Poetry: A Psychological Journey* (1986),
or Stephen Black, *Whitman's Journeys into Chaos: A Psychoanalytic Study
of the Poetic Process* (1975) fault the poet for failing to cross the bridge
(as so many of his boys did) into healthy, heterosexual matrimonial
bliss. But the happiest of his boys (despite his separation from Whitman) was Peter Doyle, who never married. The ones who married and
raised families wrote pathetic letters detailing their burdens and ennui
in (what the psychos call) "maturity."

With the adolescent rough trade, Whitman's sexuality remained
primarily oral. Edward Carpenter in 1923 demonstrated to the young
Gavin Arthur just how Walt Whitman gave a blow job. "He snuggled
up to me and kissed my ear. His beard tickled my neck. He smelled
like the leaves and ferns and soil of autumn woods. . . . I just lay there
in the moonlight that poured in at the window and gave myself up to
the loving old man's marvelous petting. . . . At last his hand was moving between my legs and his tongue was in my belly-button. And then
when he was tickling my fundament just behind the balls and I could
not hold it any longer, his mouth closed just over the head of my penis
and I could feel my young vitality flowing into his old age" (*Gay
Sunshine Interviews,* 1:128).

Whitman was a great kisser. The Adam and Calamus clusters contain many kisses. Whitman had even projected a "Poem of Kisses—the
kisses of love—of death—of betrayal—" (*Notebooks,* 1344–5). In "To
What You Said," the poet responds "I am that rough and simple person/
I am he who kisses his comrade lightly on the lips at parting, and I am

one who is kissed in return,/ ... Behold the received models of the
parlors — What are they to me?/ What to these young men that travel
with me?" Or in "Behold This Swarthy Face," the "timid" handshake
is rejected by Whitman and Fred Vaughan as they meet in public:
"Comes one a Manhattanese and ever at parting kisses me lightly on
the lips with robust love,/ And I, in the public room, or on the
crossing of the street or on the ship's deck, give a kiss in return,/ We
observe that salute of American comrades, land and sea,/ We are those
two natural and nonchalant persons." During the Civil War, Whitman
delighted in leaving the soldiers with long, deeply held and lingering
kisses, which he felt were better medicine than anything else.

Although he uses more oral than anal images, Whitman doesn't
entirely neglect the asshole in his writings. In "Earth! my likeness!"
Basil de Selincourt sees butt-fucking: "Though you look so impassive,
ample and spheric there,/ I now suspect there is something terrible in
you, ready to break forth,/ For an athlete loves me, and I him . . ." And
in the *United States Review* (1855) Whitman wrote (again anonymously)
of himself, "He will have the earth receive and return his affection; he
will stay with it as the bridegroom stays with the bride. The cool
breath'd ground, the slumbering and liquid trees, the just-gone sunset,
the vitreous pour of the full moon, the tender and growing night, he
salutes and touches, and they touch him."

Emphasis on cocksucking has been called a peculiarly American
penchant; other parts of the world have been more into butt-fucking.
Whitman demonstrates part of his Americanness by placing cocksucking at the center of *Leaves of Grass*. Often hailed as the central mystical
moment of Whitman's poetic ecstasy and mystical enlightenment,
section 5 of "Song of Myself" celebrates more than the soul:

> I mind how we lay in June, such a transparent summer morning:
> You settled your head athwart my hips and gently turned over upon
> me,
> And parted the shirt from my bosom-bone, and plunged your tongue
> to my barestrip heart,
> And reached till you felt my beard, and reached till you held my feet.

Isn't this cocksucking plain and simple? With your mouth kissing
and sucking the cock, you can easily reach your hands to the beard and
to the feet; in no other position is this an easy gesture. Cocksucking
can't be excluded from any reading of this passage; and, once recognized, fellatio opens up much deeper understanding of the poet's voice.
When Whitman wrote — "I am the poet of the body/ And I am the poet

of the soul" — he began with the body; his implicit argument is that the only way to spiritual ecstasy comes through the body. Those who begin with the soul (New England transcendentals quite notably) will never find any soul. Whitman entered the gates of ecstasy through both his and his partner's mouth and cock.

* * *

Walt Whitman has a reputation for telling everything and excluding nothing from his poetry. In "Song of Myself," the poet promises to speak from where word had not been heard before: "Through me many long dumb voices,/ Voices of the interminable generations of slaves,/ Voices of prostitutes, and of deformed persons,/ Voices of diseased and despairing, and of thieves and dwarfs . . ." In particular, the poet promised to open forbidden sexes and lusts: "Voices . . . veiled, and I remove the veil,/ Voices indecent, by me clarified and transfigured." On the question of cocksucking, however, such candor cannot be found. Whitman includes clues, hints and indirections, but too often the cock stays in the mouth.

The sexual prudery movement had achieved one of its triumphs only a year before Whitman's birth when Thomas Bowdler in 1818 produced a clean edition of Shakespeare "in which . . . those words and expressions are omitted which cannot with propriety be read aloud in a family." Bowdler and his genteel cohorts viewed cock and cunt as indecencies, which must be hidden or veiled. Transfiguring and sacralizing the genitalia, Whitman followed an opposite tack: "I do not press my finger across my mouth,/ I keep as delicate around the bowels as around the head and heart,/ Copulation is no more rank to me than death is."

Whitman never sought out controversy or scandal, but throughout his life the prurient purity movement kept finding him out. In 1865, the Methodist Secretary of the Interior immediately fired him after searching the poet's desk and finding a copy of *Leaves of Grass*. After Victoria Woodhull ran for president of the United States on a Free Love platform, Anthony Comstock got an anti-obscenity law through Congress in 1873. Woodhull was soon arrested in New York, and Ezra Heywood went to jail in Boston for mailing his pamphlet, *Cupid's Yokes*. By 1882 Harvard College had put *Leaves of Grass* under lock and key, the Boston D.A threatened prosecution if another edition were printed in Boston, and the Boston postmaster declared *Leaves of Grass* unmailable. After Comstock arrested Heywood for publishing "A Woman Waits for Me" and "To a Common Prostitute," Whitman responded cautiously. He would not expurgate *Leaves of Grass* as he had made clear to Emerson in 1860, but he would also avoid baiting what Wilhelm Reich has called the "Emotional Plague."

For his time, Whitman was remarkably open. In 1889 he told Horace Traubel, "Sex: sex: sex: whether you sing or make a machine, or go to the North Pole, or love your mother, or build a house, or black shoes, or anything—anything at all—it's sex, sex, sex: sex is the root of it all: . . . always immanent: here with us discredited—not suffered: rejected from our art: yet still, sex, sex: the root of roots: the life below the life!" (*With W. W.*, III, 452–3). Still, when that sex was with other men, the pleasure is veiled—the contact more screened than disrobed. Avoiding vindictive heterosexuals, Whitman communicated to "the life below the life" in other gay men through an indirect form of discourse: "I perceive that you pick me out by secret and divine signs. . . . Ah lover and perfect equal,/ I meant that you should discover me so by faint indirections,/ And I when I meet you mean to discover you by the same in you."

The word "gay" could be and was used by the poet and his friends with a double meaning—one word to enemies, another to lovers. When Whitman wrote a passionate love letter to Sergeant Tom Sawyer, he used "gay." He significantly changed "celestial" to "gay" in discussing the weather in Falmouth, Virginia: ". . . it must have been gay down there about Falmouth—didn't you want some *ice cream* about last Sunday? My dearest comrade, I cannot, though I attempt it, put in a letter the feelings of my heart—. . ." (May 27, 1863). Whitman underlined "ice cream"—a word which has now become such a cliché for cum that the gay liberation journal *Fag Rag* automatically rejects every "ice cream" poem. The metaphorical interchange of weather and sex ("celestial"/"gay") also appeared in a *Notebook* entry of "heavenly" after a soldier "slept with me last night" (October 9, 1863).

Whitman's correspondents used the word "gay" with special connotations. In a letter, December 22, 1863, Alonzo Bush wrote about Lewy Brown (Tom Sawyer's boy-friend): "The fellow that went down on your B[UC]K, both so often with me. I wished that I could see him this evening and go in the Ward Master's Room and have some fun for he is a gay boy." Later the next summer, when Brown was out of the Washington hospital, the "gay boy" himself wrote Whitman about two other soldiers, whom he lived with after the war, "I have not seen Jo Harris or [Adrian] Bartlett for over a weak but I believe they are both well they went to Baltimore on a spree on the 4 of July and had what they call a regular gay time" (July 18, 1864). In 1870, a friend wrote Whitman about Peter Doyle, "I suppose by Pete's letters that he was as gay as usual" (Edward "Ned" Stewart, February 25, 1870).

While Whitman was gay, his sexuality remained circumspect. Thus in his published writings, when he used the word "gay," Whitman went out of his way to attach some "manly" accoutrement. In his *Notebooks*, he might describe a group of soldiers with sexual overtones and use the word "gay": "Handsome, reckless American young men, some eighty of them gaily riding up the avenue . . ." (*Notebooks,* 726). In the published and public *Specimen Days,* however, Whitman describes the troops not less gaily but with butch modifiers: "*June 29* [1863]. — Just before sundown this evening a very large cavalry force went by — a fine sight. . . . It was a pronouncedly warlike and gay show. . . ." Nonetheless, Whitman could sometimes be remarkably explicit. In *Good-Bye My Fancy* (1891), a short note on "Gay-Heartedness" suggests some of today's usage but Whitman shifts the responsibility to a foreigner:

> . . . a squad of laughing young black girls pass'd us — then two copper-color'd boys, one good-looking lad 15 or 16, barefoot, running after — "What *gay creatures* they all appear to be," said Mr. M. Then we fell to talking about the general lack of buoyant animal spirits. "I think," said Mr. M., "that in all my travels, and all my intercourse with people of every and any class, especially the cultivated ones, (the literary and fashionable folks,) I have never yet come across what I should call a really GAY-HEARTED MAN." [Italics and caps Whitman's.]

Whenever confronted with the question: "Are you queer?" Whitman avoided the inquiry even to the point of lying and misrepresenting himself. His notation on a letter from a soldier convalescing in Louisville, Kentucky, provides an early example of an overt lie. Nicholas Palmer wrote June 24, 1865, offering to come live with Whitman and receive support for sexual favors. Although he didn't write the soldier, Whitman (June 28, 1865) scribbled a strange note on the back of Palmer's letter: ". . . he came one rainy night to my room & stopt with me — I am completely in the dark as to what 'such houses as we were talking about,' are — — upon the whole not to be answered — (& yet I itch to satisfy my curiosity as to what this young man can have really taken me for)." What one does on a rainy night doesn't necessarily predicate living together. Part of the gay ambiance is to reveal yourself only to potential and desirable partners. In the *Leaves of Grass,* Whitman had written: "My words itch at your ears till you understand them!" Nicholas Palmer, however, was not someone with whom he wanted an understanding. To another soldier, he responded but warned him not to be so explicit in his writing: "I wish things were situated so you could be with me, & we could be together for a while, where we could enjoy each others society & sweet friendship & you could talk freely. . . . but [I] will not at present say much to you on the subject, in writing" (April 12, 1867 to Benton H. Wilson).

Another curious disguise appears in the 1870 notebook entry concerning Peter Doyle. To consider only the deception of this entry: Whitman erased all the masculine pronouns and changed them to feminine. And he changed Peter Doyle's initials, P.D., to 16.4. (P is the sixteenth letter and D the fourth letter of the alphabet. Whitman's code was not broken until 1950.) Here the off-coding of the author and the misreading of the readers are almost more interesting than what was being hidden. Whitman was having problems with his lover, his aging, his poetry; he was panicky. He had reached one of those moments in which the splendid joys of young male beauty were turning into the headaches of an overpossessive lover. He wanted to save the record of his turmoil but he wanted that account cloaked.

In light of such deceptions, Whitman's now famous letter to John Addington Symonds (August 19, 1890) can be better understood. In response to Symonds' twenty-year effort to get him to come out more openly, Whitman refused to acknowledge any specifically sexual connotations in the Calamus poems: ". . . that the calamus part has even allowed the possibility of such construction as mentioned is terrible — I am fain to hope the pages themselves are not to be even mentioned for such gratuitous and quite at the time entirely undreamed & unrecked possibility of morbid inferences — wh' are disavowed by me & seem damnable. Then one great difference between you and me, temperament & theory, is *restraint* . . ."

Each correspondent knew that the other had sex with men; Symonds said as much in his letters to Whitman. And Symonds knew Carpenter who had got a hot blow job from Whitman. Whitman in grumbling to Traubel didn't deny homosexual passion in Calamus: "What does Calamus mean? What do the poems come to in the round-up? This is worrying him a good deal — their involvement, as he suspects, is the passional relations of men with men — the thing he reads so much of in the literatures of southern Europe and sees something of in his own experience" (*With W. W.*, 1:73). The correspondence thus involved more than a simple consumer inquiry about Calamus.

Whitman rightly smelled a rat in Symonds. The Englishman pointedly mentioned his three children, talked about his fancy education and family tree. Symonds' high social standing (despite pleas of

Walt Whitman at the Camden, New Jersey, docks with his male nurse, Warren Fritzenger, 1890. Courtesy of the Library of Congress

humility) did not fool Whitman. The Englishman never came out openly to Whitman so why should Whitman come out to him? Through Carpenter, Whitman may have known of Symonds' using a love-letter to get his Harrow headmaster fired. Moreover, after Whitman's death, Symonds threatened legal action if his own letters were published. He wrote Horace Traubel (November 13, 1892), "I am aware that on one occasion I told Whitman things about my own past life (with the object of showing how he had helped me) which were not meant for the eyes of the public & the diffusion of which would not only cause me great pain, but would also provoke me to a violent attack on Whitman's literary executors."

In understanding this exchange of letters between Whitman and Symonds, the position of Horace Traubel remains obscure but important. Whitman had first picked up Traubel as a fifteen-year-old, had kissed him and forgotten him, but in 1888 he welcomed him into his house as a full-fledged disciple. Whitman may have been incapable of sexual intercourse in 1888 (when he was practically bed-ridden until his death in March 1892) but he did enjoy playing with Traubel. First he presented him with Symonds' letters, which dated back to 1871, when Symonds (around thirty) was about the same age as Traubel in 1888. Very indirectly and discreetly, Whitman used the Symonds correspondence to feel out Traubel's gayness.

Whitman had become by that time somewhat vatic—his body and his creativity had collapsed. And to keep the attention of his handsome disciple, he used devices. He reminded Traubel in 1889 of Symonds' fame, "of the literati . . . among the most distinguished . . . credited with authority by the London Times, the reviews, big quarterlies, men of distinct literary note . . ." (*With W.W.*, VI:51). Then he intrigued Traubel with confused hints about mysterious liaisons with mysterious women and vaguely defined children of his own. Traubel's curiosity led Whitman to tease Symonds and repay the Englishman for his three children. The poet concluded his now famous 1890 letter to Symonds with an enormous lie: "My life, young manhood, mid-age, times South, &c: have all been jolly, bodily, and probably open to criticism— Tho' always unmarried I have had six children—two are dead—One living southern grandchild, fine boy, who writes to me occasionally." To continue the fiction, Whitman even told Traubel that a grandson had come to Camden for a visit. That Whitman during his quarter-year stay in New Orleans produced six children with a Southern woman from a wealthy planter or quadroon background which prohibited marriage is biologically possible (sextuplets) but not likely. If Symonds had three children, Whitman had six; American queers are more fertile.

Whitman recognized latent hostility in Symonds' inquiries. The Englishman was playing doctor as it were, but Whitman would not submit to the game. As he told Traubel, "I like to cross-examine, but I don't like to be cross-examined." And another time he retreated into the poet's cocoon, "It always makes me a little testy to be catechized about the Leaves — I prefer to have the book answer for itself." After all, "What right has he to ask questions anyway?" Who then should catechize whom? "Symonds has got into our group in spite of his culture: I tell you we don't give away places in our crowd easy — a man has to sweat to get in" (*With W.W.*, 1:102, 203, 388).

Whitman explained that "What lies behind *Leaves of Grass* is something that few, very few . . . are in a position to seize. It lies behind almost every line; but concealed, studiedly concealed; some passages left purposely obscure." Being arch if not artful, the poet was laying his Easter eggs: "There is something in my nature *furtive* like an old hen! You see a hen wandering up and down a hedgerow, looking apparently quite unconcerned, but presently she finds a concealed spot, and furtively lays an egg, and comes away as though nothing had happened!" (Edward Carpenter, *Days with Walt Whitman*, 43). Some of his coding was less protective than playful. Whitman wrote Anne Gilchrist, February 22, 1878, "At least two hours forenoon, & two afternoon, down by the *creek* — Passed between *sauntering* — the *hickory saplings* — & '*Honor* is the *subject* of my story' — (for explanation of the last three lines, ask Herby —)." Edwin Miller suggests that "Hickory Saplings" and "Honor Subject" (underlined by Whitman) are code for H.S. or Harry Stafford, Whitman's teenage boyfriend. The intricacy of such a conceit would appeal to Gilchrist who was the world authority on William Blake and should serve to caution anyone who thinks everything is obvious in Whitman's life or poetry.

Although he was hesitant in answering literary ghouls, Whitman's sexual politics in *Leaves of Grass* comes through clearly. He defined poetry as itself supremely political; the poet, a political figure. The true poet must extend liberty and democracy everywhere. And while Whitman claimed to be the poet of everyone, he was preeminently the poet of the working classes. In the concluding section of "Starting from Paumanok (O Camerado Close!)," Whitman links his sexuality, politics and poetry: "O to be relieved of distinctions! To make as much of vices as of virtues!/ To level occupations and the sexes! To bring all to common ground!/ O adhesiveness! O the pensive aching to be together . . ." In his 1855 *Leaves of Grass* preface, he declared that "the attitude of great poets is to cheer up slaves and horrify despots." He had no sympathy for an art separated from either life or sex. "There is a still better, higher school," Whitman wrote, "for him who would kindle his fire from coal from the altar of the loftiest and purest art. It is the school of all grand actions and grand virtues, of heroism, of the death of captives and martyrs . . . Read well the death of Socrates. . . . Read how slaves have battled against their oppressors — how the bullets of tyrants have, since the first king ruled, never been able to put down the unquenchable thirst of man for his rights."

Although Whitman wasn't ready to join Symonds in a crusade for gay rights, he praised the Englishman's poem "Love and Death," which became the first entry in the posthumous *Re Walt Whitman* (1893). Symonds celebrated two Athenian lovers who sacrificed themselves in the war against Sparta. Comrade love was thus presented as less selfish than family love, which was concerned with procreation more than community. In *Democratic Vistas* Whitman preached that "adhesiveness," the love of comrades, would redeem mass culture and democracy from Gilded Age corruptions. He looked to "a time when there will be seen, running like a half-hid warp through all the myriad audible and visible worldly interests of America, threads of manly friendship, fond and loving, pure and sweet, strong and life-long, carried to degrees hitherto unknown — not only giving tone to individual character, and making it unprecedently emotional, muscular, heroic, and refined, but having the deepest relations to general politics." Sexual politics was at the core of Whitman's poetry; his problem with Symonds was that the Englishman wasn't enough of a democrat.

Whitman predicted that "fervid comradeship" or "adhesive love" would equal if not go beyond "the amative love hitherto possessing imaginative literature." The Calamus cluster and parts of "Song of Myself" are generally recognized as filling Whitman's criterion for establishing an "imaginative literature" of "fervid comradeship," which we now call "gay" or "homosexual." Robert K. Martin explains the importance of recognizing such poems: "It has been, and continues to be, necessary to insist upon the homosexuality of a homosexual poem because it has so often been ignored or invalidated. It is essential, then, for a better (more accurate) reading of the poem, not because it makes the poem better" (*The Homosexual Tradition in American Poetry*, 1979).

*　　*　　*

None of Whitman's poems can be understood without a gay perspective. As examples let me trace the vascular, sexual, homosexual arteries in two classics, "Out of the Cradle Endlessly Rocking" and "When Lilacs Last in the Dooryard Bloomed." Both poems are meditations on death; one the young boy and the male bird contemplating the nest without a mother; the other, an elegy for Abraham Lincoln. I pass over the Freudian suggestions that any mention of death is always a disguised Oedipal difficulty, an incapacity or fear of fucking a woman. Although Whitman did say after his mother's death, "Nelly Death has become to me a familiar thing." And I set aside the more luxuriant sentimental context of nineteenth-century writing where virtue was demonstrated by crying over dead birds, babies, flowers and lovers. The Freudian analysis is not so much false as boring because the psychoanalyst homogenizes homosexuals. Likewise the fact that literally millions of deaths occurred in poems around 1855 — while not without interest — homogenizes all poems and poets.

"Out of the Cradle Endlessly Rocking" was first published December 24, 1859, and was written in the same year as most of the Calamus Poems, which I argue were triggered by Fred Vaughan (see Chapter 2 below). While there is considerable evidence of Whitman's homosexual liaisons as early as 1836, there were no lovers until Vaughan. For two men to take each other as lovers creates many difficulties unique to men. Some problems are common with heterosexual couples: shock at discovering a fantasy collapse under close scrutiny, loss of freedom, loss of sexual interest, and changes brought on by time. But for many generations past — if not in the future — each male homosexual has had to find his way virtually alone. That isolation — cruel enough in itself — becomes compounded by taking lovers. For a heterosexual, taking a spouse eliminates a whole series of social problems; for a homosexual, the same act with a person of the same sex — particularly two men — compounds rather than diminishes difficulties.

Thus the boy and the bird singing together are not playing the usual game of birds & bees:

> Demon or bird! (said the boy's soul,)
> Is it indeed toward your mate you sing? or is it really to me?
> For I, that was a child, my tongue's use sleeping, now I have heard you,
> Now in a moment I know what I am for, I awake
> And already a thousand singers, a thousand songs, clearer, louder and more sorrowful than yours,
> A thousand warbling echoes have started to life within me, never to die.

These lines suggest a male lover finding another male, but that discovery brings as they say new agonies and ecstasies:

> O you singer solitary, singing by yourself, projecting me,
> O solitary me listening, never more shall I cease perpetuating you,
> Never more shall I escape, never more the reverberations,
> Never more the cries of unsatisfied love be absent from me,
> Never again leave me to the peaceful child I was before what there in
>   the night,
> By the sea under the yellow and sagging moon,
> The messenger there aroused, the fire, the sweet hell within,
> The unknown want, the destiny of me.

"Out of the Cradle Endlessly Rocking" utilizes Grand Opera machinery with arias, solos and music combined with high drama. Henry James read "Death, death, death, death, death" like the opening notes in Beethoven's Fifth Symphony. The beating notes of "death" —"That strong and delicious word which, creeping to my feet, . . . / The sea whispered me"— might be compared to Whitman's "Sex, sex, sex, sex, sex" quoted above. The Demon or bird sex/love brought deadly disappointments. With Fred Vaughan Whitman found that appearances deceive because after all no one will ever love you for yourself alone — and another man shatters that expectation and possibility particularly rapidly. Our bright prince teaches a hard lesson: "O you singer solitary, singing by yourself, projecting me,/ O solitary me listening, never more shall I cease perpetuating you . . ." "The unknown want, the destiny of me" is familiar to every faggot lover. Within any couple the hostile but repressed feelings of wanting to strangle the partner are always present, and occasionally husbands and wives do kill each other. Homosexuals more often separate than murder each other. After Fred Vaughan got married in 1862 and began raising a family, Whitman departed south and became a Florence Nightingale bird of mercy to the solitary soldiers.

The Civil War provided a powerful outlet for combining love and death, whose profound expression Whitman eventually realized in his poem for Lincoln and his attachment to Peter Doyle. During the war, Whitman's 1855 line "I am the man . . . I was there . . . I suffered" came to be fulfilled as he passed among dying and wounded soldiers dropping kisses and tokens of his love on their cots. Whitman's description (January 5, 1864) of sitting up with Lewy Brown is a powerful prose poem.

> Today, after dinner, Lewy Brown had his left leg amputated five
> inches below the knee—(the surgeon in charge had examined it the

day before & decided to [cut])—I was present at the operation, most
of the time in the door, [waiting]. The surgeon in charge amputated,
but did not finish the operation being called away as he was stitching
it up. Lewy came out of the influence of the ether. It bled & they
thought an artery had opened. . . . I could hear his cries sometimes
quite loud, & half-coherent talk & caught glimpses of him through
the open door. At length they finished, & they brought the boy in on
his cot, & took it to its place. I sat down by him. . . . About 7 oclock
in the evening, he dozed into a sleep, quite good for a couple of
hours. The rest of the night was very bad. I remained all night, slept
on the adjoining cot.

While this might not appear erotic on the surface, the case of Oscar
Cunningham is less ambiguous. By the soldier's name, Whitman wrote
in his *Notebook* about "the profuse beauty of the young men's hair,
damp with the spotted blood, their shining hair, red with the sticky
blood . . ." The description of Cunningham leaves no doubt about how
appealing the poet found the combination of beauty, blood and death:
". . . a young Ohio boy . . . badly wounded . . . has been here nearly a
year—He & I have been quite intimate all that time. When he was
brought here I thought he ought to have been taken by a sculptor to
model for an emblematical figure of the west, he was such a handsome
young giant, over 6 feet high, a great head of brown yellowy shining
hair thick & longish & a manly noble manner & talk—he has suffered
very much." After Cunningham died in 1864, Whitman retained keep-
sakes from him, including a letter to Oscar from another soldier,
asking "If your friend Whitman can come up I would be gratified to
see him" (W. J. Ward to Oscar Cunningham, May 17, 1864).

Edmund Wilson titled his Civil War study *Patriotic Gore*. The hospital death, flesh and sex exhausted Whitman (see below, "Many Soldiers' Kisses"). While he was recuperating with his mother in Brooklyn, news arrived of the assassination of Abraham Lincoln, April 14,
1865. While some have found homosexual themes in Lincoln's life, I
doubt Whitman slept over at the White House; however, he did cruise
the area by moonlight and he certainly had a crush on the Illinois Rail-
Splitter. On November 1, 1863, Whitman visited the White House
and "saw Mr Lincoln standing, talking with a gentleman, apparently a
dear friend . . . his face & manner have an expression & are inexpres-
sibly sweet—one hand on his friends shoulder the other holding his
hand. I love the President personally."

When Lincoln was assassinated, Whitman felt the bullet and wrote
the poem out of the same fountainhead as "Out of the Cradle Endlessly

Rocking." "Lilac blooming perennial and dropping star in the west,/
And thought of him I love"—a trio remarkably similar to the he-bird,
boy and ocean. And "him I love" mixes demon-like with the solitary
thrush singing from "the swamp in secluded recesses . . . warbling a
song." Part 7 mixes the vegetation, the love and the death ("death
sweet death"):

> Nor for you, for one alone,
> Blossoms and branches green to coffins all I bring,
> For fresh as the morning, thus would I chant a song for you
>   O sane and sacred death.
>
> All over bouquets of roses,
> O death, I cover you over with roses and early lilies,
> But mostly and now the lilac that blooms the first,
> Copious I break, I break the sprigs from the bushes,
> With loaded arms I come, pouring for you,
> For you and the coffins all of you O death.

The lilacs function not unlike the live-oak & moss in Louisiana or the
calamus on Long Island. In "These I Singing in Spring," written before
1860, Whitman enumerated these tokens:

> Some walk by my side and some behind, and some embrace my arms
>   or neck,
> They the spirits of dear friends dead or alive, thicker they came, a
>   great crowd, and I in the middle
> . . . Plucking something for tokens, tossing toward whoever is near me,
> Here, lilac, with a branch of pine,
> Here out of my pocket, some moss which I pulled off a live-oak,
> Here, some pinks and laurel leaves, and a handful of sage,
> And here what I now draw from the water, wading in the pond-side,
> (O there I saw him that tenderly loves me, and never separates
>   from me,
> Therefore, this shall be the special token of comrades, this calamus-
>   root shall,
> Interchange it, youths, with each other! Let none render it back!)

Lilacs, growing in bunches as they do, resemble pendant cocks and
balls and were always among the special tokens of camerados. Among
whom now lay the fallen captain. We might debate whether Lincoln
deserved all Whitman's lilacs, whether any head of state were worthy
of this great outpouring. If Lincoln reciprocated the kisses, I say give
him the poem and more.

On the evening Lincoln was shot, Peter Doyle, a former Confederate
soldier working in Washington on the horsecars, witnessed the assassi-

nation and later told Whitman what had happened in Ford's Theater. Doyle's account became the one Whitman used in lecturing on Lincoln's death. Something of the war suffering and deaths rubbed off on Doyle and became incorporated into his love with Whitman. The two men met at the time Whitman was writing "When Lilacs Last in the Dooryard Bloomed." Whitman signed the photograph of the two in a love seat: "Washington, D.C., 1865 — Walt Whitman & his rebel soldier friend Pete Doyle." Peter Doyle and Walt Whitman remained a couple for about ten years and then went their separate ways (see "Whirled among Sophistications" below). When Doyle came to Whitman's funeral in 1892, he was almost excluded before Horace Traubel recognized him.

Although only spiritually accurate, Guillaume Apollinaire published the best account of Whitman's funeral. On April 1, 1913 (April Fool's Day, that great gay holiday), Apollinaire wrote that a circus was set up with food, drink and coffin tents; thirty-five hundred people showed up uninvited. There were brass bands, speeches, all sorts of people, according to Apollinaire, including "cameradoes (he used this word which he thought was Spanish to designate the young men that he loved in his old age, and he did not conceal his taste)." (In Spanish *camerada* has only the feminine form; Whitman invented *camerado*.)

The festivity lasted from dawn to dark; fifty people were arrested for brawling and drunkenness. "Pederasts came in crowds. The one who received most attention was a young man twenty to twenty-two years old, famous for his beauty, Peter Connolly [Doyle], an Irish train conductor, first at Washington, afterwards at Philadelphia, whom Whitman loved above all others. Everyone remembered having often seen Walt Whitman and Peter Connolly sitting on the edge of the sidewalk eating watermelon." In his *Notebooks,* Whitman included melons with the calamus, "Sweet flag Sweet fern illuminated face clarified unpolluted flour-corn aromatic Calamus sweet-green bulb and melons with bulbs grateful to the hand/ . . . Coarse things/ The sweet Trickling Sap flows from the end of the manly maple tooth of delight tooth prong — time/ . . . Living bulbs, melons with polished rinds that smooth to the soothing hand/ Bulbs of life-lilies, polished melons flavored for the gentlest hand that shall reach." Like lilacs, melons in the poem suggest big, sweaty balls.

Whitman slips into history on melon skins; the crowds come and go, but as long as there are pederasts, he will have lovers. Every time a boy gets his cock sucked a bird sings in Walt's throat and whispers:

As I lay with my head in your lap camerado,
The confession I made I resume, what I said to you and the open air I
  resume,
I know I am restless and make others so,
I know my words are weapons full of danger, full of death,
For I confront peace, security, and all the settled laws to unsettle
  them,
I am more resolute because all have denied me than I could ever have
  been had all accepted me,
I heed not and have never heeded either experience, cautions, majori-
  ties, nor ridicule,
And the threat of what is called hell is little or nothing to me,
And the lure of what is called heaven is little or nothing to me;
Dear camerado! I confess I have urged you onward with me, and still
  urge you, without the least idea what is our destination,
Or whether we shall be victorious, or utterly quelled and defeated.

In 1860, Whitman proceeded "to tell the secret of my nights and days,/ To celebrate the need of the love of comrades." His procedure, his secret, his celebration remain no less a struggle, no less a need a century and more later. By 2060, *Leaves of Grass* may again be censored. Or readers may wonder how anyone would have had to disguise the Calamus revelations. In 1986, we stand on a divide. What we read, how we act and love will carry on a struggle Walt Whitman wrestled with when he walked on Boston Common with Ralph Waldo Emerson in 1860; Emerson said delete; Whitman stood his ground. Camerado, take my hand, the road is before us.

CHAPTER TWO

Calamus Lover

Fred Vaughan

FRED VAUGHAN COMBINED (not unlike many teenagers) a blend of boldness and shyness, assertion and uncertainty. Although never so physically cocky as some of the boys, Fred loved to splash, dive and wrestle among the nude swimmers in the East River waters off Brooklyn. Especially he loved to throw water in the face of Walt Whitman (who had a hairy chest, big body, and pendant cock and balls) and then have the man admonish him by dunking him under the water and when he reached for the man's cock, pulling him too under water. Walt would respond by goosing the boy. An editorial in the Brooklyn *Daily Times,* July 27, 1858, caught the fun of water-sporting: "Every morning and evening the East and North Rivers ought to show not hundreds but thousands of persons, engaged in these manly, wholesome, and luxurious ablutions. . . . To be a daily swimmer during the warm season, to acquire that ease, muscle, litheness, of physical action, so fostered by the free movements of the limbs in the water — Who is not inspirited by the thought?"

Many older men came to watch with eager eyes. They had to seek out the nude bathers who stayed away from the Brooklyn Ferry dock at the end of Fulton Street and other busy places. Not all lookers, however, could be trusted. There were the ludicrous Brooklyn police. Not that there were very many of them nor that they were very effective in stopping crime; but fearing the more heavily armed rough types (all fully clothed), the police loved to go after the nude bathers. Were they excited by all the cocks (some only half soft), balls and bare asses? Or were they afraid of all the fun and laughter — especially the giggles? There was after all an ordinance "against all bathing between sun rise and sun set." Bathtubs hardly existed then; the first one was installed in the White House after 1852; there were some efforts — supported by Whitman — to establish public bathhouses in Brooklyn — but that is another story . . . An ordinance once established had to be enforced. In an editorial (July 20, 1857), Whitman denounced "the mock-vigilance of the Policemen, who pounce upon parties of young men and boys — arresting them and carrying them to the station houses, for the frightful crime of bathing!" Wasn't this just "filthy modesty . . . terrified at the neighborhood of a few people at their agreeable and wholesome sports in the water?" At the end of his days, Whitman was still at odds with the authorities. In Camden he complained, "That miserable wretch, the mayor of this town, has forbidden the boys to bathe in the river. He thinks there is something objectionable in their stripping off their clothes and jumping into the water!" (*Visits to Walt Whitman in 1890-1891*).

Cocksucking and bathing go together. Doubtless bathing itself is an invention of cocksuckers. And while faggots have many tastes — some are only into ass fucking, others have to have smegma to be happy, and some may only want to kiss in the dark — nonetheless, bathing has a special relationship to the feet, cock, armpits, balls, asshole and other aromatic parts of the body. "Scented herbage of my breast . . . in your pink tinged roots . . . calamus-root . . . stems of currants, and plumb-blows, and the aromatic cedar" drawn "from the water by the pond-side." Odor — one of the five primary senses where faggot sexuality concentrates. Walt Whitman taught his lovers both cleanliness — at the time a by no means common habit — and the joys of cocksucking. Again and again, commentators note how scrupulously clean (although admittedly sloppy) Whitman was.

Besides swimming in the river there was play in Washington Park and the pastures just outside the settled areas of Brooklyn. From its inception Washington Park (as it does today) drew lovers in search of one another. Whitman described the park in the *Daily Times:* "For grandeur of situation, we doubt if there is a finer public ground in the world than Washington Park on Myrtle Avenue. The views from some of its elevated points sweep over a wide distance, comprehending city and country, houses, shipping, and steamers, sea and land, hill and hollow" (April 17, 1858). If the tourists there were too numerous or the order too cultivated, you could leave the city easily enough. Brooklyn Heights along the river was then unsettled, "commanding a wide view of bays, shores, rivers, and island of New York, with all their moving life." Whitman and Fred would spend many days in finding out nooks and crannies ("in paths untrodden") along the edges of the city where they could be alone and give their bodies to one another: "We two boys together clinging, One the other never leaving . . . Fulfilling our foray."

Fred Vaughan and Walt Whitman not only swam together and ran together in the wild, they also lived together, sharing a room with three erotic prints of Hercules, a Bacchus, and a satyr—the equivalent of today's Athletic Model Guild photos—which piqued Bronson Alcott's curiosity during a visit. Fifteen years later, Fred Vaughan wrote Walt that he had "been down past our old home several times this summer" and recalled a letter from Emerson "while we were living in Classon Ave." (Nov. 16, 1874). Walt Whitman and his extended family moved into Classon Avenue May 1, 1856, and left there May 1, 1859. In those days, young boys were not expected to stay at home; in Whitman's and Vaughan's class, boys were either formally or informally apprenticed out to an older man (who would teach them something about the world and about work). Fourteen was commonly the age for apprenticing, and while the formal contracts of a century earlier had largely lapsed— except in a few trades—the practice of getting rid of children as soon as possible continued. In most states, at that time, the age of consent for sexual acts was ten years. Thus, for Walt Whitman to take in a young boy to sleep with him was not considered anything unusual. Fred just fitted in with Walt's mother and other siblings.

The two became more than buddies romping in the woods; what generated the electricity—not completely dead even when Fred made his last visit to Walt in 1890—was the way they echoed each other. Fred recalled: "Years ago Dear Walt . . . Father used to tell me I was lazy. Mother denied it—and . . . I used to tell your Mother you was lazy and she denied it . . ." (Nov. 16, 1874). I don't think a more concise statement of what makes men lovers—rather than casual sexual partners—could be given.

Fred Vaughan in his letter to Walt clearly shows that Whitman was his first and perhaps most profound love. Fred inspired Whitman to write the Calamus poems—perhaps the most intense and successful celebration of gay love in our language. In 1870, when Whitman was having problems with a later lover (Peter Doyle, whom he met in 1865), he wrote in his notebook: "Depress the adhesive [i.e., homosexual] nature—It is in excess—making life a torment . . . Remember Fred Vaughan." Scholars have previously identified "some specific emotional experience" and rather precisely dated the composition of the Calamus poems. The most fervent of the Calamus poems were written when Whitman and Vaughan were living together on Classon Avenue; the sadder, departure Calamus poems were written after Fred moved out. The Calamus manuscripts that survive can be rather neatly dated between May 1, 1857, and May 1, 1859 (Fredson Bowers, *Whitman's Manuscripts*, Chicago, 1955). The change in the relationship between Walt and Fred can be read between the manuscript and the final text as published in 1860. In the manuscript Walt wrote, "I have found him who loves me, / as I him, in perfect love . . ." The 1860 printing (first publication of the Calamus section) reads, "One who loves me is jealous of me, and withdraws me from all but love . . ." In the cooler, later time, Whitman wrote, "Whoever you are holding me now in hand . . . I am not what you supposed, but far different." Or "Not Heaving from my Ribb'd Breast Only" is filled with brooding "rage dissatisfied" "clenched teeth" "Ill-supprest" "beating and pounding" "many a hungry wish" "defiances" "murmers" "dismiss you continually" — all these words to salute "adhesiveness"! — Whitman's word for gay love. Part (but only part) of the cooling of Whitman's ardor comes from his attempt to clean up (i.e., hide) what was on his mind. Thus the mansucript read "I dreamed in a dream of a city where all the men were like brothers, O I saw them tenderly love each other — I often saw them, in numbers, walking hand in hand . . .," while the printed version read: "I dreamed in a dream, I saw a city invincible to the attacks of the whole of the rest of the earth / I dreamed that was the new City of Friends . . ."

Whitman's relationship to Fred Vaughan was that of teacher, mentor and lover. ("To the young man, many things to absorb, to engraft, to develop. I teach, that he be my élève . . ."). What Whitman loved, Fred became; and what Fred loved, Whitman became. Through his mentor, Fred got jobs working on the Fulton Ferry and then on the Manhattan coaches. Walt Whitman taught him reading and writing. They studied together the precious letters from Ralph Waldo Emerson to Walt Whitman — one of which Whitman evidently got rid of as Emerson pleaded "impecuniosity" against his need for a loan. Fred went to hear Emerson lecture on Friendship and concluded that Emerson was one of their nature; he wrote Walt that the elder philosopher "said that a man whose heart was filled with a warm, ever enduring not to be shaken by anything Friendship was one to be set on one side apart from other men, and almost to be worshipped as a saint. — There Walt, how do you like that? What do you think of them setting you & myself . . . up in some public place, with an immense placard on our breasts, reading *Sincere Freinds*!!!"

Fred however learned his lessons too well; when Whitman wrote "But if through him speed not the blood of friendship, hot and red — If he be not silently selected by lovers, and do not silently select lovers — of what use were it for him to seek to become élève of mine?" Well and good to say, but when the élève — pupil, student, disciple, apprentice — finds other lovers, the expansive teacher might falter at the loss. At any rate, as Fred was moving around finding lovers (both men and women) Whitman's position changed. They no longer lived together; Fred lived with another man — Bob Cooper — and his mother; as Fred wrote, "Bob and I had quite a long walk together in Central park last Sunday. We talked much of you, and in anticipation had some long, long strolls together in the Park this summer."

Walt and Fred still saw each other regularly; only now they met in the semi-gay bar Pfaff's located near Bleecker and Broadway in the Village. When Walt Whitman went to Boston in the spring of 1860 to proofread and put final touches on the third edition of the *Leaves of Grass,* Fred tried to catch him at Pfaff's before he caught the train to Boston. And after 1859, Whitman wrote his poem about meeting with Fred in the bar: "Of a youth who loves me, and whom I love, silently approaching, and seating himself near, that he may hold me by the hand; A long while, amid the noises of coming and going — of drinking and oath and smutty jest, There we two, content, happy in being together, speaking little, perhaps not a word." Neither Fred nor Whitman realized how much they meant to each other until they were separated. In the short time Whitman was in Boston, Fred wrote at least seven letters — which have survived — and Walt wrote as many back; none of these have been located. The anxiety in his last letter before Whitman's return rings a familiar sound of separated lovers: "Walt, I hope you will be home soon. I want to see you very much indeed. I have never thought more frequently about you than during the time you have been in Boston. Make it your business to call and see me as soon as you arrive in New York, and we can make an appointment to pass some hours together. As I have much, very much to talk to you about."

Separated lovers leave more memories than those together. Back from Boston, Walt resumed some ties with Fred — although the two did not live together again, they did not stop loving each other. The final excruciating break came two years later. Fred Vaughan had got a woman pregnant; Walt never favored abortions; the necessary thing was marriage. Fred sent Walt Whitman a note May 2, 1862, to attend the marriage ceremony: "I shall have no show! I have invited no

the marriage ceremony: "I shall have no show! I have invited no company. *I want you to be there.*" The pupil had graduated into adulthood; now in his twenties, a husband, soon to be a father. Exactly what the mentor would want. But he was so crushed that he used the first opportunity/excuse he could find to leave his beloved Manhattan and Brooklyn. In December 1862, when he went to find his wounded brother near Washington, D.C., Walt left New York permanently; he did not look back; henceforth he lived either in Washington or Camden, New Jersey. With Fred's marriage a chapter ended in Whitman's life.

Nonetheless, he saved Fred Vaughan's letters and the two kept in touch through the years. Fred never seems to have prospered; he had at least four boys; drank heavily; tried being an insurance agent for a time; ran an elevator; married life was not much fun. After Walt's stroke, Fred wrote two deeply heartfelt letters in 1874, and in 1876 traveled to Camden to visit the poet; in 1876, Whitman checked up on Fred when he visited Manhattan, and they evidently wrote back and forth during the 1880s (though none of the correspondence after 1874 survives). In 1885, Whitman recorded Fred's address at the Franklin Hotel in Harrisburg, Pennsylvania. And finally in 1890, Fred came to Camden to visit Walt for a final tribute before the poet's death.

Perhaps Vaughan's most touching testimonial to his lover was the poem-monologue he sent in an 1874 letter (see pp. 48–49 below). Fred Vaughan's erotic images — barefoot sailors, "the laugh and wrangle of the boys in swimming," linked to "a remembrance of thee dear Walt"—all cast new light on Whitman's own "Crossing Brooklyn Ferry." The two lovers shared "sailors at work in the riging, or out astride the sparr"; they shared a love that could not be forgotten but like the East River kept moving along: "Flow on, river! flow with the flood-tide, and ebb with the ebb-tide." The élève had indeed grown up, had indeed learned the hard lesson of separation and departure.

Fred Vaughan Letters

Fred Vaughan to WW, New York, March 19, 1860

Dear Walt,

    I am sorry I could not see you previous to your departure for Boston. I called in at Pfaffs two evenings in successsion but did not find you on hand.

I am quite anxious to hear about how matters are progressing with you.

Write to me as soon as you can make it convenient.   Care of Man-[hattan] Ex[press] Co. 140 Chamber St., New York.

Every thing remains as usual in New York. I have seen the *Atlantic* for April. "good, bully for you." —

Yours as Ever, Fred

Fred Vaughan to WW, New York, March 21, 1860

Your letter in answer to my note came to hand this a.m. I was very glad to hear from you, Walt, and hope you will continue to write often while you stay in Boston. It will be a good way for you to pass some leisure time as I do not doubt you will have plenty of it on your hands.

Walt, I am glad, very glad, you have got things fairly squared. I do not care so much about the style the book comes out in. I want to see it out and have no doubt the style, writing, etc. will be no disgrace to *Boston*. You know I have always had a very high opinion of the people of the *City of Notions*.

I have not seen any of the folks up town, but they will undoubtedly be very glad of your success.

You are well off in Boston this weather, Walt. I cannot see across the streets. The dust is moving in a dense mass through the streets as dust in no other city but NY can move. — It is actually sickening.

I want you to look closely into the Municipal affairs of Boston, and comparing them with those of New York, give me the conclusion you arrive at regarding their respective good and bad qualities. —

If you want to form the acquaintence of any Boston Stage men, get on one of those stages running to Charlestown Bridge, or Chelsea Ferry, & enquire for Charley Hollis or Ed Morgan, mention my name, and introduce yourself as my friend. —

I am obliged to you for your kind offer of sending me a few of the sheets in advance of Publication, and hope you will not forget it. —

Bob and I had quite a long walk together in Central Park last Sunday. We talked much of you, and in anticipation had some long, long strolls together in the Park this summer. It is a noble place, and Boston can no longer point exultingly to their common as the finest park in America.

By the way, what do you think of the common?

I must go out, good bye, Fred.

Fred Vaughan to WW, New York, March 27, 1860

Walt, I received your kind letter the day after you mailed it, and immediately wrote you again. But finding some trouble in procuring a stamp, I sent it down to Frank Moran to have him mail it for me. It appears Frank was taken ill that day, and oblidged to go home; and has not been out of the house since. I did not find it out until today. — But of course my letter to you was not mailed, and now I have once more to reply to yours. —

I am glad you like Boston Walt, you know I have said much to you in praise both of the city and its people. — It is true the first is quite *crooked*, but it is generally clean, and the latter, though a little too straight-laced for such free thinkers as you and I are, a very hospitable, friendly lot of folks. — You tell me Mr. Emmerson (one m to many I guess?) came to see you and was very kind. — I heard him lecture in Fr. Chapins church on Friday evening last, on the subject of *manners,* and though very much pleased with the *matter,* I did not at all like his delivery. It appeared to me to be strained, and there was a certain hesitation in his speech and occasional repetition of words that did not affect the hearer very well. —

But, Walt, when I looked upon the man, & thought that it was but a very few days before that he had been so kind and attentive to you, I assure you I did not think much of his *bad delivery,* but on the contrary, my heat warmed towards him very much. I think he has *that* in him which makes men capable of strong friendships. — This theme he also touched on, and said that a man whose heart was filled with a warm, ever enduring *not to be shaken by anything* Friendship was one to be set on one side apart from other men, and almost to be worshipped as a saint. — There Walt, how do you like that? What do you think of them setting you & myself, and one or two others we know up in some public place, with an immense placard on our breast, reading *Sincere Freinds*!!! Good doctrine that but I think the theory preferable to the practice. — I am glad very glad Walt to hear you are succeeding so well with your book. — I hope you will not forget the promise you made of sending me on some of the first proof sheets you have. — I am quite anxious to see them. —

There is nothing new here, Walt. Everything remains about he same. I suppose of course you see the New York papers every day. Our streets are just about as dirty as ever, but the dirt is not allowed to remain long in one place, this March wind picks it up and scatters it

New York, March 27/69

Walt. I received your this letter
the day after you mailed it, and immediately
wrote you again. But finding some trouble
in procuring a stamp I kept it down
to Frank Sherman to have him mail it
for me. It appears Frank was taken with that
day, and refused to go home, and has
not been out of the house since. I did
not just it out & sent to day. But of course and now
suppose too you was not afraid. And now
I have sure now to reply to you. —

Dear Walt
I am glad you like Boston Walt.
now know I have said much to you in
praise both of the city and its people. —
It is true the first is quite crooked. but
it is generally clean, and the latter though
a little to straight-laced for such like
Trustees as you and I are a very little
friendly, set of folks. You tell me

It appeared to me to be strained, and
then was a certain hesitation in his speech
and received repetition of words, that
did not affect the hearer very well. —
But Walt when I looked upon the man, I
thought that it was but a very few days
before that he had been so kind and attentive
to you, I assure you I did not think
much of his fastidiousness, but on the
contrary, my heart warmed towards him
very much. I think he has that in
him which make men capable of
strong friendships. He then he also
touched on and said that a man whose
heart was filled with a warm, enduring
yet to be shaken by anything friendship
was one to be set on and set apart from
other men, and almost to be worshipped as
a saint. — Now Walt how do you like that?
What do you think of them setting you, I
B. well. And me or two other we know
up, no some public place, with an
immense placard on our breast. Reading
Sincere Freinds!!!. God doctrin' that
but I thank the many disposable to the
plastic. I am glad very glad that
to hear you are succeeding so well
with your topic. I hope you will get

with a perfect looseness in your eyes, ears, mouth, and nose. It penetrates to the house, covering the floor, the furniture and even the beds in a manner not at all agreeable to persons who have any idea of cleanliness. — Monuments erected in mud to the honour of the street inspector have to be regularily wet down, or like riches, and birds they take to themselves wings and fly away. — I have an idea that "There is a better time coming" But so far have been unable to find any one who could satisfactorily *fix the date*. Robert is drinking tea, Mrs Cooper is moving around the room as usual ready to wait upon Bob even before he needs it. They both join me in wishes for the best success to you, and Mrs Cooper says if you will make love to her you had better do so personally the next time you call, as she cannot put much faith in a profession made in a letter to an outside party.

Write me a good long letter Walt, as I am anxious to hear from you. Yours, Fred.

Fred Vaughan to WW, New York, April 9, 1860

How is this, Walt? I have written to you twice since I heard from you. Why don't you answer? How about them proof sheets? I have not seen any of them yet. Come, Walt, remember I take a deep interest in all that concerns you and must naturally be anxious to hear from you. Mrs Cooper and Robert keep asking me every evening "if I have heard from Walt yet." and if you do not write to me soon I am afraid I shall be under the *painful* necessity of telling a lie to keep up your reputation. —

There is nothing new here. — The weather was disgusting both yesterday and today wet, muddy and chilly. — Did you see the Sunday Courier of April first? It contains an article on "Yankee Bards and New York Critics." — Get it if you can there, if not let me know & I will send it to you. It gives a good description of the Bohemian Club at Pfaffs in which you are set down as the grand master of ceremonies. Our folks have shifted me once more. I am now back again in my old position at 168 Broadway, behind the desk. — So please address me here. — Mrs. Cooper and Robert send their love and best wishes. — Write soon and do not forget those sheets. Your friend, "Fred."

Fred Vaughan to WW, New York, April 30, 1860

Walt,

I was very glad indeed to hear from you in answer to my last, and you know I could not but be gratified to find your business was progressing so favorably, —

In accordance with not only your wishes, but my own I went to Brooklyn yesterday and saw your Mother. — I found her alone, Matt & Jeff out walking. Eddy at church, and George out somewhere's else I suppose. She did not remember me at first but as soon as she did she was very much pleased. I had a long talk, and settled the old $2.00 affair of Matts. I came away before she and Jeff returned. Walt, Mother says she feels first rate, is not at all sick, and I think she looks as well now as she did while I was living over there. — There is no news new Walt. The last fight, the Japenese Embassy, and the Charleston Democratic Convention, fill the papers to the exclusion of Every thing else. — Dunn, the ex stage driver is in Boston with that Circus Co. I think he will call upon you as I gave him your address. — If you come on here this [week] Be sure and make it your business to call and see me. Do not neglect it please Walt, for I want to see you very much. Mrs. Cooper & Robert send their loves. Ever yours, In a Hurry! Fred.

Fred Vaughan to WW, New York, May 7, 1860

Dear Walt. —
What the devil is the matter? Nothing serious I hope. — It seems mighty queer that I cannot succeed in having one word from you. — I swear I would have thought you would be the last man in this world to neglect me. — But I am afraid. —
Lizzie is married!, Johnny is dead! Walt has forgotten.
Such is life, Yours, Fred.

Fred Vaughan to WW, New York, May 21, 1860

Dear Walt,
I received your note this a.m. and I was very very much pleased to hear from you. I am right glad to hear your mission to Boston has terminated so successfully. I hope to God it may be not only a success as regards its typography, appearance and real worth, but also pecuniarily a success. For you know, "A well filled pocket, now & then, is relished by the best of men." Walt, I hope you will be home soon. I want to see you very much indeed. I have never thought more frequently about you than during the time you have been in Boston. Make it your business to call and see me as soon as you arrive in New York, and we can make an appointment to pass some hours together. As I have much, very much to talk to you about. Robt and Mrs. Cooper send their love, Yours truly, Fred.

Fred Vaughan to WW, New York, May 2, 1862

Walt,

I am to be marri'd tomorrow, Saturday at 3 o'cl[ock] at 213 W. 43rd St. — near 8th Ave.

I shall have no show! I have invited no company. —

I want you to be there. —

Do not fail please, as I am very axious you should come. —

Truly yours, Fred

Fred Vaughan to WW, Brooklyn, August 11, 1874

Walt,

I enclose you one of the very many letters I write to you. I think I have written to you at least once a week for the past four years — sometimes I write long letters, sometimes short ones. But so you know my dear friend they are all real to me — and I often keep them months before I destroy them. —

Many and many a mile have I rode on a Locomotive while in charge of a Freight-train and had you by my side in conversation — which to me was as really a *presence* as in years gone by on the box of a Broadway stage — or asleep and lounge on the deck of a Fulton Ferry Boat —

Walt in all your sorrows that has been made public, I have sorrowed with you — most especially in the death of Dear Mother and your own illness.

If you can Dear Walt write to me and acknowledge the receipt of this. — If you cannot, I shall still keep writing in my own way,

As Ever & always, Yours, Fred. care [of] Levine's & Weeber, 164 Fulton St., Brooklyn

This undated meditation was enclosed in a separate envelope with the letter of August 11, 1874. Since the envelope is addressed to Walt Whitman on Portland Ave., near Myrtle Ave., Brooklyn, it must have been written before Whitman's mother moved to Camden, New Jersey, in 1872.

Walt

Driver hour. I loafing in a Lumber Yard at foot of 35th St — Under the shade of a pile of Lumber and sitting on a lower pile. — Opposite and close to me at the pier head a Barque. In the forerigging flapping lazily in the summer breese are a few sailors clothes. From the galley-pipe between the Main and the foremast issues a cloud of smoke. — One of the men in blue shirt and bare footed has just come from alooft — where he has been loosening the Mainsail which seems to be wet. He has now gone below I suppose to his dinner.— On the opposite side of the river W[illia]msb[ur]gh—between the ever plying ferryboats, the tugs, the Harlem Boats, and mingled with the splash of the paddle wheels—the murmur of the sailors at dinner.—the lazy flap of the sails. the screech of the steam whistle of the tugs, the laugh and wrangle of the boys in swimming—comes a remembrance of thee dear Walt—

With WmsBgh & Brooklyn—with the ferries and the vessels with the Lumber piles and the docks. From among all out of all. Connected with all and yet distinct from all arrises thee Dear Walt. Walt—my life has turned out a poor miserable failure. I am not a drunkard nor a teetotaler—I am neither honest or dishonest. I have my family in Brooklyn and am supporting them.—I never stole, robbed, cheate, nor defrauded any person out of anything, and yet I feels that I have not been honest to myself—my family nor my friends

---

One Oclock, the Barque is laden with coal and the carts have come. The old old Poem Walt. The cart backs up, the bucket comes up full and goes down empty—The men argue and swear. The wind blows the coal dust over man & beast and now it reaches me. —

Fred Vaughan   Atlantic Ave. 2nd door above Classon Ave. Brooklyn

Fred Vaughan to WW, Brooklyn, November 16, 1874

Dear Walt—

I promised to write to you a week ago Sunday evening and did not do it. —I have no apology to offer. —Years ago Dear Walt—(and looking back over the tombstones it seems centuries)—Father used to tell me I was lazy. Mother denied it—and in latter years—(but O' my friend still looking over tombstones). —I used to tell your Mother you was lazy and she denied it. —You have assented yourself. I have confirmed my Father. —O, Walt, what recollections will crowd upon us both individually and in company from the above. To me the home so long long past—the brother—sisters—the sea—the return—New York, the Stage box—Broadway. —Walt—the Press—the Railroad. Marriage. Express—Babies—trouble. *Rum,* more trouble—more *Rum* —estrangement from you. More *Rum.* —Good intentions, sobriety. Misunderstanding and more *Rum.* Up and down, down and up. The innate manly nature of myself at times getting the best of it and at other times entirely submerged. Now praying now cursing. —Yet ever hoping—and even now my friend after loosing my hold of the highest rung of the ladder of fortune I ever reached and dropping slowly but surely from rung to rung until I have almost reached the bottom, I still hope—From causes too numerous and complex to explain *except verbally,* I found myself in June last in Brooklyn possesed of a wife and four boys—ages 12—9—4 years—and one of 8 months—no money, no credit—no friends of a/c and no furniture—Well, I am writing with my own pen, ink and paper on my own table, in a hired room, warmed by my own fire and lighted by my own oil—my wife sleeping on a bed near me and the Boys in an adjoining room. —

I have just got through supper after a hard days work and have to start again in the morning at 7 o'clock and am glad of it. —I am living on Atlantic ave one door above Classon ave and have been down past our old home several times this summer taking Freddie with me. —

There is never a day passes but what I think of you. So much have you left to be remembered by a Broadway stage—a Fulton ferry boat, a bale of cotton on the dock. The "Brooklyn Daily Times"—a ship loading or unloading at the wharf. —a poor man fallen from the roof of a new building, a woman & child suffocated by smoke in a burning tenement house. All—all to me speak of thee Dear Walt. —Seeing them my friend the part thou occupiest in my spiritual nature—I feel assured you will forgive my remissness of me in writing—My love my Walt—is with you always. —

I earnestly pray God that he may see fit to assuage your sufferings and in due time restore your wonted health and strength owing to *"impecuniosity"* (The first time I ever seen that word was in a letter from R.W. Emerson to you while we were living in Classon Ave, excusing himself as I now do). I cannot promise to come and see you soon. But, Walt should you become seriously ill, promise to telegraph to me immediately.

My Father is dead. Brother Burke is dead. I have not heard from Mother in 10 months. —My wife is faithful-loving-honest. true. and one you could dearly love. Ever yours, —Fred. —

Walt—please do not criticize my grammer, nor phraseology—it was written too heartfelt to alter. Fred.

CHAPTER THREE

Myriads of
New Experiences

Whitman's Notebooks
and Daybooks

WALT WHITMAN'S ENERGY and sexuality flowed like his poems— sprawling every which way. Insistently trying to exclude noth- ing, the poet's passion incorporated "myriads of new experiences"— mountains, valleys, transportation/communication networks, entire states, rivers, thieves, politicians, parsons—whatever came along but most insistently, most desperately the roughs, the sailors, boatmen, farmers, roustabouts—in short, the common man in a common land. Many of these interests and enthusiasms appear in the recent collection of his *Notebooks and Unpublished Prose Manuscripts.* Meticulously edited by Edward Grier and published in six volumes (1984) by New York University Press, the Whitman *Notebooks* gather a great mass of ad- dresses, notes, memoranda and other records of the poet in two thou- sand three hundred and fifty-four pages. William White, *Daybooks and Notebooks* (New York University Press, three volumes, 1978) contains a somewhat more orderly calendar of days from 1876 to 1891 in the first two volumes. The former is cited here as *Notebooks;* the latter, *Daybooks.*

These manuscripts contain no stunning revelations about sexual liaisons. Whitman specifically records a half dozen or so men and boys that he "slept with"; most of these were published in Jonathan Katz's *Gay American History* (1976). There are a few odd symbols, some enigmatic numerical entries, but Whitman doubtless meant to leave little evidence behind. What he has not disguised (as in the now famous code 16.4 = P.D. = Peter Doyle) or destroyed has probably been

subsequently eliminated by librarians or editors. A leather-bound notebook of 1862 suffered many disasters over the years; the original, as
Edward Grier explains, "has disappeared," which is something of a
euphemism. Grier has had to reconstruct a text from photostats, type-
scripts, notes and other sources, but slippage could easily occur along
the way. Other notebooks which have not "disappeared" have been cut
up and mounted into albums so that their original form can not be
entirely certain.

These *Notebooks* even if we had them intact and complete from
Whitman's hand doubtless never contained anything like Roger Casement's *Secret Diaries*. The differences are instructive. I see nothing
of guilt or remorse in Whitman's record. Casement's entries suggest
naughtiness in his sexual interest: July 13, 1903: "At State beach
photoed pier and Loanaga—about 9 [inches]." February 28, 1910:
"Deep screw and to hilt. X 'poquino.' Mario in Rio 8½+6 [inches]
40$. Hospedaria, Rua do Hospico. 3$ only FINE room shut window
lovely, young 18 and glorious. Biggest since Lisbon July 1904 and as
big. Perfectly huge. 'nunca veio maior!' Nunca." His enthusiasm that
"I have seen none greater, None!" sounds somewhat tarnished—not
because he's such a size queen but because he feels he's doing wrong,
getting away with something.

Whitman's entries are remarkably innocent by contrast. Thus October 9, 1863: "Jerry Taylor, (NJ.) of 2d dist. reg't slept with me last
night   weather soft, cool enough, warm enough heavenly." The sex,
the weather and the concluding, concise "heavenly" neither falsely
titillates nor hides nor elevates the experience with Jerry Taylor. Casement's precision on cock inches suggests less than Whitman's winsome
comments on the weather. Another weather scene of Whitman's carries
some of the same matter-of-factness combined with ecstasy in the entry
for December 28, 1861: "Saturday night Mike Ellis—wandering at the
cor of Lexington av. & 32d st.—took him home to 150 37th street,—
4th story back room—bitter cold night—works in Stevenson's Carriage factory."

Whitman's *Notebooks* and *Daybooks* were those of a newspaper re-
porter as well as of a poet and of a homosexual. He tried to get it all
down in the fewest possible words. Thus: "Wm Culver, boy in bath,
aged 18 (gone to California '56 [)]" just above "Tom Egbert, conductor
Myrtle av. open neck, sailor looking." Uncoding the references here is
simple for any homosexual; the fantasies or types haven't changed that
much over the last century. Casement's *Diary* contains some similar
types, although he shows a condescension toward his objects of love

Matthew Brady photograph of Walt Whitman, 1862. Courtesy of the New York Public Library

which never appears in Whitman: August 8, 1910: "Arr. Para at 2, alongside 3.30. Tea and at 5 with Pogson to Paz Cafe. Lovely moco. Then after dinner to Valda Peso, two types, also to gardens of Pracao Republica, 2 types, Baptista Campos one type. Then Senate Square and Caboclo (boy 16–17) seized hard. Young stiff, thin, others offered later, on board at 12 midnight." Whitman did have a preference for blonds, but his tastes were eclectic. He recognized and loved a true queen in "James Lennon (Leonard), age 21 Spanish looking—I met on the ferry—night Aug 16 [1879]—lives toward Cooper's Point—learning machinists' trade—'fond of music, poetry and flowers.'" The last phrase sounds like a personal ad from today's gay papers.

The comparison to Roger Casement does suggest a similar plenitude. So many men, so many muscles, so many liaisons. The poet's notebooks resemble Casement's in their bulk of numbers and exceed Casement's in their loving details of the boys. Whitman tried never to uniform (even his soldiers) but to find what was unique and noteworthy in those he loved. Casement gives only the size, time and cost of his boys; Whitman is more of a pre-industrial craftsman in his recordings.

Finally, Whitman's *Notebooks* and *Daybooks* as clearly as the Calamus poems and as clearly as Casement's *Secret Diaries* present deep homoerotic images. What is most extraordinary in Whitman is the sheer number of men mentioned usually with some identifying fantasy tags. And likewise the few women mentioned by both diarists. Neither man was a woman-hater, but their sexual imaginations were stirred only by males. Whitman's lover Peter Doyle recalled, "I never knew a case of Walt's being bothered up by a woman. . . . His disposition was different. Woman in that sense never came into his head." Whitman had great respect for women, enjoyed their company and admired their achievements, but they appear most often in his notes as mothers, sisters, nurses, but never as lovers. He was thus the opposite of Virginia Woolf, who wrote that "women alone stir my imagination."

Entries from Whitman's Notebooks

March 10th '54   Bill Guess, died aged 22. A thoughless, strong, generous animal nature, fond of direct pleasures, eating, drinking, women, fun &c. —Taken sick with the small-pox, had the bad disorder and was furious with the delirium tremens. —Was with me in the Crystal Palace, —a large broad fellow, weighed over 200. —Was a thoughtless good fellow. —/

Manuscript page from Walt Whitman's notebooks, July 15, 1870; the initials P.D. for Peter Doyle have been changed to 16.4, and the pronoun "him" changed to "her." See pages 16 and 102. Courtesy of the Library of Congress

Peter—large, strong-boned youn[g] fellow, driver. —Should weigh 180. —Free and candid to me the very first time he saw me. —Man of strong self-will, powerful coarse feelings and appetites—had a quarrel, —borrowed $300—left his father's, somewhere in the interior of the state—fell in with a couple of gamblers—hadn't been home or written there in seven years. —I liked his refreshing wickedness, as it would be called by the orthodox. —He seemed to feel a perfect independence, dashed with a little resentment, toward the world in general. —I never met a man that seemed to me, as far as I could tell in 40 minutes, more open, coarse, self-willed, strong, and free from the sickly desire to be on society's lines and points—/

George Fitch.—Yankee boy—Driver. —Fine nature, amiable, of sensitive feelings, a natural gentleman—of quite a reflective turn. Left his home because his father was perpetually "down on him." —When he told me of his mother, his eyes watered. —Good looking, tall, curly haired, black-eyed fellow, age about 23 or 4—slender, face with a smile—trousers tucked in his boots—cap with the front-piece turned behind. —

Bloom. —Broad-shouldered, six-footer, with a hare-lip. —Clever fellow, and by no means bad looking. —(George Fitch has roomed with him a year, and tells me, there is no more honorable man breathing.)— Direct, plain-spoken, natural-hearted, gentle-tempered, but awful when roused—cartman, with a horse, cart &c, of his own—drives for a store in Maiden lane. —

Dec 28 [1861]—Saturday night Mike Ellis—wandering at the cor of Lexington av. & 32d st. —took him home to 150 37th street, —4th story back room—bitter cold night—works in Stevenson's Carriage factory./

Wm Culver, boy in bath, aged 18 (gone to California '56.

Tom Egbert, conductor Myrtle av. open neck, sailor looking

Lindenmuller's Halle 201 Bowery—large—lager beer. . . . The young fellows are good loking—and still they waltz, waltz, waltz. Some till they are red in the face, a gay assembly—a dance hall, perfectly respectable, I should think—some officers.

Thursday evening April 17th '62 The hour or two with Henry W. Moore, evening, in Broadway, walking up—and in Bleecker street. — the brief 15 minutes, night July 18th '62, from Houston st. up from a five blocks through Bleecker street

Sunday, May 25th '62 — Fort Hamilton/ *William Wylie*, Co E 5th (Jackson) Artillery sentry — at the south gate of the Fort — talk &c in the evening — English lad, 23 yr's old/

Mark Ward — young fellow on fort Greene — talk from 10 to 12 — May 23d '62

John Sweeten — tall, well-tann'd, born in New Jersey, — driver 40 4th av. May 27 '62, — was a boy, in Philadelphia riots of '44 (Aug 19 drives 23)/

Dan'l Spencer (Spencer, pere, 214 44th st. & 59 William somewhat feminine — 5TH av (44) (May 29th) — told me he had never been in a fight and did not drink at all gone in 2d N.Y. Lt Artillery deserted, returned to it   slept with me Sept 3d,

Wm Miller 8th st (has powder slightly in his face.)

Aaron B. Cohn — talk with — he was from Fort Edward Institute [upstate N.Y.] — appears to be 19 years old — fresh and affectionate young man — spoke much of a young man named *Gilbert L. Bill* (of Lyme, Connecticut) who thought deeply about Leaves of Grass, and wished to see me.

Theodore M Carr — Deserted Capt. Dawson's Co. C. Monitors Co. C. Col Conks 139th Reg. N.Y. Vol — met on Fort Greene forenoon Aug. 28 — and came to the house with me — is from Greenville Green County 15 miles from Coxsacki left Sept 11th '62

James Sloan (night of Sept 18 '62) 23rd year of age — born and always lived in N.Y. is an only son — lives with his mother and two young sisters — plain homely, American — No 7 on 23rd street — has driven cart and hack —

John McNelly night Oct 7 young man, drunk, walk'd up Fulton & High st. home   works in Brooklyn flour mills had been with some friends return'd from the war

David Wilson — night of Oct. 11, '62, walking up from Middagh — slept with me — works in blacksmith shop in Navy Yard — lives in Hampden st. — walks together Sunday afternoon & night — is about 19 —

Horace Ostrander Oct. 22 '62   24 2th av. from Otsego co. 60 miles west of Albany was in the hospital to see Chas. Green) about 28 yr's of age — about 1855 went on voyage to Liverpool — his experiences as a green hand (Nov. 22 16 4th av.) slept with him Dec 4th '62/

October 9, 1863, Jerry Taylor, (NJ.) of 2d dist reg't slept with me last night weather soft, cool enough, warm enough, heavenly.

Friday Feb 13th 1863 . . . met Lucien Cole, first walked around together a little, rode up in cars — he got out with me — his parents live in Washington — he is a miller, works somewhere in a flour mill between here and Baltimore)

Tuesday, Feb 17th 1863 . . . beautiful yesterday, I stood on the platform, rode down to the Capitol and back   I rode with yesterday, and felt I loved that boy, from the first, and saw he returned it,)

The Army Hospitals Feb. 21, 1863. . . . There is enough to repel, but one soon becomes powerfully attracted also.

Janus Mafield, (bed 59, Ward 6 Camp[bell] Hosp.) about 18 years old, 7th Virginia Vol. Has three brothers also in the Union Army. Illiterate, but cute — can neither read nor write. Has been very sick and low, but now recovering. have visited him regularly for two weeks, given him money, fruit, candy, &c.

Ward G Armory May 12 [1863] William Williams co F. 27th Indiana/ wounded seriously in shoulder — he lay naked to the waist on acc't of the heat — I never saw a more superb development of chest, & limbs, neck &c a perfect model of manly strength — seemed awful to take such God's masterpeice / nearest friend Mr. J. C. Williams Lafayette Tippecanoe co. Indiana

Albion F Hubbard – Ward C bed 7   Co F 1st Mass Cavalry/ been in the service one year — has had two carbuncles one on arm, one on ankle, healing at present yet great holes left, stuffed with rags — worked on a farm 8 years before enlisting — wrote letter — for him to the man he lived with/ died June 20th '63

Ward K Armory Sq Hosp . . . a young Ohio boy, Oscar Cunningham badly wounded in right leg — his history is a sad one — he has been here nearly a year — He & I have been quite intimate all that time. When he was brought here I thought he ought to have been taken by a sculptor to model for an emblematical figure of the west, he was such a handsome young giant, over 6 feet high, a great head of brown yellowy shining hair thick & longish & a manly noble manner & talk — he has suffered very much, since the doctors have been trying to save his leg but it will probably have to be taken off yet. He wants it done, but I think [he] is too weak at present.

MYRIADS OF NEW EXPERIENCES

April 7, 1864 . . . a cavalry company, evidently service-hardened men. Mark their upright posture in their saddles, their bronzed & bearded young faces, their easy swaying to the motion of their horses, their carbines, in their [holsters] by their right knees—Handsome, reckless American young men, some eighty of them gaily riding up the avenue then the tinkling bells of the cars. . . .

Wm B. Douglass, "Billy" running & walking—Washington/

John Elverson, young man on Fulton ferry—tall, sandy July '72

William Sydnor, driver car boy on Pittsburgh's car 7th st /

Dick Smith—driver 14th st. blonde/

John Ferguson driver 14th st—tall & slender/

James Amos aged 17 young Maryland man conductor 7th st March '69/

C. Edw'd Stevens—young man 20—red hair one I lent "Poliuto" to/

Camden Wm M Cauley, boy that brings Tribune/

John B. Ward—21, blacksmith no father, mother married again—/

Tom Eastlake, left hand off.

James McLaughlin. cor Morris & Henry./

David Fender—redhaired young man/

W.W. Bazarth, 921 Broadway, next to Church. Spruce st (carpenter) /

Camden, May 20. '75 Elijah Jeffers, (or Jeffries) boy of 14, Stevens st. cor 4th convoy'd me home from car

Eugene Burdine young man 19 or 20, works in printer, Treasury, lives on Capitol Hill

Frank Howard boy that asked for [illegible] cents to get his mother some meal

Baalam Murdock cond.—No. 12—(March 1870) / Marylander by birth—parents neither living—half-brothers only/—went to school several years but with little profit/

Lewellyn Harbaugh driver No. 4. aged about 25, was in the rebel army all through the war—was a cadet at Lexington Va. (aged 16) mother, brother &c. here (is of German or Swiss stock)/

Tom Riley, boy of 24 Irish at Shillingtons/

Lieut. Mews, marine corps tall, slender.—comes in to see Blakie

Emerson Campbell cond. Myrtle ave. aged 24—from Schoharie July '71

A Crawford Crook, Alexandria boy/ young man 19 or 20—in Entwistles drug store grey clothes

Young man got on car at bridge at night—Wm Smith friend of Jack Saunders

Car 32—Wash'n—Wm. Preston Williamson cond.—West Va—wishes he "could pick up some nice girl"/

Dick Smith blonde, driver 14th st—meet at office every night—at 1/2 past 8.

March 16 '69 Wm. J. Murray, works in Mach. Shop Navy Yard Monday Tuesday & Friday evening engaged

John Laughlin youth, hill boy, Treasury hill July 28 '69

Lloyd—young man in M St. bet. 10th & 11th /

Traverce Hedgeman young slight fair feminine conductor 7th/

Willy Halers, drumer boy in marine band/

John L Sanders, 30 depot—6 Navy Yard.

Eicholtz 274 D St near 13/Hinton east of I 434 D. 1 door below 4th Monday evening/

Wallace Loyd policeman on Av bet 12 & 13

James Delay—laborer Treasury building says he has known me 9 years/

James Farnum man in Bank 7th st. restaurant acquaintance/

Townsend Clement other young man in Smith & Strong frame shop

Stacey Potts, cond 13 aged 28—boyish looking

June 16th 78 . . . Alonzo Sprague, 33 years of age western—been 2 years with Frank Aiken the actor

[1879] Michael Healy Olive st cars Cincinnati (Maryland by birth) been with shows—(left home at 14)

[1885] Robert Pearson boy of 13 sandy Milliette's printing office, April 30 (boat). George, 30 hostler/ Zeke Lukens driver 15/ Daniel Lelkens German birth Orphan 16—born in Baltimore

Entries from Whitman's Daybooks

Hugh Harrop   boy 17   fresh Irish   wool sorter

Harry White Adams Ex   Phil — (in Race st)

Phila: Market st. 28th to 32nd — hill boy —

Alfred Childs Aug '79

Wm Clayton boy 13 or 14 on the cars nights — (gets out at Stevens &
2d) April '81

young Irishman, on the boat   Matthew Kelly   works at night on
the Phil: freight wharf

Frank Oakley, deck hand on Camden, blonde, (one eye def:

Thomas Colston ("Charley Ross") young on 122 car Union Line Phil

Thos: Woolston, young (19) cashier at Ridgeway House

Harry Garrison, my R R young man, sandy compl: at Ferry

James Lennon (Leonard) age 21 Spanish looking — I met on the
ferry — night Aug 16 [1879] — lives toward Cooper's Point — learning
machinists' trade — "fond of music, poetry and flowers"

Robt Wolf, boy of 10 or 12 rough   at the ferry   lives cor 4th &
Market

Wm C Pine — "Walt Whitman sociable"

Percy Ives, Mrs Legget's grandson, age 16, a student intends to be
an artist — lives bachelor's hall fashion in Philadelphia — reads Emerson, Carlyle, &c

Clark Hilton extra conductor on 105 Market st. — I came down with
(age 23-or '4) April 23, '81

Sammy Cox   boy 17 or 18 — Dick Davis's nephew — butter & cheese
business in market stand — ice cream — Apr' 81

Tasker Lay, boy 15 or 16, with Mr Lee

little black-eyed Post boy at ferry, Paddy Connelly

Alex: Anderson, cond: on 110 night of June 25

Walter Borton, charcoal driver   young man Kirkwood

Wm Stein, gun maker, Federal St. (tall young man at ball Dec. 8
'81)

Charlie McLean, driver, Stevens st.   looks like Harry Stafford

Jo McHenry 92 Market st. ("tripper") age 22 — Dec 9 '81   leaves ferry abt 4^{10} & 6 pm admires the sunset

In the car paid no fare   756 Mt Vernon St : Walter Dean   lad 14 or 15 (in Wanamakers.) Dec 12 met him again, March 21 — he is a fine boy

Harry Caulfield, 19, printer, "the Sentinel" — father dead, 8yr's, has mother & two sisters — is from Harrisburgh

Howard Atkinson, tall, sandy, young, country fied   Dec. '81 driver, Stevens — also 5th

Clement — — boy Stevens st cars — night

CHAPTER FOUR

Many Soldiers' Kisses

Tom Sawyer, Lewis Brown, Alonzo Bush, and Elijah Douglass Fox

THE UNITED STATES CIVIL WAR stands somewhere between the campaigns of Napoleon and those of World Wars I and II in extending mass production to human slaughter. In servicing soldiers, Walt Whitman participated in the massification of love and war. Opposed to slavery, a fervid supporter of the Union and of Lincoln, Whitman did not himself kill but instead worked as a free-lance nurse — a role fitting both his love of men and his Quaker background. In *Specimen Days* (1882), Whitman gathered some of his Civil War notes. Summing up three years (1862–5) in the hospitals, he recalled attending "eighty thousand to a hundred thousand of the wounded and sick." (Two soldiers died of disease for every one killed in battle.) Holding their hands and kissing their lips, Whitman sat beside many among the hundreds of thousands who died. His three years brought "the greatest privilege and satisfaction, (with all their feverish excitements and physical deprivations and lamentable sights)"; the war aroused in him "undreamed-of depths of emotion."

Gone With the Wind (either film or novel) doesn't tell everything about the Civil War. And despite the billions of words spent so far, most of the war remains unrecorded. Whitman himself prophesized that "the real war will never get in the books . . . Its interior history will not only never be written — its practicality, minutiae of deeds and passions, will never be even suggested . . .—perhaps must not and should not be." Constance McLaughlin Green in *The Secret City: A History of Race Relations in the Nation's Capital* (1967) has documented much that was hidden about Afro-Americans during and after the Civil War. The secret city of men who loved men has yet to be written; Walt Whitman is a primary witness of what happened during his years in Washington.

Allan Berube with the San Francisco History Project has been collecting accounts of homosexuals during World War II; this history has always been there, but before the recent wave of women's and gay liberation no one had recorded the wonderful new opportunities lesbians and gay men found during the 1940s. With the millions of homosexuals surviving from the Second World War, historians can still capture stories which would otherwise have been lost. Not a single person alive during the Civil War survives today; there can no longer be any direct interrogation of those who lived through that great struggle. Nonetheless, I think students of the Civil War can learn a lot from Berube's research. Virtually everything he has uncovered has parallels during the 1860s.

Certainly both the Civil War and the Second World War opened new gates of eroticism and opportunities for sexual liaisons. Not all men were queer but the armies were all same-sex; the concentration of male genitals often led one into another. And young boys separated from the pressures of marriage or family had unique opportunities to find new ways of expressing their passion. Michael Barton's profiles composed from published letters and diaries of four hundred soldiers do not fit Whitman's correspondents (*Goodmen: The Character of Civil War Soldiers*, 1981). Comparing Union and Confederate officers and enlisted men, he concluded that the Union enlisted men were the most laconic, least verbose and least expressive among the four groups. All of Whitman's soldier-correspondents violated these norms, including Tom Sawyer (the only officer), who inversely enough was Whitman's most laconic lover!

In *Specimen Days*, Whitman explained how the different could identify and ultimately find ways into each other's arms. He recalled, "Every now and then, in hospital or camp, there are beings I meet—specimens of unworldliness, disinterestedness, and animal purity and heroism. . . ." Externally they couldn't be distinguished—"marching, soldiering, fighting, foraging, cooking, working on farms or at some trade before the war—unaware of their own nature, (as to that, who is aware of his own nature?) their companions only understanding that they are different from the rest, more silent, 'something odd about them,' and apt to go off and meditate and muse in solitude" (*Specimen Days*). From a German-speaking companion, Whitman picked up the word, a word which seemed to capture something of this special quality. His comrade translated *Gemüthlich* as "full of soul heart manliness affection" (*Notebooks*, 728).

Whitman's procedures for finding such men were quite simple — the boys wanted and needed him as he needed them. In the "Summer of 1864" section of *Specimen Days*, he noted: "Some of the poor chaps, away from home for the first time in their lives, hunger and thirst for affection; this is sometimes the only thing that will reach their condition." His method of cruising the hospital wards was first developed in New York City. Describing the Broadway Hospital, Whitman wrote in the New York *Leader* (March 15, 1862) about Green: "This young man, while working as a driver on Broadway . . . was run over, and his leg broken in one place and badly mashed in another." While visiting Green, Whitman picked up another driver who was at the hospital. In the *Notebooks*, Whitman wrote: "Horace Ostrander Oct. 22 '62 24 4th av. from Otsego ca. 60 miles west of Albany [(]was in the hospital to see Chas. Green) about 28 yrs's of age — about 1855 went on voyage to Liverpool — his experiences as a green hand (Nov. 22 16 4th av.) slept with him Dec 4th '62/."

Washington provided special opportunities for picking up men because of its unsettled and overpopulated condition during the war. The city was not only the nerve center of the war command but was also directly on the battlefront; both the North and the South believed they had to capture the other's capital (Richmond and Washington respectively). Some of the bloodiest campaigns of the war were consequently fought in the relatively short distance between the two cities. Ulysses S. Grant's notoriously bloody Wilderness Campaign filled the hospitals with the wounded; seven thousand Union soldiers were killed in a few hours at Cold Harbor, Virginia, June 3, 1864: in the two-month battle, Grant lost sixty thousand men; Lee, twenty thousand.

Washington became a transient city on the grandest scale as seven thousand might march off to die in one day; twice that many return wounded to the hospitals. There were deserters, bounty jumpers, spies, Southern sympathizers, contractors, government workers, foreign diplomats, Southern soldiers who had been captured and paroled to the street and thousands of uncounted and unaccounted-for people thronging the city streets. A soldier wrote Whitman, "We are A compound mixture of all sorts Stage Drivers, Policemen, Hotel &

steam Boat runners. Old Sports in hard luck   Dry Goods Clerks & Broken Down merchants all mixed together & on the most friendly terms with each other."

For cruising, this was the perfect milieu. In a letter to soldier Tom Sawyer, Whitman wrote (April 21, 1863), "I guess I enjoy a kind of vagabond life any how. I go around some, nights, when the spirit moves me, sometimes to the gay places, just to see the sights." In May of 1865, Whitman described the scene: "The streets, the public buildings and grounds of Washington, still swarm with soldiers. . . . I am continually meeting and talking with them. They often speak to me first, and always show great sociability, and glad to have a good interchange of chat." And they "are continually looking at you as they pass in the street." They could be approached almost anywhere, Whitman said: "I always feel drawn toward the men, and like their personal contact when we are crowded close together, as frequently these days in the street-cars." Whitman describes in one of his *Notebooks*, Friday, Feb. 13, 1863, one of his street encounters: he "met Lucien Cole, first walked around together a little, rode up in cars—he got out with me—his parents live in Washington—he is a miller, works somewhere in a flour mill between here and Baltimore."

Whitman liked to go for walks in the country around the city, where security was surprisingly lax; Lewy Brown, a soldier comrade, wrote about riding out on the street-cars to one of the battles with a full car of curious civilians. The suburban woods provided many bushes and opportunities for love-making. Whitman also describes cruising Lafayette Park, the area opposite the White House, where I myself sucked a passing stranger's cock on a bench over a hundred years later. "*February 24th* [1863]. — A spell of fine soft weather. I wander about a good deal, sometimes at night under the moon. To-night took a long look at the President's house."

The boys often came back to his room, where there was more privacy. Whitman records in his *Notebooks* taking Justus Boyd home; the boy "went back to the hospital at dark," and a few days later (February 25, 1863), "When I came to L. street, to dinner, found Justus Boyd, waiting for me!" Boyd had been discharged and was on his way home but stopped by for a few parting kisses from his loving comrade. After the war (October 28, 1867), Whitman wrote another "Dear boy & Comrade" that he was "living at a boarding house, the same place where you come to see me, but new landlord & landlady— 472 M st. — it is quite pleasant—mostly young people, full of life & gayety."

Not all the soldiers would come up to his room, even after they had promised. The one whom Whitman claimed to love the most, Tom Sawyer, stood him up, and the poet wrote, April 26, 1863, "I was sorry you did not come up to my room to get the shirt & other things you promised to accept from me and take when you went away. I got them all ready, a good strong blue shirt, a pair of drawers & socks, and it would have been a satisfaction to me if you had accepted them." As Virginia Woolf remarked, "To Whitman there was nothing unbefitting the dignity of a human being in the acceptance either of money or of underwear, but he said that there is no need to speak of these things as gifts" (*Granite and Rainbow*). These were more than gifts, they were physical tokens; the underwear which Whitman had touched would then touch Tom's bulging crotch. The poet fantasized to his comrade, "I should have often thought now Tom may be wearing around his body something from *me*, & that it might contribute to your comfort, down there in camp on picket, or sleeping in your tent." He ends the letter with a question, "Well, Tom, how did you stand the gay old rain storm of Thursday & Friday last?"

Although he spent time street cruising and bringing the boys home, Whitman concentrated on the hospital wards. He wrote his mother, September 8, 1863, "I believe no men ever loved each other as I & some of these poor wounded, sick & dying men love each other." And in a letter to a friend, October 11, 1863, Whitman explained his soldier passion: "poor fellows, how young they are, lying their with their pale faces, & that mute look in their eyes. O how one gets to love them, often, particular cases, so suffering, so good, so manly & affectionate . . . lots of them have grown to expect as I leave at night that we should kiss each other, sometimes quite a number, I have to go round — poor boys, there is little petting in a soldier's life in the field. . . ." Whitman felt the boys needed spiritual as well as physical love, which he communicated in long, deep kisses. He believed his "boundless love" would cure their maladies: "The men feel such love, always, more than anything else. I have met very few persons who realize the importance of humoring the yearnings for love and friendship" (*New York Times*, December 11, 1864).

Whitman was well aware of the sexual current in his contacts with the wounded soldiers. He criticized those visitors who chose only attractive soldiers for their love: "Some hospital visitors, especially the women, pick out the handsomest-looking soldiers, or have a few pets. Of course, some will attract you more than others, and some will need more attention than others; but be careful not to ignore any patient"

View of Armory Square Hospital, Ward K, c. 1863–4. *The Photographic History of the Civil War* (1911). This is the ward that Whitman frequently visited.

(*ibid.*). During the eighteenth century, "mollies" had accompanied the soldiers; they were nurses, cooks and sexual companions. "Molly" could be either a man or a woman. Appointed superintendent of nurses in June, 1861, Dorothea Dix tried to cut down the erotic content of nursing by specifying that women nurses must be over thirty and "plain in appearance." Whitman heartily encouraged this trend. Even so, among the nurses about seventy-five percent were men. Around himself Whitman organized an erotic circle of male nurses, soldiers and patients who found time and places to play with each other.

Whitman throughout his life seems to have been a master politician/lover in balancing the needs and loves of his various companions who were often quite jealous. Among the thousands of soldiers, this problem was particularly acute since they often lay side by side in beds nearly touching: telling one he was the most loved could inevitably be overheard by others. In his relations with other soldiers, Whitman soon found an indispensable ambassador, Lewis K. Brown. A poor farm boy from Maryland, Brown had been wounded August 19, 1862, at the battle of Rappahannock, and lay several days in distress on the battlefield before being taken to the Washington hospitals, where he stayed many months. In his *Notebook,* Whitman recorded attending Brown during the boy's ordeal in January, 1864, when the boy's leg was "amputated five inches below the knee."

Through Lewis K. Brown, Whitman not only met other compatible soldiers, but Brown also served as a message carrier and go-between with all the boys. Brown seems to have been the center of a group of sexually inclined soldiers who managed to make out in the wards. Making out could not have been easy; the men were plopped down on cots with as many as sixty in a room. However, each ward had a captain's room, which provided some privacy. Alonzo Bush, a comrade soldier, wrote Whitman, "I am glad to know that you are once more in the hotbed City of Washington so that you can go often and see that Friend of ours at Armory Square, L[ewis] K. B[rown]. The fellow that went down on your BK, both so often with me. I wished that I could see him this evening and go in the Ward Master's Room and have some fun for he is a gay boy" (December 22, 1863). I tentatively identify "BK" as "buck," which in regional dialect can mean as a noun "cock" and as a verb "fuck." The initials may stand for a person or hospital bed. Other possible readings suggested by friends: "book," "basket," "bended knee," "beak," "bunk," "back," "buttock" and "big cock." However the initials are rendered, the scene is clear enough: the gay boys went into the ward master's office for sex. Brown was in Ward K where the Ward Captain was quite friendly. In another ward, Whitman was chased away by the master but begged back by a soldier, who wrote, "I hope that dont keep you away what the ward master told you that night" (William Stewart to WW, Washington, July 17, 1865).

Much of the male sexual interchange was justified only as a substitute during wartime for the more domestic, but unavailable male-female romance. Thus Bethuel Smith wrote Whitman, September 28, 1863, from a Pennsylvania hospital, "Carlisle is miserablaer than washington for women. I think friend walt I would like to Come & see you verry much." Comradeship could thus be seen as only situational, temporary. Whitman himself discouraged one veteran of Ward K who wrote him suggestive letters. Benton Wilson's letter of January, 1867, said, "I wrote to you a year and more ago that I was married but did not receive any reply, so I did not know but you was displeased with it. . . . I remain as ever your Boy Friend with Love." On April 7, he wrote that "I have got a good Woman and I love her dearly but I seem to lack patience or something. I think I had ought to live alone, but I had not ought to feel so." In love with Peter Doyle by then, Whitman replied cautiously: ". . . we must take things as they are. I have thought over some passages in the letter, but will not at present say much to you on the subject, in writing." Whitman didn't want Wilson to leave his pregnant wife and come to live with him; consequently, he concluded "that it is every way the best & most natural condition for a young man to be married. . . ." Learning his lesson, Wilson concluded on April 21, "I shall have to be more guarded in my letters to you."

Nonetheless, Whitman did not always see man-woman marriage as always "the best & most natural condition." He recognized and admired men lovers forming a kind of marriage. Thus in the summer of 1862, Whitman met a "fresh and affectionate young man" in New York, who "spoke much of a young man named *Gilbert L. Bill* (of Lyme, Connecticut) who thought deeply about Leaves of Grass, and wished to see me" (*Notebooks*, 487–8). And among the captured Southerners, Whitman spotted many soldier-comrades, some of whom may have been lovers: "Feb. 23, '65 — I saw a large procession of young men from the rebel army, . . . Several of the couples trudged along with their arms about each other . . . as if they were afraid they might somehow get separated" (*Specimen Days*).

Many of the soldiers lived as lovers during and after the war. Thus Alonzo Bush wrote in 1863 that "Johny Strain my companion wishes to be remembered to all   I am sorry to inform you that he met with another misfortune after he got here he was thrown from his Horse and had his arm broken but is getting along very well at presant." And Anson Ryder brought his fellow soldier home with him to Cedar Lake, New York; he wrote Whitman, August 9, 1865, "Wood is with [me] here at my old home says it is not very natural here does not seem at all like an hospital." And that "gay boy Lewis K. Brown," when he got out of the hospital, boarded in Washington "with Joseph Harris (who by the way sens his love to you). . . . Jo is not enjoying good health he is sick nearly half of his time. he did not know your address or he would of writen to you e'er this probily he will write & send some with this. Adrian Bartlett is boarding there allso & we will have a pleasant time of it" (LKB to WW, September 5, 1864). Three years later, Whitman wrote another soldier, "Brown is well. I see him often" (WW to Hiram Sholes, May 30, 1867).

Walt Whitman himself followed the dream inscribed inside Mary Todd Lincoln's wedding ring: "Love is eternal." His declarations to Tom Sawyer were unequivocal: "Dear comrade, you must not forget me, for I never shall you. My love you have in life or death for-ever. . . . my soul could never be entirely happy, even in the world to come, without you, dear comrade." And he always made clear that this sergeant was first in his heart: "Tom, I wish you was here. Somehow I don't find the comrade that suits me to a dot — and I won't have any other, not for good" (April 21, 1863). Tom Sawyer was a nearly illite-rate soapmaker from Cambridge, Massachusetts. The Sawyer family had come from rural Lancaster, a New England town, where farming was being abandoned as fertile western lands were brought into cultiva-tion. Walt Whitman may have met him in 1860 when he visited John Trowbridge, who shared Whitman's love of men and lived very near Sawyer. Trowbridge visited Washington in 1864. Those who suggest that Sawyer was uneasy about Whitman's passion misread the reserved response. Sawyer was a country Yankee boy descended from Puritans and not accustomed to passionate outbursts; expression of any kind was alien to him. He hated to write letters and got someone else to help him with his correspondence. Moreover, he was a minor officer, whose position dictated a certain formality. Nonetheless, he did re-ciprocate Whitman's advances; he wrote Lewis K. Brown on April 12, 1863, "I want you to give my love to Walter Whitman."

But he did not expect to come live with Whitman for the rest of his life. Whitman essentially proposed to him "that if you should come safe out of this war, we should come together again in some place, where we could make our living, and be true comrades and never be separated while life lasts — and take Lew Brown too, and never separate from him." And in another letter, Whitman proposed a common estate for his threesome: "I should feel it a comfort to share with Lewy whatever I might have—& indeed if I ever have the means, he shall never want" (May 27, 1863). Whitman made the same proposal to Lewy, "You speak of being here in Washington again about the last of August—O Lewy, how glad I should be to see you, to have you with me—I have thought if it could be so that you, & one other person & myself could be where we could work & live together, & have each other's society, we three, I should like it so much—but it is probably a dream . . ." (August 1, 1863).

The dream was fulfilled in a Rebel soldier boy, Peter Doyle, whom Whitman met in 1865 and the two became lovers for nearly a decade. While Doyle and Whitman were hardly inseparable, Doyle did see Whitman for the last time at the poet's funeral. Whitman kept in touch with the "gay boy" Lewy Brown, but Tom Sawyer passed out of sight. In 1867, Whitman wrote that "Tom Sawyer, (Lewy Brown's friend), passed safe through the war—but we have not heard from him now for two years."

War Letters

Thomas P. Sawyer to Lewis K. Brown, Camp near Falmouth, Virginia, April 12, 1863

Friend Lewis,

On my mussels and I have just got home from Pickett and I feel very tired but for all that I am agoin[g] to try and pen you a few lines to find out how you are getting along for it is over a week now since I rote to you and I have not received eny answer and I feel very anxious and want you to write   if you cant your self get Miss Smith or some one else to for you   I received a short letter from Walter yesterday but he did not say enything about you or Hiram so I have come to the conclusion that they have gon back on you and him but I hope not but there is one that never will go bad on you and that is Tom Sawyer   I suppose you [k]now him and now I should like to have send me word just how you are getting along for we are agoin to moove here soon and there is agoin to be a big Battle and I am agoin to have a hand in it to help crush this wicked Rebelion. I want you to give my love to Walter Whitman and tell him I am very sorry that I could not live up to my Prommice because I came away so soon that it sliped my mind and I am very sorry for it   tell him also that I shall write to him my self in

a few days   give him my love and best wishes for ever and tell him that I have got that little Book in witch he gave me, and I shall always keep it for old acquaintence sake. Lewis when you write home remember me to you Father and Mother and tell them that I have not forgotten my Promis, for if I live to get through this wicked war I shall go to Elkton and see you and them, give my love to Miss Smith and Slater and all the rest who may enquire of me and when I get any soap I shall send you some for what you lent me have when I came away and now I will tell you how I am getting along   well in the first Place I am in the best of health and so is Charles Robinson but we have him on pickett for 4 days and have just come home and I feel very tired and you must excuse this writing this time and I will try and do better next time so I shall bring this to a close hooping soon to here from you   I send you all that a friend can desire and wish your wound would get well. So good by for the preasant   I reman the same true friend
    Serg Thomas P. Sawyer
to Lewis R. Brown good night. Right soon

WW to Thomas P. Sawyer, Washington, April 21, 1863

 . . . Tom, I was at Armory last evening, saw Lewy Brown, sat with him a good while, he was very cheerful, told me how he laid out to do, when he got well enough to go from hospital, (which he expects soon), says he intends to go home to Maryland, go to school, and learn to write better, and learn a little bookeeping, &c. — so that he can be fit for some light employment. Lew is so good, so affectionate — when I came away, he reached up his face, I put my arm around him, and we gave each other a long kiss, half a minute long. We talked about you while I was there. . . . Tom, I do not know who you was most intimate with in the Hospital, or I would write you about them.
 . . . I guess I enjoy a kind of vagabond life any how. I go around some, nights, when the spirit moves me, sometimes to the gay places, just to see the sights. Tom, I wish you was here. Somehow I don't find the comrade that suits me to a dot — and I won't have any other, not for good.
 . . . Tom, you tell the boys of your company there is an old pirate up in Washington, with the white wool growing all down his neck — an old comrade who thinks about you & them every day, for all he don't know them, and will probably never see them, but thinks about them as comrades & younger brothers of his, just the same.
 . . . Dear comrade, you must not forget me, for I never shall you. My

love you have in life or death forever. I don't know how you feel about it, but it is the wish of my heart to have your friendship, and also that if you should come safe out of this war, we should come together again in some place, where we could make our living, and be true comrades and never be separated while life lasts — and take Lew Brown too, and never separate from him. Or if things are not so to be — if you get these lines, my dear, darling comrade, and any thing should go wrong, so that we do not meet again, here on earth, it seems to me, (the way I feel now,) that my soul could never be entirely happy, even in the world to come, without you, dear comrade. (What I have written is pretty strong talk, I suppose, but I mean exactly what I say.)

Thomas P. Sawyer to WW, Camp, April 26, 1863

Dear Brother,

As you have given me permission I have taken the liberty to address you as above, and I assure you I fully reciprocate your friendship as expressed in your letter and it will afford me great pleasure to meet you after the war will have terminated or sooner if circumstances will permit.

I am much pleased that Lewy is so cheerful and happy, and I trust he will be successful in his hopes and desires and be prosperous and happy and enjoy life to a good old age. I am sorry very sorry that Hiram has not improved. I was in hopes that ere this he would be sufficiently recovered to go Home and I sincerely hope that it will not be long until he can do so. It is [my] sincere wish that Johny Makey will survive the operation. and ultimately recover. I hope you will be more fortunate and procure a good berth, and be ever prosperous. We in the Army feel our reserves at Charleston and Vicksburg very deeply as yet we have not had a chance to strike a blow in our vicinity but as you say that time is near at hand and I hope we will be successful at any rate we will do out utmost and endeavor to give the Rebels the biggest thrashing they have yet received. Let the Government Officials in Washinsgton mind their own biz. let Hooker alone and the Army of the Potomac will be triuimphant but as long as they will continue to interfere with our Gen[era]ls arrangements, dictate to him when he shall move, and when he shall halt, just so long will the Army of the Potomac be of little avail. It is composed of good material, and all ready for a forward movement. then let Hooker have the reins, and he will soon drive the Rebs to Richmond and far beyond it.

Yes my dear Brother, You have my friendship as fully as you can desire, and I hope we will meet again.

Having nothing more of importance to communicate, I will conclude with my best wishes for your health and happiness and believe me to be Yours sincerely, Thos P. Sawyer

WW to Thomas P. Sawyer, Washington, April 26, 1863

...I was sorry you did not come up to my room to get the shirt & other things you promised to accept fom me and take when you went away. I got them all ready, a good strong blue shirt, a pair of drawers & socks, and it would have been a satisfaction to me if you had accepted them. I should have often thought now Tom may be wearing around his body something from *me*, & that it might contribute to your comfort, down there in camp on picket, or sleeping in your tent.

...Well, Tom, how did you stand the gay old rain storm of Thursday & Friday last?

...Not a day passes, nor a night but I think of you. Now, my dearest comrade, I will bid you *so long*, & hope God will put it in your heart to bear toward me a little at least of the feeling I have about you. If it is only a quarter as much I shall be satisfied.

WW to Thomas P. Sawyer, Washington, May 27, 1863

...Lewy Brown seems to be getting along pretty well. I hope he will be up & around before long — he is a good boy, & has my love, & when he is discharged, I should feel it a comfort to share with Lewy whatever I might have — & indeed if I ever have the means, he shall never want.

...My dearest comrade, I cannot, though I attempt it, put in a letter the feelings of my heart — I suppose my letters sound strange & unusual to you as it is, but as I am only expressing the truth in them, I do not trouble myself on that account. As I intimated before, I do not expect you to return for me the same degree of love I have for you.

WW to Lewis K. Brown, Washington, August 1, 1863

Both your letters have been received, Lewy — the second one came this morning & was welcome as any thing from you will always be, & the sight of your face welcomer than all, my darling — I see you write in good spirits, & appear to have first-rate times — Lew, you must not go around too much, nor eat & drink too promiscuous, but be careful & moderate, & not let the kindness of friends carry you away, lest you break down again, dear son —

...You speak of being here in Washington again about the last of August—O Lewy, how glad I should be to see you, to have you with me—I have thought if it could be so that you, & one other person & myself could be where we could work & live together, & have each other's society, we three, I should like it so much—but it is probably a dream—

...Dear son, you must write me whenever you can—take opportunity when you have nothing to do, & write me a good long letter—your letters & your love for me are very precious to me, for I appreciate it all, Lew, & give you the like in return.

Lewis K. Brown to WW, Maryland, August 10, 1863

My Dear Friend Walter,

Your very kind and long looked for letter of Aug 1st came to hand on the 6th & I was verry glad to hear from you but was verry sorry to hear that you wer so sick & I think that it would be much better for your health if you would give your self that furlou but I think that the boys about the Hospital could ill spare you, if you are as good to them as you wer to me. I shal never for get you for your kindness to me while I was a suffering so mutch, and if you do not get your reward in this world you will in Heaven.

Now I will put in a word for myself my leg still continues to mend verry slow but I hope sure, and I have ben enjoying my self as well as I could with my sore leg I have bin a way on a visit for a week & I have enjoyed my sel[f] verry much (for a wounded soldier is something hear I tell you) for the people wer so kind to me. Walter, we have a good many copperheads hear and some of them are verry rank I can tell you, and I have bin insulted by them twice since I came home, but I manage them verry well, I believe if I was in a battle & see a copperhead & a Reblle I would shoot the copperhead first, and to tell you the truth I am proud of my *wound* for I think that it is an honor to be wounded in this Cause. If I was able to enlist again, I would willingly do it. But we want first such men as you to stay at home and battle with treason in our midst, for I think that [a] good able Newspaper's correspondent dos a great deal to put down this rebelion & if we all leave home the rebbles will get to bold about home so I think that it is better as it is.

Well Walter how mutch I would like to see you out hear it is not near so warm out hear in the country and fruit is a getting ripe. Appels & Pairs & Peaches. & they are so nice to pull them of[f] of the trees them selves.

Walter I cannot write any thing that will interest you but I will try and fill up with something. The farmers are most all don Harvisting the crops are all light the wheat mostly was verry thin on the ground but well filled the Oats are verry light hardly worth a cutting (in fact there is a good many that wont cut them at all) the flax is allso short but there will be quite a lot of seed. Corn looks verry promising I dont remember of ever seeing it look better at this time of year. We have plenty of green corn to eat and it is very nice.

My Dear friend I hardly know what to put in this to interest you for I have wrot most everything that I can think of so I will give you a discription of My Fathers little place there is about 4 acres in it but the most of it is woodland we have a small stone hous about 18 by 24 ft. it has bin built about 6 years we are a going to build an end to it this fall about the same sise as it is too small, we have a nice little stable. We keep 1 horse and two cows and two hogs we have in a nice little field of corn & we had a nice little field of wheat & a pack of Irish Tralas, Water melons and cantilops, and every thing that is good & last though not least and a exelant spring of watter close to the door

Well I think I will have to fetch my letters to a close and you must not be angry for writing so much foolishness for you know that I am young and foolish all I have to add is my love to you good by and write soon from your ever faithful friend & companion,

L. Brown

WW to Lewis K. Brown, Washington, August 15, 1863

. . . Lewy, I feel as if I could love any one that uses you well, & does you a kindness — but what kind of heart must that man have that would treat otherwise, or say any thing insulting, to a crippled young soldier, hurt in fighting for this union & flag? (Well I should say damned little man or heart in the business) —

. . . Lew, you speak in your letter how you would like to see me — well, my darling, I wonder if there is not somebody who would be gratified to see you, & always will be wherever he is — Dear comrade, I was highly pleased at your telling me in your letter about your folks' place, the house & land & all the items — you say I must excuse you for writing so much foolishness — nothing of the kind — My darling boy, when you write to me, you must write without ceremony, I like to hear every little thing about yourself & your affairs — you need never care how you write to me, Lewy, if you will only — I never think about literary perfection in letters either, it is the *man* & the *feeling* . . .

WW to Thomas P. Sawyer, Washington, August, 1863

. . . I see Lewy Brown always, he has returned from his furlough, he told me a few days ago he had writen to you, & had sent you my best respects — I told him he must never send my respects to you but always my love. Lewy's leg has not healed, gives him trouble yet. He goes around with crutches, but not very far. He is the same good young man as ever, & always will be.

. . . Dear brother, how I should like to see you — & would like to know how things have gone with you for three months past. I cant understand why you have ceased to correspond with me. Any how I hope we shall meet again, & have some good times. So, dearest comrade, good bye for present . . .

WW to Lewis K. Brown, Brooklyn, November 8–9, 1863

. . . I am now home at my mother's in Brooklyn, N Y — I am in good health as ever & eat my rations without missing one time — Lew, I wish you was here with me, & I wish my dear comrade Elijah Fox in Ward G was here with me . . .

Lewy, I was very glad to get your letter of the 5th — I want you to tell Oscar Cunningham in your ward that I sent him my love & he must try to keep up good courage while he is confined there with his wound. Lewy, I want you to give my love to Charley Cate [ward master] & all the boys in War K & to Benton if he is [there still] — . . .

Lew, I wish you would go to Ward G & find a very dear friend of mine in bed ii, Elijah D. Fox, if he is still there. Tell him I sent him my best love, & that I make reckoning of meeting him again, & that he must not forget me, though that I know he never will — I want to hear how he is, & whether he has got his papers through yet — Lewy, I wish you would go to him first & let him have this letter to read if he is there — Lewy, I would like you to give my love to a young man named Burns in Ward I, & to all the boys in Ward I — & indeed in every ward, from A, to K inclusive, & all through the hospital, as I find I cannot particularize without being tedious — so I send my love sincerely to each & all, for every sick & wounded soldier is dear to me as a son or brother.

. . . My loving comrades, I am scribbling all this in my room in my mother's house. It is Monday forenoon — I have now been home about a week in the midst of relations, & many friends, many young men, some I have known from childhod, many I love very much.

. . . Lewy, dear son, I think I shall remain here ten or twelve days longer, & then I will try to be with you once again. If you feel like it I would like to have you write me soon, tell me about the boys, especially James Stilwell, Pleasant Barley, Cunningham, & from the calvary boy Edwin in ward B—tell me whether Elijah Fox in ward G has gone home—Lew, when you write to Tom Sawyer you know what to say from me—he is one I love in my heart, & always shall till death, & afterwards too—...

So, Lew, I have given you a lot of messages but you can take your time to do them, only I wish each of the boys I have mentioned to have my letter that wishes it, & read it at leisure for themselves, & then pass to another.

Elijah Douglass Fox to WW, Washington, November 10, 1863

Dear Father

You will allow me to call you Father wont you. I do not know that I told you that both of my parents were dead but it is true and now Walt you will be a second Father to me wont you, for my love for you is hardly less than my love for my natural parent. I have never before met with a man that I could love as I do you   still there is nothing strange about it for "to know you is to love you" and how any person could know you and not love you is a wonder to me. Your letter found me still here and not yet ready to start home   my Papers have not yet returned from headquarters. I almost wish at times that they would not return until you come back. Were it not for the great love for my wife I would stop until you returned but I still think I shall come back eer long. I think my papers will be in tomorrow certain.

Dear Comrade do not feel bad about anything you did or did not do while here. You did *much* and that which I prized most of all you gave me was your love and your company. One of these I know I have and for both I would charge all the riches in the world. As for your not coming to see me I felt bad about it then but now I think it only taught me how much I should miss you and also what a vacancy there would be in my affections were I to be deprived of your love as well as your company. I have not yet seen your letter to Brown as I did not get this until nearly dark but I will go up there in the morning and see if he has received it.

I suppose you have heard that we received some 90 wounded men Sunday night a number of which were Rebels. Among the wounded were the Col and the Maj. of the 6th Wisconsin Regt. and quite a number of privates a great many of them were very badly wounded, more so than any lot I have seen come in, eight of them died while on the way. And now Dear Comarade I must bid you good by hoping you will enjoy your visit and when you return have a pleasant and safe journey be assured you will meet with a warm welcome from many in Armory Square. You will yet be rewarded for your kindness to the Soldiers. (You can direct your next either as you did the last or direct to Portage Kalamazoo Co. Mich) if it comes here it will be forwarded to me. I shall start as soon as my papers come. My love to you and now Dear Father good by for the present. Douglass

WW to Thomas P. Sawyer, Brooklyn, November 20, 1863

. . . I shall be back in Washington next Tuesday. My room is 456 Sixth street. But my letters are still addrest care of Major Hapgood, paymaster U S A, Washington D C.

Well, comrade I must close. I do not know why you do not write to me. Do you wish to shake me off? That I cannot believe, for I have the same love for you that I exprest in my letters last spring, & I am confident you have the same for me. Anyhow I go on my own gait, & wherever I am in this world, while I have a meal, or a dollar, or if I should have some shanty of my own, no living man will ever be more welcome there than Tom Sawyer. So good by, dear comrade, & God bless you, & if fortune should keep you from me here, in this world, it must not hereafter.

WW to Elijah Douglass Fox, Brooklyn, November 21, 1863

. . . I am still here at my mother's, & feel as if [I] have had enough of going around New York — enough of amusements, suppers, drinking, & what is called *pleasure* . . . I cannot bear the thought of being separated from you — I know I am a great fool about such things, but I tell you the truth, dear son. I do not think one night has passed in New York or Brooklyn when I have been at the theatre or opera or afterward to some supper party or carouse made by the young fellows for me, but what amid the play of the singing, I would perhaps suddenly think of you — & the same at the gayest supper party, of men, where all was fun & noise & laughing & drinking, of a dozen young men, & I among them, I would see your face before me in my thought as I have seen it so often there in Ward G, & my amusement or drink would be all turned to nothing, & I would realize how happy it would be if I could leave all the fun & noise & the crowd & be with you . . .

Douglass, I will tell you the truth, you are so much closer to me

than any of them that there is no comparison — there has never passed
so much between them & me as we have — besides there is something
that takes down all artificial accomplishments, & that is a manly &
loving soul . . .

Elijah Douglass Fox to WW, Wyoming, Illinois, December 9, 1863

I expect to go into business here with Brother but do not know certain. . . . Since coming here I have often thought of what you told me
when I said to you I am certain I will come back to Washington. you
said to me then that a gret many of the boys had said the same but none
had returned. I am sorry it is so but after I had thought it over I
concluded it would be better for me to go into some business that
would be a periminent thing.

Alonzo S. Bush to WW, Glymont, Maryland, December 22, 1863

Friend Walt,
    Sir I am happy to announce the arrival of Your Kind and verry
wellcom Epistel and I can assure you that the contents ware persued
with all the pleasure immaginable. I am glad to Know that you are
once more in the hotbed City of Washington So that you can go often
and See that Friend of ours at Armory Square, L[ewis] K. B[rown]. The
fellow that went down on your BK, both So often with me. I wished
that I could See him this evening and go in the Ward Master's Room
and have Some fun for he is a gay boy. I am very Sorry indeed to here
that after laying So long that he is about to loose his leg, it is to bad,
but I Suppose that the Lords will must be done and We must submit.
Walter I Suppose that you had a nice time while at Home. I am glad to
report that I enjoyed my Self finely and had a gay time. Generaly I am
now paying up for the good times I had at Armory Square & at Home.
Just immagin that you see me at the dead Hour of night Standing
picket on the Potomac looking to see how things are going on and
pick up Deserters it is amusing to See how Sly they are in getting
over they come on rafts logs & any thing that will bear there weight
with oars muffled and as still as possible. And you may guess that they
are Some what suppriz[ed] on landing to find an escort of the first Ind
Cav waiting to See them Safe to Washington. We have caught over a
hundred in the last 2 months. They all Seam to be flush with money
and that goes to Show they are Sub[stitutes.] They come for money &
not country. We have verry good Quarters and plenty of Grub. Our
Shantys are of Logs and are very comfort[able.] Our Horses can not be

beat for they are fat and in Splend[id] Condition our Stables are made
of pine boughs and covered With Straw which turns rain and snow very
well considering

When off duty the boys enjoy them selves by Horse racing & Hunt-
ing Game is very plenty down Here ducks Quail Squirl & fox are the
chief ones Coons & opoposms are als[o] numerous. We have a good
pack of Hounds now and are training our Horses for a grand fox Hunt
on the 25th of this month   I wish you and Some of the boys ware here
to take a hand, as there will be fun, that you may depend on. I have
been waiting for a comission Ever cince I came Here but as yet I have
not Seen it. I expected to be in Washington before this on my way
Home to get my rights, if I dont get it I will not come to Washington
till the latter part of Jan or the first of Feb—and when I do come I will
be sure to give you a call. I want you to give my best wishes to the Lady
Nurse of Ward K also to W[ard] M[aster] Cate, Brown, Billy Clem-
ents, Miss Felton & all the rest . . .

Please to tell them each & every one that I would like to write to
them all but am So Situated that I can not but will call on them the
first time I come up. Tell Miss Lowell that her kindness to the Solders
undr her charge While I was there I never Shall forget and that I often
think of the games we used to play   Tell Miss Felton that I never will
forget the Watter cooler of Ward P. and as there are some of my Friends
that I have omited on account of names I hope you will as[k] Pardon in
my behalf. tell Brown to remember me to Joseph of the Starr.

Johny Strain my companion wishes to be remembred to all   I am
sorry to inform you that He met with another misfortune after he got
Here he was thrown from his Horse and had his arm broken but is
getting along very well at presant. My Love & best Wishes to all I will
close Hoping to Here from you soon.

I remain your True Friend, Alonzo Bush

Thomas P. Sawyer to WW, Camp near Brandy Station, Virginia, January 21, 1864

Dear Brother Walter,

As I have just written to Lewis I thought I would try and pen you a
few lines hooping that they will [find] you in the best of health and
enjoying your self—and I wish I was there with you.

Dear brother I hardly know what to say to you in this letter for it is
my first one to you but it will not be my last   I should have written to
you before but I am not a great hand at written and I have ben very

buisy fixing my tent for this winter and I hope you will forgive me and in the future I will do better and I hope we may meet again in this world and now as it is getting very late you must ecuse this short letter this time — and I hope to here from [you] soon. I send you my love and best wishes. Good by from

Your Brother, Sergt Thomas P Sawyer

P.S. if I knew your addrss I should not send it this Way. Good by Brother.

Lewis K. Brown to WW, Washington, July 6, 1864

Dear Walter,

I take my pen in hand as a final resort to find out where you are. as it appears to me it has bin six months since I seen you, I would like very much to see you & if I knew where you wer I would come & see you for I can never forget your love and friendship to me while I was in the Armory Square Hosp. It would be ungreatful in me to forget you & all you[r] many kindnesses to me. I have not herd from you for some time the last time I herd from you Jo Harris was telling me that you [weren't] well & that you wer on the Avinue & had a room there. I am still here & will stay untill August   I get out now most every day untill six oclock but I never see you   I have got my Artificial leg but cant walk very well on it but I think that practice will make me more perfect. I would like very much to see you come in here & spend the evening as you usd to do at the old Armory but alas I never see your [old] familliar in the threshold of my old tent.

The boys feels sadly at a loss not to have some one to come in and set awhile with them for there is no one here to do so, as you usd to at Armory Square. There is a great many wounded in the Hospital here & in this ward there is three very bad cases one of the Gangereene & two of the Erysipelas they wer removed from one of the other wards.

I am not going to write much to you but will come & see you as soon as I find out where you are at.

No more at preasant, but remain you[r] loving Solder,

L. K. Brown

WW to Lewis K. Brown, Brooklyn, July 11, 1864

Dear Comrade

I have rec'd your letter of the 6th as it has been sent on to me by Major Hapgood. My dear comrade, I have been very sick, and have been brought on home nearly three weeks ago, after being sick some ten days in Washington—The doctors say my sickness is from having too deeply imbibed poison into my system from the hospitals—I had spells of deathly faintness, & the disease also attacked my head & throat pretty seriously. . . .

Elijah Douglass Fox to WW, West Jersey, Illinois, July 14, 1864

Dear Comrade

I received your kind letter, and it will be impossible for me to tell how glad I was to hear from you again though very sorry to hear that you had been sick. Oh! I should like to have been with you so I could have nursed you back to health & strength, but if you were with your mother no doubt you were taken care of better than I could have done for you but I would liked to have been with you anyway I could have read to you and talked *with* you if nothing more   I am afraid I shall never be able to recompense you for your kind care and the trouble I made you while I was sick in the hospital unless you are already paid by knowing you have helped the sick and suffering soldiers many of them will never cease to remember you and to ask God's blessing to rest upon you while you and they live   there is no one such as you at least I have often thought of you and wondered where you were if you were still visiting Armory Square Hospt   I believe I wrote to you that you had two Children instead of one, you know I used to call you Father or "Pa," and I still think of you as such for I am sure no Father could have cared for their own child, better than you did me, if you could see your other child I think you would like her better than you did me for I do. I have *also* been very sick since you heard from me, for two weeks I knew nothing, was perfectly insane. I was taken with some kind of spasm and for two or three days many said I could not live but I had a good Doctor and have almost regained my health but think I shall never be able to do hard work again   Mary sends her love to you she often talks about you   she sends her thanks to you for your kindness to me and hopes you may soon regain your health, but I must stop for this time   write soon and often   the reason I did not write was that I wrote once and received no answer   I thought you had left there but now you shall hear from me often   no more   I remain your Son & Comrade   E. D. Fox

Lewis K. Brown to WW, Washington, July 18, 1864

My dear Friend

Your kind letter came to hand yesterday. I was very much supprised to hear that you wer in Brooklin I was also very sory to hear of your illness & to think that it was brought on by your unselfish kindness to the Soldiers There is a many a soldier now that never thinks of you but with emotions of the greatest gratitude & I know that the soldiers that you have bin so kind to have a great big warm place in their heart for you. I never think of you but it makes my heart glad to think that I have bin permited to know one so good.

I hope you will soon be enjoying good health again for it is one of God's greatest blessings I should like very much to see you back here but I suppose you must stay whear it suits your health best but I will still write to you for I can never forget your great kindness to me.

I have got my leg but I think that I will never be able to walk much on it as my stump is so short but if I cant I can go on my crutches for they appear to be a part of myself for I have bin on them so long I have not seen Jo Harris or Bartlett for over a weak but I believe they are both well they went to Baltimore on a spree on the 4 of July had had what they call a regular gay time, they wer prety hard looking after they got back,

Now a word for myself. I have not succeeded in getting a position in any of the Depts yet thoug my M.C. tried quite hard Gov Hicks tried also but there is so many aplicants for such positions that there is not much chance but I will still try for I do not like to give up after so much trouble.

I suppose you herd that J. A. Tabor was killed. he was killed in the wilderness the second days battle. I seen some men out of his company & they say that he fell dead when he was shot. The Hospitals are not so full now as they have bin transferring the men north as fast as they get able all the men in the Hospitals that are fit for duty are sent off to their regiments

The 4 of July pased of[f] here as usual there was a national salute fired from the surrounding forts & there was any amount of sky rockets. they comenced celebrating the 4th on Sunday evening after dark & they kept it up until morning I could not sleep a partical all night there being so much noise

Dear Walt I expect that I will tire you by writing so much but I must write & tell you about the rebs while they wer here if you get tired you must rest & begin again

They first maid their appearence on Sunday night some few miles from the City. On Monday there was great excitement in the City, the citizens armed them selves & went out to hold the rebs, in check, the soldiers that wer in the Hospitals wer formed into companys, & marched out to the fortifications & put in the Rifle pits, & there was some little skirmishing within about 1000 yards of fort Stephens, & some in front of fo[r]t Slocum. On Monday night the part of the 6th Army Corps came up and went out & part of the 19th Army corps came also; on Tuesday morning the excitement was intence the citizens in the Q.M. Dept & some in the War Dept wer armed and hurried out to the front 3 miles from the City limits. On Tuesday morning soon as I got my breakfast, George McArthur & I went & took the 1st cars & went out as far as they went then we walked out to fort Stephens (& it was a long walk for me on my crutches but I was eagre to see the fight if there was to be any) the guard let us through so we went up to the advance line of battle & seen the picquets firing the Rebs balls whistling over our heads (there was a motly set there for there was citizens women & Niggers all mixed up in a bunch) at last there was one of the rebel bullets struck a man in the head by my side & killed him that started some of the Citiznes to the rear with the women but I staid there untill there was another one of our men killed the ball striking him in the abdomen he expired in a few minuts at the same time the Colonel of the 98th Pa. (Blair) was brought in off of the skirmish line wounded in the head & thy[gh] & arm (I think that he was wounded in all three places) I then left the fort & went back in the woods in the shade. but prety soon the military ordered all non-combatants to the rear. some of the citizens took a gun & said that they wer determined to stay & see it out. So then I took my passage in a returnd ammunition train & came back to the Hospt on the same day the balance of the 6th & 19th Corps came & the Johnies got up & disstd for the rear they are now going back to rebeldon with their plunder with our arm[y] is following them.

After I came back I took sick the hot sun was to much for me & I have bin sick ever since but am able to be up—

No more at preasant but hoping very soon to hear from you, very affectionately yours,

L.K.Brown

Lewis K. Brown to WW, Washington, September 5, 1864

I once more after a long delay will endeavor to converse with you with the aid of pens & paper. I received a answer to my first letter stating that you wer at home sick. I was *very very* sorry to hear of it indeed, for it appears to be very hard for you to be sick, after being amongst it so much in the Hospitals & doing so much to seas [cease?] it among the suffering & sick Soldiers, but if it is the will of God I suppose it is for the best. I hope by the time this reaches you that you will be in the enjoyment of good health. I have got my discharge from the Hospitals about 3 weeks ago & am now employed in the Provost Marshall office at the corner of 18th & I St at the enrolling office I like the place very well but I dont know how long I will stay here. The salery is $3.00 per day & the work is very easy. We are allmost ready for the draft to come off I guess that by tomorrow Morning we will have all the cards wrote. there is over 2000 men to come out of the district & that is going to fetch some of the *old rats out of their holes.* There is a great deal of swindling done here now in the way of getting in substitutes they get some in that a[i]nt 15 years [old.] Some of the Brokers will make a man drunk & when he gets sober he will be a Soldier with the uniform on him. One of the detectives arrested a deserter belonging to the 14th Broklin Regiment that deserted at the first Battle of Bulls Run he has bin working for Adams & Co. Express here ever since until the detective got after him. he is now in Forrest Hall Georgetown. He will be assigned to some other regiment to serve the remainder of his time.

I was down at the Armory Square Hospital. things have changed very much there Dr. Bliss he charge. The amiable Miss Lowell is still there & will be untill the end of the *Chapter.* Cate is Ward Master. Benedict is M.C. little Billy is still there but his time is out the offices in the Ward each give him $5.00 per week to stay & dress their wounds for them

I Board down in the city with Joseph Harris (who by the way sens his love to you). I have bin boarding up on 18th & H st untill Saturday I moved down. Jo is not enjoying good health he is sick nearly half of his time. he did not know your address or he would of writen to you e'er this probily he will write & send some with this. Adrian Bartlett is boarding there allso & we will have a pleasant time of it he is still in the tresaury & I think probibly will stay for some time.

Well I must stop & go to work now I will finish after while.

Noon. I will now write some more. I took a trip down to Alexander a few days ago I went down in the Morning about 10 A.M. & came home about 4 P.M. I had a very pleasant time only I broke my *leg* just as I got ready to come home & had some little difficulty in getting home without my cruches I got so I could walk quite well on my leg only last week my stump took a notion to brake out & there has bin two small pieces of bone come out but I think in a little while I will be ready to wear my leg again.

The weather here has bin very bad but until within this last few days it has moderated & is now very pleasant. It looks very much like rain to day but I dont know whither it will get it down or not

I guess I have wrote about all I can think of this [time] so I must close hoping very soon to hear from you I remain very affectionately your most sincear friend Hoping you will forgive all mistake &c I am as ever yours

"Fall In for Soup," engraving by Edwin Forbes, c. 1862. The *Walt Whitman Quarterly Review* (Fall 1985) identifies the third man in line as possibly the poet.

Hustling the Good Gay Poet

Nicholas Palmer

IN HIS 1855 PREFACE to *Leaves of Grass*, Whitman wrote, "If the savage or felon is wise it is well . . . if the greatest poet or savan is wise it is simply the same . . . if the President or chief justice is wise it is the same . . . if the young mechanic or farmer is wise it is no more or less . . . if the prostitute is wise it is no more nor less" (Whitman's ellipses). The poet had an abiding interest in prostitution, but heretofore critics have assumed that all Whitman's prostitutes were women. That illusion should have been dispelled by his lines in the 1856 *Leaves of Grass* about "the she-harlots and the he-harlots." One letter to Whitman presents new evidence about male prostitution in the nineteenth century, about prostitution in *Leaves of Grass* and about Whitman's curious sexual disguises. Nicholas Palmer wrote Whitman June 24, 1865, from a Union army camp near Louisville, Kentucky. His letter suggests that male hustling may have been no less organized in Lincoln's time than now.

The last Confederate troops surrendered May 26th, and the young soldier was worried about employment after his discharge. Many soldiers faced problems of returning to civilian life. Thousands stayed in the army, which went West and attacked polygamy and Indians. General Sherman, who had commanded Palmer, is famous for saying, "The only good Indian is a dead Indian." Several soldiers wrote Whitman for assistance and he did what he could in most cases. Some correspondents offered curious propositions. Justus F. Boyd, whom the poet had brought to his rooms in Washington, now wrote from Detroit, asking for an exchange of photographs, and concluding: "Now Mr. Whitman if you could get me a situation as Bookeeper or Clerk . . . I will pay you any price your a mind to ask" (September 18, 1864).

Nicholas Palmer's 1865 letter is only a more explicit and specific solicitation. Palmer said he was experienced in the "variety of ways of making a living." Hard work did not appeal to him, so he makes a clear proposition: "Name anything you Please and if I do not Propose to accept: that is as far as it will Go. I will *blow* on no one." By "blow" he meant "blow the whistle," of course, but the underlining suggests the word meant what it does today, fellatio. And when he writes "I have been over the world," is he perhaps suggesting today's gay slang "going around the world"?

The poet immediately wrote a long note on the letter—a message intended for posterity, not Palmer, who received no reply. Whitman's attempt to dissociate himself from the soldier only corroborates Palmer's suggestions. Whitman acknowledges he met him in Washington and that Palmer "came one rainy night to my room & stopt with me—" Whitman worked among the soldiers as a volunteer; he held no position as military nurse and worked during the day in the army Paymaster's office. Thus when he took the boy "to my room" at "night," he was doing more than comforting a lonely serviceman far from home. The phrase "stopt with me" carries sexual overtones. Stops within *Leaves of Grass* often have erotic suggestions. Thus in "The Wound-Dresser":

> . . . I stop,
> With hinged knees and steady hand to dress wounds,
> I am firm with each, the pangs are sharp yet unavoidable,
> One turns to me his appealing eyes—poor boy! I never knew you,
> Yet I think I could not refuse this moment to die for you,
>   if that would save you.

While the nurse acknowledged bringing the soldier-boy back to his room, he pretended to be scandalized by Palmer's question, "What about Such houses as we were talking about?" Just the asking of the question, however, provides some significant clues to the grounds of the discourse. Obviously both Whitman and Palmer knew instantly that "Such houses" were houses of prostitution, houses of prostitution for boys. In his note, Whitman uses the word "curiosity" twice, but his amazement is not at the suggestion that such houses existed, his amazement is that the soldier was trying to con him. As he says, "& yet I itch to satisfy my curiosity as to what this young man can have really taken me for." Male hustlers sometimes offer more trouble than pleasure.

Houses of prostitution operated quite openly in New York throughout the time Whitman was there. They were centered first in the notorious Five Points area (near the Williamsburgh ferry, later bridge) and subsequently expanded into the Bowery. And virtually every bar and many of the balconies at operas provided assignation spaces. Judge John M. Murtagh and Sara Harris in their study *Cast the First Stone* (1957) describe some of the houses: "Kit Burns's place, Sportsman's Hall, occupied the whole of a three-story frame house on Water Street and featured, among other attractions, and in addition to young girl prostitutes, Jack, the Rat, Kit's son-in-law, who would decapitate a live mouse for ten cents and a rat for a quarter. One-armed Charley Monell, assisted by Gallus Mag, a giant Englishwoman who always kept her skirts up with men's suspenders and dragged obstreperous customers out by their ears, ran the Hole-in-the-Wall at the corner of Dover Street. Big Sue, the Turtle, a 350-pound Negro woman, ran a thirty-five-cent house for seamen and fishermen on Arch Street between Broome and Grand." As the city expanded, the houses multiplied; a complex in the area between Fifth and Seventh avenues and 24th and 40th streets came to be known as Satan's Circus. In 1866, one bellowing minister asked his congregation whether they were "aware that there are more prostitutes than Methodists in our city?"

Walt Whitman was fully aware of all these activities, and he sympathized with the prostitutes, not the Methodists. He calculated that nineteen out of twenty young men had visited a prostitute. In the Brooklyn *Daily Times,* Whitman praised Dr. William Sanger's book on prostitution and denounced the Brooklyn authorities for not answering the doctor's questionnaire. Whitman complained of the "pseudo modesty of this hypocritical age [which] shrouds [prostitution] with darkness, and refuses to look at it" (December 9, 1858). When the New York police responded to the publication of Sanger's book by attacking prostitutes, Whitman denounced the government policy: "The police . . . neither vigorously put down all such places, nor tolerate them, under inspection; but every now and then make a descent on a particular quarter, destroy the last vestige of self-respect in the unhappy outcasts by herding them with thieves in the Tombs and on the Island, rendering them more promiscuous in their associations thereafter, and more liable to incur and propagate disease." The police and politicians, nonetheless, made big money on their operations through "a mere system of black mail and favoritism, neither vindicating law and public decency, nor guarding the young from demoralization, nor affording any chance of reclaiming the unfortunates themselves" (June 20, 1859).

"What about Such houses as we were talking about?" Most writing on brothels has been about women — and most likely men passing as women. There are reports of boy houses in the Middle East, and of the molly houses in eighteenth-century England. During the 1890s, Earl Lind (Jennie June) cruised the Five Points and Bowery areas where he paid young rough boys for sexual favors. During World War II, the Senator from Massachusetts and chair of the Naval Committee, David Ignatius Walsh, was caught — along with composer Virgil Thomson — in a raid on a boy whorehouse in Brooklyn. President Roosevelt used war censorship powers to keep the story out of the newspapers (*Fag Rag* no. 8).

There was a vast population of young boys — many lonely and homeless — thronging the rapidly expanding cities such as New York. The famous newsboys — for instance — whom Horatio Alger courted and celebrated — and the somewhat older boys living in boarding houses. Allan Berube has identified the streets of Horatio Alger's *Rugged Dick* as rendezvous points for hustlers and older men. The New York houses were developing specialties to appeal to those wanting French sex (blow jobs) or English sex (spankings). Wouldn't a boy-house be altogether easy to arrange? A madam could set up a "boarding house," which those "in the know" could visit. If they did not exist in New York City, can one imagine New Orleans without such houses? Walt Whitman lived and worked there between February and May, 1848. And if there were no boy-houses, there must have been boys dressed as women, who passed as women and who specialized in the increasingly popular French pleasure of fellatio. Earl Lind's *Autobiography of an Androgyne* (1918) and *The Female Impersonators* (1922) document the close ties between heterosexual and homosexual prostitution.

The idea of boy houses of prostitution puts Whitman's own writings and dealings with prostitutes in a new light. Some Whitman students believe they have identified Mlle. Sophie Farvacer — whose address appears twice in his address/notebook in early 1863 — as a "woman" he had sex with. Mlle. Farvacer was listed in the Washington, D..C. directory as an "artiste." What if she were in fact a drag queen who gave French sex — blow jobs — as part of her artistry? Bruce Rogers' *gay talk* (1979) gives the following usage: "I'm not a queer, you moronic prig; I'm an artiste par excellence!" Edward Grier first identified Farvacer and suggested that she might be a "member of the anonymous 'Ballet of Feminine Loveliness' "—an obvious showplace for those seeking assignations with men. Whitman preferred the butch transport workers, but 1863 was a trying time—war, dying, amputations. He had just fallen in love with Sergeant Tom Sawyer who was exposed to enemy fire in the notoriously deadly Wilderness Campaigns. What better time for him to try something unusual?

If in fact Mlle. Sophie Farvacer was a drag queen who used a French name to let customers know she gave blow jobs, the correspondence with Will Wallace takes on a whole new light. Wallace was himself a nurse stationed in a Tennessee hospital. Wallace hailed Whitman as the Prince of Bohemians, and urged him to come visit the hospital in Tennessee. Wallace wrote in a letter, "I have never had better health in my life, perhaps I can explain it to you. I have five young ladies who act in the capacity of nurses—i e, one of them is French, young and beautiful to set your eyes upon. Can you not visit us and note for yourself?" (April 5, 1863). Whitman's reply is lost, but evidently he referred to Mlle. Farvacer, his artiste, who may have given him VD and whom he had stopped seeing. Wallace wrote back, "I am surprised at your frenchy leaving you in such a deplorable state, but you are not alone. I had to dismiss mine to save the reputation of the Hospital and your humble servant." *gay talk* defines "frenchy" as "cocksucker" or "artiste." And provides an example of usage—"I'm Irish by birth and French by injection." Whitman himself was most Frenchy in the 1860 edition of *Leaves of Grass,* which first included the Calamus poems. The poet added many French titles: "Salutation" became "Salut Au Monde!" The amative love section "Enfans d'Adam" became "Children of Adam" in subsequent editions.

Thus the correspondence with both Nicholas Palmer and Will Wallace might be working on the same line, indeed might possibly be traced to one drag queen. Certainly, as every homosexual knows, the quickest way to get into the pants of a straight boy is to start talking about women who give blow jobs. Once this pleasure is established as desirable, the next move is to ask what difference there is between a boy's and a girl's mouth. Throats, except for the Adam's apple, are gender-free sexual organs. If there's no difference, then why not drop your pants?

The close connections between homosexuals and whores are being lost in some circles, who seek respectability, but before 1969—if not now as well—our fates and paths have been intertwined. "Gay" itself probably derives from a French word for prostitute. Gay/lesbian/whore bars have almost always been in the same neighborhoods, have been

Inscribed in soldier's hand: "Walt! I am Will W. Wallace." Wallace was a cocky Whitman correspondent during the war. Courtesy of the Library of Congress

operated by the same families, and have shared the same harassment from politicians, clergy, police and purity crusaders. Pfaff's — Whitman's favorite New York bar before he went to Washington in 1862 — was in part just such a rendezvous place for fags, whores, artists, writers and others of a bohemian nature. The Bowery was a busy prostitute area during the 1860s and in the 1890s at least one gay bar in the neighborhood (which allowed prostitution) was raided.

A curious dichotomy developed after the 1830s — at least among the middle classes. The ideology of Pure Womanhood contained both a harsh, vindictive attitude toward so-called fallen women and at the same time sentimentalized the prostitute. On the harsh side, there was the snobbery of Mrs. Jonathan Starr, who was outraged that a woman she took to be a prostitute was better dressed then herself. She denounced the lady with a floppy green hat and gathered together the Female Benevolent Society, which began an unsuccessful ministry to fallen women. The wealthy Lewis Tappan hired a man from Princeton, who stole four thousand dollars, to redeem the Mary Magdalenes, but all that came out of this effort was the ravingly insane "Awful Disclosures of Maria Monk," which blamed prostitution on convents and Catholicism. Lewis Tappan nearly went bankrupt in the depression of 1837 and his project was abandoned, but the condescension of the middle class grew even greater.

The sentimentalization of prostitution was more prominent in European literature, but many in the United States thrilled to the trials of Camille, first in the translation of the younger Dumas's novel and then in stage productions in 1853, 1857 and 1874. Walt Whitman attended the 1857 production and he also caught Verdi's *La Traviata* in 1858. The plot of the novel, play and opera is quite simple — the courtesan gives up the one man she loves in order not to ruin family's advancement into the middle class. She then returns to her supposedly shallow rounds of frivolities and, of course, soon dies to many tears. Walt Whitman started to write a "Poem on a Prostitute's Funeral" and sketched out a plot outline for a prostitute story similar to *La Traviata*. The Camille fate still appeals to homosexuals. *gay talk* defines Camille as a "homosexual who goes from one tragic love episode to another. Most often sarcastically directed at one who over-exaggerates and therefore, perhaps, delights in his misfortune: 'That one's a real Camille, never has one happy thing to talk about.' "

Whitman's experiences as a homosexual cannot help but have shaped his poem, "To a Common Prostitute," which first appeared in the 1860 edition lumped as a Messenger Leaf with "To Him that was Crucified,"

"To one shortly to Die," and "To a Cantatrice." "To a Common Prostitute" seems to have upset the censors most; Ralph Waldo Emerson
wanted it out in 1860, and in 1882, the Boston District Attorney
banned the book in part because of this loose poem. Ezra Heywood
was arrested and served time in prison for publishing the poem. Emerson, at least, could understand the "Calamus" poems as sweet flag
flowery friendship such as he himself felt for beautiful young men, but
he did not want that love connected with something so disgusting as a
"common prostitute." Here there could be no ambiguity — at least so it
seemed. But the first manuscript for the poem did not use "My girl,"
but instead the more ambiguous "My love." Thus Whitman's first
thought may not have been of a woman at all. "My love" could have
been — indeed, almost certainly was — "My boy." Later, as he saw the
boys — literally dying as he tended their wounds — he told at least one
of them the story about a house which offered boys; and when one took
up the suggestion, he was quite unhappy to be so callously hustled.
So he concluded by writing, "& yet I itch to satisfy my curiosity as to
what this young man can have really taken me for." This might have
been a good time for him to reread "To a Common Prostitute":

> Be composed — be at ease with me — I am Walt Whitman,
>   liberal and lusty as Nature,
> Not till the sun excludes you do I exclude you,
> Not till the waters refuse to glisten for you
>   and the leaves to rustle for you,
>   do my words refuse to glisten
>   and rustle for you.
>
> My love I appoint with you an appointment,
>   and I charge you that you make preparation
>   to be worthy to meet me,
> And I charge you that you be patient and perfect till I come.
>
> Till then I salute you with a kiss on your lips that you do not forget me.

Johns still talk about love, but they want you to remain patient and
perfect till they come.

Nicholas Palmer Letter

Nicholas Palmer to WW, Camp near Louisville, June 24, 1865

Mr. Whitman, Dear Friend,
   I concluded I would talk a few words to you, through this instrument. I am well and hope the safe arrival of this may find you the same. There is not much talk of the Vetterans Getting Out. Yet if you have any thing in the way of advice to Give Concerning my imployment when I am Discharged, names talk Plain to me Mr. Whitman. I have been over the world more Perhaps than you would imagine. There are a grat many cruel turns and there are a variety of ways of making A living. Leaving hard work out of the Books, I'd have thought that there were bigger fools than me making a living Very Easy. Although I admit my Education is Limited, name any thing you Please and if I do not Propose to accept: that is as far as it will Go. I will *blow* on no one. What about Such houses are we were talking about? And [What?] if it Could be made agreeable for me to take up Lodgeing in Close Proximity with yours? I Should be Pleased in the Superlative Degree. Please write amediately after you receive this and Give me Some advice No matter what Sort. I conclude hoping to hear from you soon. Until then, I remain your Friend, as Ever, Nicholas D. Palmer

Note in WW's hand:

June 28th, '65. I have rec'd many curious letters in my time from one & another of those persons (women & mothers) who have been reading "Leaves of Grass"—& some singular ones from soldiers—but never before one of this description—I keep it as a *curiosity.* The writer was one of the soldiers in Sherman's army last of [May]—one of the hundreds I talked with & occasionally showed some little kindness to—I met him, talked with him some.—he came one rainy night to my room & stopt with me—I am completely in the dark as to what "such houses as were were talking about," are—
   —upon the whole not to be answered—(& yet I itch to satisfy my curiosity as to what this young man can have really taken me for)

Inscribed in Whitman's hand: "Washington, D.C. 1865 — Walt Whitman & his rebel soldier friend Pete Doyle." Courtesy of the Library of Congress

Whirled among Sophistications

Peter Doyle

AMONG WHITMAN'S working-class lovers, Peter George Doyle left more trace than any other. Dr. Richard Maurice Bucke published an introduction, interview and Whitman's letters to Doyle in *Calamus, A Series of Letters Written during the Years 1868–1880 by Walt Whitman to a Young Friend (Peter Doyle)* (Boston, 1897). Whitman didn't meet Doyle until 1865 (five years after first publication of the Calamus poems); nonetheless, by filling so many of the poet's fantasies, Doyle is commonly remembered as Whitman's Calamus lover. Prefigurations of Doyle appear in Whitman's notes and correspondence. In February, 1863, Whitman cruised a cute, streetcar number, a passenger on the same line where he later met Doyle: "beautiful yesterday, I stood on the platform, rode down to the Capitol and back[.] I rode with yesterday, and felt I loved that boy, from the first, and saw he returned it" (*Notebooks,* 561). In a letter, March, 1863, to "my darlings, my gossips," the poet described his love for a Confederate soldier: "a young Mississippi captain (about 19) that we took prisoner . . . poor boy, he has suffered a great deal, and still suffers — has eyes bright as hawk, but face pale — our affection is quite an affair, quite romantic — sometimes when I lean over to say I am going, he puts his arm round my neck, draws my face down, &c. quite a scene for the New Bowery" (*Correspondence,* 1:81–2). Doyle himself had worn the Confederate grey.

Two characteristics of Doyle appealed to Whitman's sensibilities: the blarney and the suffering — common elements in much gay culture. Doyle had many stories of his past, which varied according to circumstances. Thus biographers will probably never know when he was born; 1845, 1847 and 1848 are years given by Doyle; "in or near Limerick, Ireland," the probable birthplace. He suggested several dates for his arrival to the United States. Doyle always retained some of his boyish playfulness, an impishness, which can be noted in the fragments of the letter of January 20, 1878, when he promises, "If the Spirit moves me, I will give you my opinion of the book . . ." Like many gay men, Doyle liked firemen and uniforms (two of his brothers were Washington policemen). In 1868, he asked Whitman to bring him a New York Fire Brigade badge.

Although Doyle was often whimsical and light-hearted, his adversities moved Whitman deeply. During the 1857 depression, his father Peter, a blacksmith, took the family to Richmond, where several Doyles were employed by Tredegar Iron Works. Young Doyle himself became a Confederate soldier, but how he passed from the rebel army into Whitman's arms remains obscure, as does the date of their meeting. Whitman suggested that Doyle had been captured, imprisoned and/or injured, escaped and came to Washington, D.C. He was listed in the 1864 Washington Directory as a "laborer"; therefore, Doyle would have been in the city in 1863 when the directory was being compiled. Whitman autographed a photograph of himself and Doyle sitting on a love seat: "Washington, D.C., 1865 — Walt Whitman & his rebel soldier friend Pete Doyle."

Pete Doyle's love-at-first sight account of their meeting rings true to any gay ear. Forty years later, Doyle recalled the night they first met:

> It is a curious story. We felt to each other at once. I was a conductor. The night was very stormy, — he had been to see Burroughs before he came down to take the car — the storm was awful. Walt had his blanket — it was thrown round his shoulders — he seemed like an old sea-captain. He was the only passenger, it was a lonely night, so I thought I would go in and talk to him. Something in me made me do it and something in him drew me that way. He used to say there was something in me had the same effect on him. Anyway, I went into the car. We were familiar at once — I put my hand on his knee — we understood. He did not get out at the end of the trip — in fact went all the way back with me.

The shifting confusion of dates in the young man's life combined with another element to appeal to Whitman, Doyle's sorrows. As much a Calamity as a Calamus character, Doyle always had a sorrow to relate to Whitman. He told the poet that the ship carrying him from Ireland nearly brought him to the bottom of the sea: Whitman wrote in his

WHIRLED AMONG SOPHISTICATIONS

notebook: "The heavy storm & danger, Good Friday night — 1853 — almost a wreck." Doyle provided a first-hand account of Lincoln's assassination, which Whitman included in his lectures on Lincoln. Their surviving correspondence begins in 1868 and continues until they were parted by Whitman's death in 1892; the poet's running motif is encouragement for Doyle in his misfortunes. Whitman gathered stories of trains which wrecked and mailed them to Doyle; evidently melodrama and catastrophe appealed to both their sensibilities.

They were openly affectionate and in continuous contact during the early years of their relationship. John Burroughs described the two men together: "I give here a glimpse of him in Washington on a Navy Yard horse car, toward the close of the war, one summer day at sundown. The car is crowded and suffocatingly hot, with many passengers on the rear platform, and among them a bearded, florid-faced man, elderly, but agile, resting against the dash, by the side of the young conductor, and evidently his intimate friend." Whitman helped a mother whose screaming baby he held until it fell asleep, "utterly fagged out." And then when Pete needed a break, Whitman (carrying the fagged baby) conducted the car.

Another account from 1867 by William Douglas O'Connor describes the remarkable transformation which came over Whitman in his relationship with Doyle. "A change had come upon him," according to O'Connor, "The rosy color had died from his face in a clear splendor, and his form, regnant and masculine, was clothed with inspiration, as with a dazzling aureole." Whitman — "lifting his clear face, bright with deathless smiling, and wet with the sweet waters of immortal tears" — explained what had made the difference: "Love, love, love! That includes all. There is nothing in the world but that — nothing in all the world. Better than all is love. Love is better than all." In an autographed presentation copy of *Specimen Days,* Whitman in 1883 reminded Doyle of their good times together:

> Pete do you remember — (of course you do — I do well) — those great long jovial walks we had at times for years (1866-'72) out of Washington City — often moonlight nights, 'way to "Good Hope";' or, Sundays, up and down the Potomac shores, one side or the other, sometimes ten miles at a stretch? Or when you work'd on the horse-cars, and I waited for you, coming home late together — or resting chatting at the Market, corner 7th Street and the Avenue, and eating those nice musk or watermelons?

That Walt Whitman and Peter Doyle were a couple within a gay community in Washington can be glimpsed in the letter from Ned

Stewart, who was convalescing in Nova Scotia during 1870. In the letter Stewart used the word "gay" three times and used the pronoun "Her" with quotation marks. He writes about two theaters which contained drag artists in the chorus shows, "I suppose there is gay times at Met[ropolita]n & Canterbury halls, *Moses* but I wish I was there with you old Covies for awhile." Covey, coven or covenant suggests a gay circle among Whitman and his friends. Doyle had a witty sense of humor, and Ned quotes a Doyle limerick about a farmer who couldn't build his chimney high enough to prevent Tom cat's pissing on his fire. And he begs Walt Whitman to send a picture of the two lovers together.

As with all couples, when things are going smooth, there is no record; but during crises, records accumulate. The first emergency came in 1868, when Whitman went to New York on September 15th and Doyle remained in Washington. Whitman wrote Doyle regularly: September 18, 22, 25, 29; October 2, 6, 9, 14, 17, 18, 23. Among the very few Doyle letters to survive, seven of them come from 1868 (September 18, 23, 27; October 1, 5/6, 9, and 14). Why Whitman needed to spend so many weeks in New York is not entirely clear. I suspect he wanted to get away from Doyle. On October 26, Whitman was back in Washington and the correspondence temporarily ceases. Again home visiting his mother in Brooklyn in 1869, Whitman wrote Doyle, warning him against suicide: "Dear Pete, dear son, my darling boy, my young & loving brother, don't let the devil put such thoughts in your mind again — wickedness unspeakable — murder, death & disgrace here & hell's agonies hereafter — Then what would be afterward to the mother? What to *me?* — Pete, I send you some money, by Adam's Express — you use it, dearest son, & when it is gone, you shall have some more."

Everything seemed cheerful when Ned Stewart wrote in February, 1870: "I suppose by Pete's letters that he was as gay as usual, but guess the boy is coming to his senses and thinking about settling down in life and is going to benefit by the numerous oportunities which he has. How does he & the widow [Doyle's mother] pull together now, I suppose I [will] find you & Pete in the same box when I return to Washington." However, by the summer, the relationship had heated up as Whitman made his famous diary entry of July 15, 1870, in which he resolved to suppress his "adhesiveness" or love of men. But again visiting his mother, Whitman wrote Doyle affectionately on July 30th: "I never dreamed that you made so much of having me with you, nor that you could feel so downcast at losing me. I foolishly thought it was all on the other side. But all I will say further on the subject is, I now see clearly, that was all wrong."

Two unresolvable changes in their lives were brought on by time. Most gay couples undergo changes sometime between three and six years after they meet — a time when their sexual passion either cools or is transformed. When the age range is great between the couple, even more difficulties arise. Pete had been a teenager when he met Walt, who was nearing fifty. As Pete grew older, he was no longer a boy; and as Walt grew older, he began to suffer the infirmities of age. The strains of his relationship with Peter interwove with his own deteriorating health and his mother's death. Whitman suffered a stroke on January 23, 1873, in Washington. In 1889, the poet recalled Doyle and told Horace Traubel, "I wonder where he is now? He must have got another lay [sic!]. How faithful he was in those sick times — coming every day in his spare hours to my room — doing chores — going for medicine, making bed, something like that and never growling!" Convalescing from his stroke and the shock of his mother's death in May, 1873, Whitman retired to his brother's house in Camden, New Jersey. He never rejoined Peter.

Unlike several of Whitman's lovers (Vaughan, Brown, Stafford, Rogers and others), Doyle never married, lived a bachelor life, and became something of a quean. Walt Whitman told an English friend (J. W. Wallace) that Doyle hardly represented the average American because, "For years past Pete has been whirled among the sophistications." "Sophisticate" here could be a synonym for "homosexual," since as a baggage clerk Doyle hardly led the life of an esthete. Doyle thus ceased to be straight trade, but Whitman always remembered him kindly. The two remained in correspondence and made occasional visits; for instance, in 1880 Doyle traveled to Niagara Falls to accompany Whitman on his return from Ontario to New Jersey. In 1891 Whitman told one of his visitors, who asked about Doyle, "I should like to know where Pete is as I am rather uneasy about him. The cars used to come to Philadelphia, and he came here every week."

Whitman sent Doyle many letters and cards (the bulk of which Doyle preserved), but Whitman saved virtually none of Doyle's letters. One theory suggests that Whitman destroyed all of the letters; another suggests that the letters survive squirreled away. But my own suspicion is that Whitman thought Doyle's writings so worthless that he simply never saved them. Two letters (November 7, 1875, and January 20, 1878) were cut into pieces and used as scrap paper. Pete's declining favor in his lover's eyes can be traced in Whitman's wills. In 1873,

Whitman left his gold watch to his brother and the silver one to Pete:
"I wish it given to him, with my love." After the brother died and
Whitman had met young Harry Stafford, Harry was to get the gold
watch; Doyle, silver (1888); in the final codicil (1892), Horace Traubel, gold; Stafford, silver; Doyle, nothing.

Doyle was almost not admitted to Whitman's funeral in 1892, but
Whitman admirers like Traubel, Bucke and others kept track of him;
they published an 1895 interview with his letters from Whitman.
Doyle died in Philadelphia in 1907 and was buried in Washington,
D.C., in the Congressional Cemetery, at 18th & E Streets (S.E.). On
March 20, 1981, the *Washington Blade* printed a picture of Doyle's
tombstone with an article by Haviland Ferris, "Portrait of the Young
Man as Friend of the Poet."

Peter George Doyle like so many gay boys had many stories, but
among them all runs one consistent strain. He suffered greatly and
found happiness only in his love with Walt Whitman. In the 1895
interview, Doyle brought out a raglan of Whitman's and explained, "I
now and then put it on, lay down, think I am in the old times. Then
he is with me again. . . . When I get it on and stretched out on the old
sofa I am very well contented. It is like Aladdin's lamp. I do not ever
for a minute lose the old man. He is always near by." Doyle subtly
echoed the Calamus conclusion: "I that was visible am become invisible,/ . . . Fancying how happy you were if I could be with you and
become your comrade;/ . . . Fancying how happy you were if I could be
with you and become your comrade;/ Be it as if I were with you. (Be
not too certain but I am now with you.)"

Peter Doyle Letters

Peter Doyle to WW, Washington, September 18, 1868

Dear Walt,

I could not resist the inclination to write to you this morning   it
seems more than a week since i saw you   there is hardly anything of
interest transpired since you went away except occasionly some one
inquires for the *Major* or the *General* or some familiar name which no
doubt which you have heard so often   Dear Walt, I have examined that
book (Pollard's History) and i am Very much displeased with it. i find
it is quite the opposite from what i was led to believe   i thought it
mentioned the movements of the different companys & Regiments   i

Walt Whitman, 1883. Courtesy of the Library of Congress

am sorry that i made such a mistake because the Book is of no interest
to me

inclosed you will find something from this morning's Cronicle   it
seems the Washington Papers has you right for once   i am very impa-
tient to hear from you to know that you are doing well. Dave & all the
rest of the Rail Road boys is well & sends their best respects   Mother
had a very sick headache when i left home this morning   i have
to cut this short as i write a part of it while the car is in motion   farewell, Peter Doyle

Peter Doyle to WW, Washington, September 23, 1868

7 1/2 O clock Evening
Dear Walt,

As i send this I am getting ready to go to the Theater to see the
Black Crook   Nothing new today but the Weather Very Wet & Stormy
& i am afraid to Venture to work until the storm is past   just received
your letter of the 20th about ten minutes ago   i cant explain the
Pleasure i experience from your letters

Farewell my good & true Friend, Pete the Great
Alfred Goldsmith has this letter

Peter Doyle to WW, Washington, September 27, 1868

Dear Walt,

I visited the Theatre since i wrote last to see the Black Crook. i had
no idea that it was so good   Some of the scenes was magnificient.
Harry (No 11) sends you his love says he wished you would go to the
city Hall at the sheriffs office and see Michael Halloran tell him all
about him (Harry) & ask him how 48 Hose is. & if there is any chances
of getting into the Fire Department   also to give my respects to all
inquiring friends & ask him if i can get one of the old Exempt Fire
Badges. Dear Walt you have no idea how much interest the boys takes
in your letters

That second letter of yours has gone all around to them as you
mentioned   you could not think how happy it makes them to think
that you remember them. Pittsburg sends his love & would like you to
write to him   his address is Lewis Wraymond 7th St. R.R. office   i
could not see the young man Sy[d]nor   he is sick & not at work.
Jimmy the Californian on 7th St.   RR Jim Sorrill sends his love & best
respects & says he is alive & kicking but the most thing that he dont
understand is that young Lady that said you make such a good bed

fellow. also Charley Sorrill sends his love & is glad to hear you are doing so well   Towers is Very much pleased at your letter & sends his love

Henry Hurt sends his love & is very thankful for the Broadway that you sent him   I saw another game of Base Ball last friday between the Cincinatti & the Olympix   the game was all one sided   at the end of the game the score stood Olympic, 22 & the Cincinatti 9. I received your 3rd letter yesterday the 26 & also a copy of the Broadway and am Very thankful for them   in Friday Star you will find some Remarks of Mr. Hinton in some of the Equal rights associations for Females

There is nothing new here at present Congress all gone home & everything Very dull   raining continually for nearly 2 weeks and everything looking Very miserable   I have been off for a few days but i resumed operations again yesterday the 26th   all seems to be quiet along the Potomac once more except a little skirmishing between the Sailor the Superintendent & the Rail Road boys occasionaly let me know if you get the Star every evening

Walt you cant think [how] much pleasure i derive from our letters. it seems to me Very often that you are With me and that i am Speaking to you. good bye Dear Walt until i write again, yours Truly Walt, Pete

Peter Doyle to WW, Washington, October 1, 1868

[*Swann Auction Galleries, April 4–5,* 1951, *Sale* 285, #576, *lists this letter with the few lines below quoted. Who bought the letter and where it is now located are unknown.*]

i showed your letter to Jimmy Sorrill & it tickled him very much as he did not know that i told you what he said about that young lady. He sends his best love. . . . & all the rest of the boys send love. . . . I expect you will get tired of so much scribbling as it's done with a lead pencil & very often in the car.

Peter Doyle to WW, Washington, October 5/6, 1868

Dear Walt,

I should have wrote to you saturday or yesterday, but i lost the Two last [Washington] Stars paper. i had them on the car & somebody took them out   However, i will get them today & send them to you   you will find them interesting as Fridays paper contains a piece about you   the same i think that was in the NY Times & saturdays paper has got a letter from Mr. Noyes   by the way, Mr. Noyes is in town   he was on my car yesterday (sunday) & he looks first rate   i told him i sent you the star containing his letter and it seemed to please him very much. I have seen Pittsburg & showed him the letter you wrote to him   it pleased him firstrate to mention them N.y. Drivers   he told Me to send his love & also to state that Wm Sydnor is well and allright again & is at work   Jim Sorrill sends his love & says Charley's baby is well & doing first rate   Dave is well & sends you his love & says he wont go to the Springs again for a long time yet & told me to ask you if you wont take a trip with us tonight   Richings Opera troupe is drawing good houses   they bring out two new operas this week, one is your favorite, Travi[a]ta   they are also sweeping the Dust & Cobwebs out of the Walls Opera House   the[y] open tonight with Uncle Toms Cabin.

I would like to send you a Picture of Dave   as i write this, he is about two thirds asleep in one end of the car while i sit in the other end writing this letter   I received your letter of the 2nd all right on Saturday, also the N.y. Times   I sent you a letter on Friday which will explain how i am getting along   i am doing tip top at present   Yours as Ever, Pete

P.S. as i was sealing this up to send away Mr. Hart of the Cronicle stepped on the car & asked me if i sent him the Ny Times   i told him i expected it was you & he seemed Very much pleased with it   it came too late for the sunday cronicle, so he will put it in some of the Daily

Peter Doyle to WW, Washington, October 9, 1868

Dear Walt,

I received your Welcome letter on the 8 ins accompanied With a copy of New York Herald   I am Very thankful for the Paper   but i think your description of the Procession beats theirs all to pieces   I can almost imagine myself Wedged & Blocked in on a 3rd Ave car. Nothing of interest here at present   every thing looks Very Dull & Miserable   yesterday & today is Very Cold   leaves all falling off the trees strewing the ground in every direction   since i wrote last, i came across Sydnor driver of 7th St   he is well & doing first rate   he sends his love & best respect. Mr. Hart got on my car last night on my last trip. We had a long conversation about everything in general   first we commenced on home affairs   he is troubled a good deal about a house he bought & now wants to get rid of it   We next started on Politics   he would Vote for Grant but he is no Radical & last we wound up with Newspapers   he wants to start a paper here soon   he is tired of working for others   You may not be interested with his

affairs so i will come to close   excuse this short letter as my car is going
[to] start & i want [to] put this in the mail   good bye   My Dear friend
   Pete
i will write a long one next Sunday as i am off

Peter Doyle to WW, Washington, October 14, 1868

Dear Walt,
   since i received your Papers last Monday i have been Very anxious to
write to you but the Death of one of my Cousins delayed me somewhat
& yet there is nothing unusual going on here   I believe the road is
running the same as when you went away with the exception of our
new President   During Monday & Tuesday there was a good deal of
excitement over the elections in the several states but today it has got
back to old standing   there is also a report out here that there was a
Plot to assasinate the President but i dont think there is any truth in
the report   all the boys sends their love   Pete x x [indicates two big
kisses?]
I sent you a letter last sunday

WW to Peter Doyle, Brooklyn, August 21, 1869

[*In this letter Whitman reassures and upbraids his lover for having considered
suicide after the boy's face broke out in a rash, which Dr. Bucke diagnosed as
"barber's itch." Doyle feared venereal disease and Whitman's own deteriorating
health was not reassuring.*]

   I have been very sick the last three days—I dont know what to
call it—it makes me prostrated & deathly weak, & little use of my
limbs. . . .
   And now, dear Pete, for yourself. How is it with you, dearest
boy—and is there any thing different with the face? Dear Pete, you
must forgive me for being so cold the last day & evening. I was
unspeakably shocked and repelled from you by that talk & proposition
of yours—you know what—there by the fountain. It seemed indeed to
me, (for I will talk out plain to you, dearest comrade,) that the one I
love, and who had always been so manly & sensible, was gone, & a fool
& intentional murderer stood in his place. I spoke so sternly & cutting.
(Though I see now that my words might have appeared to have a
certain other meaning, which I didnt dream of, insulting to you, never
for one moment in my thoughts.) But I will say no more of this—for I
know such thoughts must have come when you was not yourself, but

in a moment of derangement—& have passed away like a bad dream.

Dearest boy, I have not a doubt but you will get well, and entirely well—& we will one day look back on these drawbacks & sufferings as things long past. The extreme cases of that malady, (as I told you before) are persons that have very deeply diseased blood, probably with syphilis in it, inherited from parentage, & confirmed by themselves— so they have no foundation to build on. *You* are of healthy stock, with a sound constitution, & good blood—& I *know* it is impossible for it to continue long. My darling, if you are not well when I come back I will get a good room or two in some quiet place, (or out of Washington, perhaps in Baltimore,) and we will live together, & devote ourselves altogether to the job of curing you, & rooting the cursed thing out entirely, & making you stronger & healthier than ever. I have had this in my mind before, but never broached it to you. I could go on with my work in the Attorney General's office just the same—& we would see that your mother should have a small sum every week to keep the pot a-boiling at home.

Dear comrade, I think of you very often. My love for you is in-destructible, & since that night & morning has returned more than before.

Dear Pete, dear son, my darling boy, my young & loving brother, don't let the devil put such thoughts in your mind again—wickedness unspeakable—murder, death & disgrace here & hell's agonies here-after—Then what would it be afterward to the mother? What to *me?*—

Pete, I send you some money, by Adam's Express—you use it, dearest son, & when it is gone, you shall have some more, for I have plenty. I will write again before long—give my love to Johnny Lee, my dear darling boy, I love him truly—(let him read these three last lines)—Dear Pete, *remember*—Walt

Edward ("Ned") Stewart to WW, Plaister Cove, Nova Scotia, February 25, 1870.

[*The use of the word "gay" three times in this letter suggests the word was used then as it is today; also the enclosing of "Her" in quotation marks suggests a gender inversion.*]

Dear Friend Walt,

Yours of the twelfth Just rec'd, was very glad to hear from you.

There is some mistake about Peters letters. I have received four or five from him, no fear of your "photo" not reaching here, wish you had have sent it   I would like very much to have yours also Peters if you have a double one of yourself & Peters I would like very much like to have that   if not, why [not] stir Pete up and make him send me his   you send yours also.

Yes you may safely put you & I down in your log as two good friends (even if one old & one young, as you say).

I suppose by Petes letters that he was as gay as usual, but guess the boy is coming to his senses and thinking about settling down in life and is going to benefit by the numerous opportunities which he has. How does he & the widow pull together now, I suppose Ile find you & Pete in the same box when I return to Washington.

I suppose there is gay times at Met[ropolita]n & Canterbury halls, *Moses* but I wish I was there with you old Covies for awhile, never mind Ile be back very soon now, think Ile stay here till August or September then will come home for a month at least if not to stay there altogether. Ive got a grand chance here with some Lady whose Pa happens to have some spare cash   think he would settle up pretty lively should I take one of his Daughters. He is the American Consul for this place so you see there's no knowing how it may turn out. I am having quite a nice time among the Elite of this place. Ive just joined the Sons & Sisters of Temperance "British Lodge" & am making fine progress. Rode the cussed Goat last night & feel quite stiff over it. I wish you could have heard me speechifying for them   you know everyone has to do that who joins. They wanted me to give them a recitation but twas no go unless they would take that familiar old piece of Peter's (Something about the Man who could not get his chimney up high Enough to keep his neighobrs Thomas cats from putting out his fire) Ha Ha, That would have been fine but the girls up this way are very modest so I got off quite an *Elaborate* address in which I expressed my Phellow Phelinx to the best of my abilities & wished the cause of Temperance Everlasting progress & said I supposed that in the course of a few more years I hoped there would be no such thing as Intemperance. (Was interrupted with "hear" "hear" and any amount of cheering & in the midst of the cheering I brought my speech to a mighty sudden close & sat down the hero of the evening.

Hows that for a Lager beer imbiber   Eh, guess it makes you open your eyes somewhat. I am still improving in health, getting more blooming every day people who saw me on my way here & who have been here within last month didnot recognize the pale youth who passed them last summer. Ime as strong as a buck. Eat as much hash & porridge as usual.

Ime going to surprise you all when I do come home   none of you

will know it   Just see if you will recognize the Boy who left Washington some time ago   Ive got over my home-sickness & am I suppose as
hard-hearted as the rest of humanity when they've left home for the
first time determined to enjoy themselves to their utmost, but for all
that there's no place like home as the song goes.

I received several challenges from several young Ladies here, through
some very flattering valentines with something like this inscription on
them. "A hand" with "If you can get   will you accept" quite a nice
thing but as it came from wrong quarter why I didn't accept.

So Ile beg you to exucse this writing which is done in a very big
hurry as i have made an Engagement to go out Driving in Sleigh with
"Her" & the time is drawing near a head   So I'll close sending you &
Peter much Love.

P.S. Tell Pete Ile answer his as soon as rec'd   Snowing here now, Adieu,
Yours Muchly, Ed C. Stewart

"Continuation"
Eleven Oclock P.M.

Well, Walt, Ive just returned from that ride I mentioned   I was
away about twenty miles on the Blue Mountains of Cape Breton   had
gay time, Saw any amount of Indians of Mickmac Tribe. Ive promised
that young Lady to show her your picture so you will not disappoint
me. Today I received two papers, from Pete I suppose, Sunday Chron-
[icle] & Balti[more] Sun.

No more at present   Yours Infernally (as Old man "Weller," says in
Pickwick, Ned

Notebook entry, July 15, 1870.

[*Walt Whitman's notebook entry might have aroused less interest had he not
disguised Peter Doyle's initials with numbers (16th letter, P; 4th, D) and
replaced "him" with "her." The poet was disguising what he called "adhesiveness." The entry appears under the title "Epictetus," the Stoic philosopher, who
is often confused among Whitman scholars (and perhaps by Whitman himself)
with Epicurus, whose teachings Whitman had admired as a young man. On
Fred Vaughan, see Chapter 2; Edward Grier, Notebooks, 890n, presents
details on Jenny Bullard (1828–1904), who lived out her life with two other
women in Ipswich, New Hampshire.*]

Cheating, childish abandonment of myself, fancying what does not
really exist in another, but is all the time in myself alone—utterly
deluded & cheated by *myself*, & my own weakness—REMEMBER WHERE

I AM MOST WEAK, & most lacking. Yet always preserve a kind spirit & demeanor to 16 [Peter]. BUT PURSUE HER[HIM] NO MORE.
A COOL, GENTLE, (LESS DEMONSTRATIVE) MORE UNIFORM DEMEA-NOR — give to poor — help any — be indulgent to the criminal & silly & to low persons generally & the ignorant, but SAY little — make no explanations — *give no confidences* — never attempt puns, or plays upon words, or utter sarcastic comments, or (under [ordinary] circum-stances) hold any discussion or arguments.
  It is IMPERATIVE that I obviate & remove myself (& my orbit) *at all hazards,* from this incessant *enormous & abnormal*
                              PERTURBATION
  TO GIVE UP ABSOLUTELY *& for good from the present hour this* FEVER-ISH, FLUCTUATING, *useless* UNDIGNIFIED PURSUIT *of* 16.4 [P.D.] — *too long, (much too long)* persevered in, — so humiliating — — *it must come at last &* had better come now — (*It cannot possibly be a success*) LET THERE FROM THIS HOUR BE NO FALTERING, NO GETTING *at all henceforth,* (NOT ONCE, UNDER *any circumstances*) — *avoid seeing her*[him], *or meeting her*[him], *or any talk or explanation* — or ANY MEETING WHATEVER, FROM
                   THIS HOUR FORTH, FOR LIFE
                                                        July 15 '70
Outline sketch of a superb calm character
his emotions &c are complete in himself, irrespective of whether his
    love, friendship &c are returned or not
He grows, blooms, like some perfect tree or flower, in Nature, whether
    viewed by admiring eyes, or in some wild or wood, entirely unkown
His analogy is as of the earth, complete in itself, enfolding in itself all
    processes of growth effusing life & power, for hidden purposes
Depress the adhesive nature/
It is in excess — making life a torment/
All this diseased, feverish disproportionate adhesiveness/
Remember Fred Vaughan/
Case of Jenny Bullard/
Sane Nature fit & full Rapport therewith/
Merlin strong & wise & beautiful at 100 years old.

WW to Peter Doyle, Brooklyn, July 30, 1870

Dear Pete,
    Well here I am home again with my mother, writing to you from Brooklyn once more. We parted there, you know, at the corner of 7th

st. Tuesday night. Pete, there was something in that hour from 10 to 11 oclock (parting though it was) that has left me pleasure & comfort for good — I never dreamed that you made so much of having me with you, nor that you could feel so downcast at losing me. I foolishly thought it was all on the other side. But all I will say further on the subject is, I now see clearly, that was all wrong. . . .

Peter Doyle to WW, Washington, November 7, 1875

[*This letter is on Baltimore and Potomac Rail Road Co. stationery, and has been cut into three pieces and used by Whitman as scrap paper for drafting another letter. Mr. Nash was Doyle's uncle.*]

Walt,
     . . . Your Welcome Letter recieved. I have just come from Mr. Nash's and had a good Square dinner. Wish you was [here]. . . . [He said] to tell you to come on and they would do the best they could to make your visit pleasant. I will meet you at the Depot   the train gets to Wash-[ington] 4:10 PM.
     i will Say no more until i see you, So Long, Pete

Peter Doyle to WW, Washington, January 20, 1878

[*This letter was cut up and used as scrap paper by Whitman for preparing his Lincoln lectures; the surviving pieces are preserved in the Library of Congress Harnet Collection.*]

Dear Walt
     Thanks for Sending [*Autumn Rivulets* (?) & "Walt Whitman in 1878," *West Jersey Press,* January 16, 1878, and] to do so soon. If the Spirit moves me, I will give you my opinion of the book when I have read it carefully that is if you should care to know my opinion. The photograph . . .

Peter Doyle Interview

[*Peter Doyle had lost contact with Walt Whitman during the last decade of the poet's life. Doyle's appearance at the funeral in 1892 piqued the interest of Dr. Richard Bucke and Horace Traubel, Whitman's literary executors. They approached Doyle and convinced him to give up letters Whitman had sent Doyle over the years. (The earliest surviving letter is from 1868.) Bucke and Traubel interviewed Doyle in 1895; they presumably used the techniques for recording*

*that Traubel had perfected in his record of conversations with Whitman begin-
ning in 1888* (With Walt Whitman in Camden, 6 *vols.* 1905–1984).
Dr. *Bucke published the letters and the interview in* Calamus: A Series of
Letters Written during the Years 1868–1880 by Walt Whitman to a
Young Friend (Peter Doyle); Edited with an Introduction *(1897). The
interview also appeared in* The Complete Writings of Walt Whitman
(1905) and is now reprinted here in its entirety.]

In May, 1895, in company with Horace L. Traubel, I visited Doyle,
whom I had known for years but had not seen for a long time. I
explained to him that it was my intention to publish these letters and
asked him if he felt there was any insuperable objection? He first
inquired—"Of what use are they?" and then, upon my assurance that
(in some measure) they would do for the world the same service they
had done for him, he further inquired: "Do you think Walt, if he were
here, if he could be asked, would be willing?" Whereupon, I, answering affirmatively, was told that I should "go ahead," doing that which
seemed to me best, since he felt "entirely safe" in my hands. It was
likewise by Doyle's consent that Mr. Traubel took notes of the conversation that ensued, and it is only after his revision that these are printed
in this volume. The conversation was desultory but serves to show what
manner of man Doyle is and by what sacred ties he feels himself still
indissolubly bound to Whitman. Mr. Doyle is reported almost absolutely in his own words. He said:—

I was born in 1847, in Ireland, and was about two years old when
brought to America. Father was a blacksmith. We lived our first years
in America at Alexandria, Virginia. Bad times came on in 1856–7.
Father went to Richmond, where he had been offered a place in an iron
foundry. While there I was a member of the Fayette Artillery, and
when the war broke out I entered the Confederate Army. Getting my
parole in Washington, forced to look out for myself, I hung round that
region with no particular object in view. I might have been more
successful somewhere else, but I was there, and so I just stuck to the
case as it was. I became a horse-car conductor. This other business came
later on. Yes, I will talk of Walt, nothing suits me better. I will
commence anywhere. When you are tired stop me. Walt never used to
take much to newspaper men in the old time. There were some few in
Washington he rather favored. They always made a good deal of him,
of course—that is, they came to him often enough for news or opinions
or such stuff. He could shut a man off in the best style, you know. He
had a freezing way in him—yet was never harsh. But people got to

know that he meant what he said. He said "no" and "no" it was. I remember one special night, we met a half-loaded fellow with some of his journalist friends — a newspaper man, since prominent, who was then pretty well acquainted with Walt. This man was offensively familiar with Walt — insisted on introducing his friends, and all that. Walt held him off — froze him out — would not be introduced. It was simply impossible for the intruder to make his point. Now, Walt was always dignified — simple enough, too — and this is a sample of the manner he showed to all alike, famous or plain folks, who stepped across what he thought his private border-line.

How different Walt was then in Washington from the Walt you knew in the later years! You would not believe it. He was an athlete — great, great. I knew him to do wonderful lifting, running, walking. You ask where I first met him? It is a curious story. We felt to each other at once. I was a conductor. The night was very stormy, — he had been over to see Burroughs before he came down to take the car — the storm was awful. Walt had his blanket — it was thrown round his shoulders — he seemed like an old sea-captain. He was the only passenger, it was a lonely night, so I thought I would go in and talk with him. Something in me made me do it and something in him drew me that way. He used to say there was something in me had the same effect on him. Anyway, I went into the car. We were familiar at once — I put my hand on his knee — we understood. He did not get out at the end of the trip — in fact went all the way back with me. I think the year of this was 1866. From that time on we were the biggest sort of friends. I stayed in Washington until 1872, when I went on the Pennsylvania Railroad. Walt was then in the Attorney-General's office. I would frequently go out to the Treasury to see Walt; Hubley Ashton was commonly there — he would be leaning familiarly on the desk where Walt would be writing. They were fast friends — talked a good deal together. Walt rode with me often — often at noon, always at night. He rode round with me on the last trip — sometimes rode for several trips. Everybody knew him. He had a way of taking the measure of the driver's hands — had calf-skin gloves made for them every winter in Georgetown — these gloves were his personal presents to the men. He saluted the men on the other cars as we passed — threw up his hand. They cried to him, "Hullo, Walt!" and he would reply, "Ah, there!" or something like. He was welcome always as the flowers in May. Everybody appreciated his attentions, and he seemed to appreciate our attentions to him. Teach the boys to read, write, and cipher? I never heard of, or saw that. There must be some mistake. He did not make much of what people call learning. But he gave us papers, books, and other such articles, too. In his habits he was very temperate. He did not smoke. People seemed to think it odd that he didn't, for everybody in Washington smoked. But he seemed to have a positive dislike for tobacco. He was a very moderate drinker. You might have thought something different, to see the ruddiness of his complexion — but his complexion had no whiskey in it. We might take a drink or two together occasionally — nothing more. It was our practice to go to a hotel on Washington Avenue after I was done with my car. I remember the place well — there on the corner. Like as not I would go to sleep — lay my head on my hands on the table. Walt would stay there, wait, watch, keep me undisturbed — would wake me up when the hour of closing came. In his eating he was vigorous, had a big appetite, but was simple in his tastes, not caring for any great dishes.

I never knew a case of Walt's being bothered up by a woman. In fact, he had nothing special to do with any woman except Mrs. O'Connor and Mrs. Burroughs. His disposition was different. Woman in that sense never came into his head. Walt was too clean, he hated anything which was not clean. No trace of any kind of dissipation in him. I ought to know about him those years — we were awful close together. In the afternoon I would go up to the Treasury building and wait for him to get through if he was busy. Then we'd stroll out together, often without any plan, going wherever we happened to get. This occurred days in and out, months running. Towards women generally Walt had a good way — he very easily attracted them. But he did that with men, too. And it was an irresistible attraction. I've had many tell me — men and women. He had an easy, gentle way — the same for all, no matter who they were or what their sex.

Walt was not at the theatre the night Lincoln was shot. It was me he got all that from in the book — they are almost my words. I heard that the President and his wife would be present and made up my mind to go. There was a great crowd in the building. I got into the second gallery. There was nothing extraordinary in the performance. I saw everything on the stage and was in a good position to see the President's box. I heard the pistol shot. I had no idea what it was, what it meant — it was sort of muffled. I really knew nothing of what had occurred until Mrs. Lincoln leaned out of the box and cried, "The President is shot!" I needn't tell you what I felt then, or saw. It is all put down in Walt's piece — that piece is exactly right. I saw Booth on the cushion of the box, saw him jump over, saw him catch his foot, which turned, saw him fall on the stage. He got up on his feet, cried

out something which I could not hear for the hubbub and disappeared.
I suppose I lingered almost the last person. A soldier came into the
gallery, saw me still there, called to me: "Get out of here! we're going
to burn this damned building down!" I said: "If that is so, I'll get out!"

We took great walks together — off towards or to Alexandria, often.
We went plodding along the road, Walt always whistling or singing.
We would talk of ordinary matters. He would recite poetry, especially
Shakespeare — he would hum airs or shout in the woods. He was always
active, happy, cheerful, good-natured. Many of our walks were taken
at night. He never seemed to tire. When we got to the ferry opposite
Alexandria I would say to myself, "I'll draw the line here — I won't go
a step further." But he would take everything for granted — we would
cross the river and walk back home on the other side. Walt knew all
about the stars. He was eloquent when he talked of them. It was
surprising what he knew of the operas, too, and the concerts of the
Marine Band always tempted him. He never failed these concerts —
we usually strayed in there together. The old man Scala led the band.
He used to play a piece called *The Rival Birds* — Walt could get it off
almost as good as the band.

He was a long time after me to go to New York, while his mother
was alive. I asked him: "Will we stop there with your mother?" He
was as little doubtful about that. We both stayed in Jersey City. The
Whitmans lived on Portland Avenue. We took our dinner with Mrs.
Whitman. We would take a bus-ride in the morning — then go to
Brooklyn and have dinner. After we had had our dinner she would
always say — "Now take a long walk to aid digestion." Mrs. Whitman
was a lovely woman. There were just the three of us eating together.
Walt and I had a week of it there in New York that time. It was always
impressed upon my mind — the opera he took me to see — *Polyato*. All
the omnibus drivers knew him. We always climbed up to the top of the
busses, our heels hanging over.

Yes, Walt often spoke to me of his books. I would tell him "I don't
know what you are trying to get at." And this is the idea I would
always arrive at from his reply. All other peoples in the world have had
their representatives in literature: here is a great big race with no
representative. He would undertake to furnish that representative. It
was also his object to get a real human being into a book. This had
never been done before. These were the two things he tried to impress
upon me every time we talked of books — especially of his books. Walt
used often to put a piece in Forney's Washington *Chronicle*. We never
really talked about politics. I was a Catholic — am still supposed to be

one. But I have not been to church for so many years I would not know
what to do there. He had pretty vigorous ideas on religion, but he
never said anything slighting the church. I don't know if he felt
different from what he spoke. He never went to church—didn't like
form, ceremonies—didn't seem to favor preachers at all. I asked him
about the hereafter. "There must be something," he said—"there can't
be a locomotive unless there is somebody to run it." I have heard him
say that if a person was a right kind of person—and I guess he thought
all persons right kind of persons—he couldn't be destroyed in the next
world or this.

Dollars and cents had no weight with Walt at all. He didn't spend
recklessly, but he spent everything—mostly on other people. Money
was a thing he didn't think of as other people thought of it. It came
and went, that was all there as to it. He didn't buy many books, but I
remember that once he bought a set of Alexander Dumas, which
afterward disappeared, I could not tell where, probably it was given
away.

I have Walt's raglan here [*goes to closet—puts it on*], I now and then
put it on, lay down, think I am in the old times. Then he is with me
again. It's the only thing I kept amongst many old things. When I get
it on and stretched out on the old sofa I am very well contented. It is
like Aladdin's lamp. I do not ever for a minute lose the old man. He is
always near by. When I am in trouble—in a crisis—I ask myself,
"What would Walt have done under these circumstances?" and whatever I decide Walt would have done that I do.

Walt's mood was very even, but I saw him mad as a March hare one
night. He was on the hind end of my car, near him stood an old fellow
(a carpet-bag senator—I don't know his name)—near-sighted, wore
glasses, peevish, lantern-jawed, dyspeptic. They rubbed against each
other. The first thing I knew there was a rumpus, the old man cussed
Walt—said, "Get out of the way, you—" and Walt only answered:
"Damn you!" the old man had a loaded stick with him—he raised
it—would have struck Walt and perhaps killed him but I came between just in time. I cried: "Get in the car, Walt!" (they were both in
the street by this time) and I was glad to see the affair ended that way.
No explanations were made. All effects of it vanished at once from
Walt's face and manner. Walt's temper was very even, it was a rare
thing for him to get angry and he must have been greatly provoked.
No man ever had better control over himself. He treated everybody
fairly, generously. He wasn't meek, but he was no fighting-cock. He
always had a few pennies for beggars along the street. I'd get out of

patience sometimes, he was so lenient. "Don't you think it's wrong?"
I'd ask him. "No," he always said—"it's never wrong, Peter." Wouldn't
they drink it away? He shook his head: "No, and if they did it
wouldn't alter the matter. For it is better to give to a dozen who do not
need what is given than to give to none at all and so miss the one that
should be fed." Walt was kind to animals. He admired them, but he
and animals never came to close quarters. His treatment of them was
always generous. I never knew him cruel to man or beast. He had a dog
once—Tip—in Camden, but he was not fond of animals for pets or
especially glad to have them round him.

In Washington Walt told me he had made up his mind to celebrate
the anniversary of the death of Lincoln every year. I have heard that he
did it until his death. He called the thing a "religious duty." Do you
remember the big black stick he carried even up to the last? I gave it to
him. It delighted him. Gifts of that sort he always valued highly—the
plainest, it might be, the most.

I once had the manuscript of *Drum Taps;* Walt made me a present of
it. But somehow, when we moved, the manuscript disappeared—was
either destroyed or stolen. Part of it was in print, but most of it was
written. All his manuscript was pieced together in that fashion. At the
time I did not appreciate it as I should now.

Walt's manners were always perfectly simple. We would tackle the
farmers who came into town, buy a water-melon, sit down on the cellar
door of Bacon's grocery, Seventh and Pennsylvania Avenue, halve it
and eat it. People would go by and laugh. Walt would only smile and
say, "They can have the laugh—we have the melon."

You couldn't get a better idea of this simplicity than if I tell you of a
visit paid him by Edmund Yates, in 1873, while he laid in the attic
there in Washington, paralyzed, I being his nurse. Yates called and sent
up his card. After some objections, mostly on my part, I referred the
matter to Walt, who instantly said: "Admit him—let him come in."
When Yates got into the room Walt saluted him by his first name and
he addressed Walt as "Mr. Whitman." No two men were ever more
different. Yates elegant, dressy, cultured—Walt plain, sick in bed, his
room all littered and poor. But both men were perfectly at home. Yates
did not seem fazed, Walt never was. In a few minutes they were in the
midst of animated talk. When Yates, after awhile, got up and said:
"Good-bye," they seemed as if they had known each other many years.

Yes, Traubel, I know who it was Walt meant when he spoke to you of
Grant's morning visits afoot to the old woman. Grant was then President. He would stroll from the White House alone. The woman he

visited in this way was a widow, well known in Washington. Walt would laugh at me trying to get the President to ride — I would motion Grant — he would shake his head. Then later on we would see him at the widow's window, outside, leaning on the sill. Grant was very fond of the old lady — in fact, she was much liked by men generally.

Garfield and Walt were very good friends. Garfield had a large manly voice; we would be going along the Avenue together — Walt and me — and we would hear Garfield's salutation at the rear. He always signalled Walt with the cry: "After all not to create only!" When we heard that we always knew who was coming. Garfield would catch up and they would enter into a talk; I would fall back sometimes. They spoke of books mainly but of every other earthly thing also. Often they would not get through the first run and would go up and down the Avenue several times together — I was out of it. Our tramping ground was between the Capitol and the Treasury.

Towards the end I saw very little of Walt, but he continued to write me. He never altered his manner toward me; here are a few more recent postal cards, you will see that they show the same old love. I know he wondered why I saw so little of him the three or four years before he died, but when I explained it to him he understood. Nevertheless, I am sorry for it now. The obstacles were too small to have made the difference I allowed. It was only this: In the old days I had always open doors to Walt — going, coming, staying, as I chose. Now, I had to run the gauntlet of Mrs. Davis and a nurse and what not. Somehow, I could not do it. It seemed as if things were not as they should have been. Then I had a mad impulse to go over and nurse him. I was his proper nurse — he understood me — I understood him. We loved each other deeply. But there were things preventing that, too. I saw them. I should have gone to see him, at least, in spite of everything. I know it now, I did not know it then, but it is all right. Walt realized I never swerved from him — he knows it now — that is enough.

I have talked a long while. Let us drink up this beer together. It's a fearful warm day. You gentlemen take the glasses, there; I will drink right from the bottle. Now, here's to the dear old man and the dear old times — and the new times, too, and every one that's to come!   R. B.

CHAPTER SEVEN

Tricks of the Trade

Jack Rogers and
Jo Baldwin

MYRIADS OF NEW EXPERIENCES" (Chapter 3) documents some of Whitman's multiple lovers and partners. Accepting Whitman's gay identity, many would then tie him to only one partner — Peter Doyle (Chapter 6) with perhaps an additional romance with Harry Stafford (Chapter 8). Doyle and Stafford were both in their way central in Whitman's life, but their importance may be exaggerated because of the amount of documentation. Whitman's more transitory but no less meaningful partners have left less evidence. Two tricks — John (Jack) Rogers and Joseph C. Baldwin — have escaped oblivion and can be partially identified. Their letters survive by chance; Whitman's letters to them are gone. While their documentation may be fuller, these two tricks are otherwise representative of many among the multitudes in his *Notebooks* and *Daybooks,* who are known only by their names.

Whitman exchanged photographs, locks of hair, rings and other mementoes with friends and lovers. (Anne Gilchrist and Harry Stafford both got rings.) After chatting about widows in Elliottstown, Illinois, where he was hiding out, having hastily fled Philadelphia, Joseph C. Baldwin wrote Whitman, "I still retain the ring you gave me and of course when I look at that I must think of you" (May 13, 1877). These rings were much like the gloves Whitman gave the drivers and boys at Christmas. In 1878, he had a list of twenty-five (including Peter Doyle) to whom he gave gloves; he couldn't even remember the names of some of the recipients. The list was expanded in 1881.

Whitman first met Jack Rogers September 21, 1870, in Brooklyn, and described him as "conductor Myrtle av. Greenport Connecticut boy, blond." Dissatisfied with Doyle and Washington, Whitman had visited his mother and family in the fall of 1870. Taking a four-month furlough from his Justice Department clerkship, the poet supervised the printing of the fourth edition of *Leaves of Grass*. Enjoying himself thoroughly, Whitman wrote to Doyle, "I have been pitching in heavy to a great dish of stewed beef & onions mother cooked for dinner—& shall presently cross over to New York & mail this letter—shall probably go to some amusement with a friend this evening—most likely Buckleys Serenaders." Jack was one of his pick-ups along the route and may have been Whitman's date for this particular evening. (Whitman possibly invented the story about the Serenaders since there is no record of their opera parodies having been performed in New York City during September, 1870).

When Whitman returned to Washington, Rogers corresponded regularly. February 27, 1871, he wrote, "I feel very greatful to you that you should take so much interist in me it makes me think of my father." Rogers sent regular details about his appearance: "am getting very Stout" (December 26, 1872) and "I have grown thin cince you last saw me" (July 24, 1875). The consistent and somewhat pathetic theme of the letters is that Jack wanted to see Whitman. He never prospered, had a hot temper, lost his job as a conductor and bounced about from job to job. In his last surviving letter, Rogers wrote, "I have thought of you a good many times I should like to see you and if God spairs our lives I hope to see you once more but God know what is best. . . . I wish that you whare that I could see you and comfort you" (February 21, 1878).

All of Whitman's letters to Rogers have been lost, but their gist was evidently to give encouragement and love along with excuses against their meeting in either Washington or New York. April 10, 1871, Jack wrote, "You say you are very busy now. I suppose this is a busy time of the year with you is it not." Rogers got married, found Christ, had a child ("Walt Whitman Rogers"!) and lived unhappily ever after as he followed odd jobs all the way to Arrendondo, Florida. Whitman regularly sent cards, newspapers and others signs of his affection to Rogers. The last unequivocal record of their contact is May 22, 1879, when the poet lists Jack's address as Battonville, Florida. Whitman did record an 1883 entry in his *Daybooks:* "John Rogers, (freight W[est] J[ersey] RR office Phil) model for studios" (*Daybooks,* 317). Perhaps Whitman was able to get Rogers a job in Philadelphia or more likely this is another trick. But, whether one or two, both the 1870 and the 1883 John Rogers physically and emotionally attracted Whitman.

After a stroke in January 1873, Whitman was nursed by Peter Doyle and other friends in Washington, but he seems not to have liked taking help from Doyle, whom he had fathered for nearly a decade. In May he returned home to his dying mother. After her funeral, he stayed on with his brother in Camden, New Jersey, where he lived until he bought his own house there on Mickle Street in 1884. Although a relatively young fifty-four in 1873, Whitman remained semi-invalid until his death in 1892. Nonetheless, he found opportunities to meet the local boys. "I have become sort of acquainted," he wrote, "with most of the carriers, ferry men, car conductors and drivers, &c. &c. they are very good indeed—help me on & off the cars, here & in Phila-delphia—they are nearly all young fellows—it all helps along. . . ." In October, 1873, he wrote Doyle of a favorite: "I am feeling quite bad to-day about a 13 year old boy, Rob Evans, I know here, next door but one—he has had his eye very badly hurt, I fear it is put out, the doctor has given it up—by an arrow yesterday, the boys playing—I thought quite a good deal of him, he would do any thing for me—his father was French, & is dead—the boy suffers very much . . ."

Jo Baldwin like Jack Rogers was a reckless and handsome boy. Whitman's *Notebook* enters "Jo Baldwin Nov 6 '73"—presumably the date of their first meeting. Whitman had suffered the stroke January 23, 1873 and his mother died May 23 in Camden, New Jersey, at brother George's house. Walt went into mourning, stayed with his brother, and slept in the bed where the mother had died. He wrote Doyle regularly, and by November 8 he had sufficiently recovered to visit Washington (where he was reunited with Doyle) and even attended a memorial service for Edgar Allen Poe in Baltimore. Thus his meeting with Baldwin took place as he was returning more fully into the world; indeed the meeting was on the Saturday night before he left Camden to rejoin Doyle in Washington after many weeks' separation.

Baldwin became much more than a passing stranger. Although he could hardly write, his letters demonstrate the strength of his passion for Whitman and his intense struggle to communicate with his elder friend. On May 13, 1877, he wrote, "Well Walt I have write a good bit but havent said much you know my capabilities is limited. . . . you tould me to write you a long and carful letter. I cant I havent got the potations." Were his potentials as a writer surpassed by his physical potencies?

Baldwin had to flee Philadelphia without saying good-bye to any-

one. "You know I could not content my self in Phila. — I was in Hot
water all the time   to come and see you before I left I Had not the
corage . . ." He went to St. Louis, Missouri, had problems with pickpockets and finally ended up as a sharecropper in Elliotstown, Illinois,
located near the railroad that went between Terre Haute and St. Louis.
Whitman was warned "dont let my address be known or less I will be
trubled to death." Exile in the middle of Illinois during one of the
worst depressions to hit the United States offered nothing but sorrows
for Baldwin. He expected a harvest of two thousands bushels of corn,
but they weren't worth much in 1877. Whitman sent ten dollars loan
on the crop.

Baldwin wanted more than Whitman's ring and money; he wanted
the poet himself. On September 11, 1877, he wrote, "I think I will pay
you a visit and we will enjoy ourselves as of old." And during the cold
winter of January 1878 he made a proposal. His letter has been lost,
but Whitman summarized the message in his *Daybook:* "He wants me
to come out there & live with him — Hon. John S. Dewey owns the
farm he works." Whitman sent cards, newspapers and other tokens to
Baldwin during 1878: February 26, March 11, April 2, April 15, May
15, June 5, August 7, September 23 and October 7. Then Baldwin
wrote October 7 that he was on his way. Baldwin seems to have moved
in with Whitman between October 29 and November 12, after which
Whitman lists Baldwin's address at his folks' place in Delaware County,
Pennsylvania.

Economic depression affected both Whitman and his boyfriends in
1873. Samuel Rezneck in "Distress, Relief, and Discontent in the
United States During the Depression of 1873–78," describes the comprehensive nature of the economic disorder: "Both foundation and
superstructure were shaken by a depression which at once revealed the
stresses of an expanding economy and intensified the uneven effects of
wartime and postwar changes upon the balance of agrarian and indus-
trial interests" (*Journal of Political Economy,* December, 1950). The
federal government instituted a reduction in staff and Whitman lost
his clerkship July 1, 1874. (After his illness, he had hired a substitute
and was able to live on the difference between what the government
paid him and what he paid the substitute.) Eventually, Whitman was
able to make a living off the sale of his books, lectures and articles, but
those opportunities expanded more after the depression. He could not
return to Washington even had he wished because he had no job;
Doyle's employment was itself precarious. Jack Rogers, Jo Baldwin,
Harry Stafford and many of the other boys he met were perplexed as

they found a world of closed economic opportunities. In their be-
wildered circumstances, they found a steady heart (if not a full purse)
in Walt Whitman.

While there are many gaps in both the Rogers and Baldwin stories,
their overall characters and their relationships with Whitman seems
fairly straightforward. Whitman provided comfort, reassurance and
fatherly love to the boys, who in return loved Whitman. Whitman's
barrage of letters, books and other tokens on one side and the constant
pleas of the boys to join him suggest a physical, sexual attachment. His
letters to Rogers and Baldwin are lost but his response was limited —
because after 1876 he was developing some hot and highly charged
contacts with a group of New Jersey farm boys. (See Chapter 8, "Timber Creek.")

John Rogers Letters

John M. Rogers to WW, Brooklyn, February 9, 1871

Dear Father, if I may call you so. I am well and hearty as ever. I
received your kind and welcomb letter and was [happy] to hear that
you are enjoying good health. I wrote answer to your letter but it got
mislaid and I did not mail it. I was looking over some letters to day and
I came acrost yours so I thought I would wright another. we have had
very cold weather here this winter and there is a great deal of Ice in
the river the Fulton Fery Boats was over an hour going across this
morning.

I am not on the cars any more. I had some word with one of the
employees and as I was in the right rather than to have any trouble I
told the Presedend I would leave as the weather was so cold and look
for something else to do, but I have found nothing as yet. I would
come to W[ashington] if I thought I could get any thing to do so good
by for the presant. I remain yours,

John

P.S. Dear Father I should like to see you very much and if you see or
hear of any one that wants to get a sober and steady young man, you
can wright for me and I will come out there with much love, I remain
your Loving Son, John M. Rogers

John M. Rogers to WW, Brooklyn, February 27, 1871

Dear Father

I receive your letter on Saturday and was glad to hear from you and that you are well and enjoying you self. I am as well as ever but I feel very uneasy at times because I am doing nothing. I have not done any thing since Jan 1st every thing is very dull here at presant. The weather is warm and pleasant here for this time of the year. We did not have a very grat time on Wahington birthday here a reg[iment] or two of Soldiers turned out in a parade was all that I see in this great City. I should like very much to come to Washinton and see you but as long as I know that you are well and enjoying your self I will try to content my self. It rained all day here yesterday and I did not go out any whare I feel very greatful to you that you should take so much interist in me it makes me think of my father all though if we think of our dear heavenly Fathe[r] he will guide and direct us in all our ways and we ought to be very thankful to him for our good health he is such a good Father to us so good by for the presant my Dear good Father, from your affecinate Son John M. Rogers

P.S. I would come out there on a visit but can not aford it Just now so good by

Johnny

John M. Rogers to WW, Brooklyn, April 6, 1871

Dear Father & Friend

What is the mater & how do you do and how are you geting along well, I hope. I am well now as can be expected after geting off of a sick bed of four weeks with a fever I wrote you letter some time ago and have not receved no answer as yet so thought I would write again. I did not know but you might be Sick.

I have lost a great deal of fleash cince you last saw me. I am looking quite thin now. I am not doing any thing yet, but I am gaing strength verry fast. I should like very much to see you again hoping to hear from you soon I remain your truly, good by

Address John M. Rogers

No. 3 Fulton St., Brooklyn, N.Y.

P.S. Write soon for I am ancious to hear from you. I remain your,

Affecinate Son, John

John M. Rogers to WW, Brooklyn, April 10, 1871

Dear Father,

I receive your kind and affecinate letter on Saturday and was glad to hear from you and that you are well and hearty. I am gaing very fast I feel beter now than I have in some time. It is very warm here to day the German People are agoing to have a great time here to day other wise things is about the same things is very quite here in the City. I should like very much to [go] to washington but I can not afford it at presant it cost me a great deal when I was sick but every thing is paid and I have a little left so I shall have to get som[eth]ing to do very quick or I shall be bankrupt with out any mony. I have not found any thing yet I started out this morning to look for work I do wish I could find something there to do so we could be togather. that would be so nice I know I should like it. You say your are very busy now. I supose this is a busy time of year with you is it not yesterday was a nice day I went to church & S. School so as I do not think of any thing more, I will close, so good by for this time I remain your affecinate Son

John M. Rogers

P.S. write Soon with love, I am yours, John

John M. Rogers to WW, Brooklyn, June 1, 1871

Dear Father,

It a long time cince I heard from you and thinking you would like to hear from me thought I wright you a line or two to see how you are geting along. I am as well as can be I should like to hear from you very much. I have got a good place and are doing well. I like it very much I will send you a card 480 Bway. I supose you will come on here soon to spend one or two months and then I shall see you. It is very warm here. yesterday we had a very hard thunder storm and it done a great deal of dammage along the North River & distroye Houses and tress and fruit things is very quite here except a murder now and then so now I will close with my love good by from your affecinate Son and Friend John M. Rogers To my Dear Father Write Soon

John M. Rogers to WW, Brooklyn, December 26, 1872

Dear friend and Father. as it is snowing here to night I was looking of some letters. I came acrost one of your letter and as it some time cince I have not seen or heard from you I thought I would write a few lines to you. I am as well as I can be and am getting very Stout but how do you do and are you well and how do you get along this cold weather   it has been very Cold here. I am now employed at the Contentatual Bank Note Co and I geting alon very nicely do much betters than I did with the wood Co. Last Sunday we had very large fire in Brooklyn. Dr. Talmage Church in Schwirharn St. was destroyed and some very large fire in New York, by Barnum's Museum, and a larg Printing Co. in Center St., but I suppose you have heard of it by this now I will close with love. I remain your   John M. Rogers

John M. Rogers to WW, New Britain, Connecticut, April, 1875

Dear Friend and Sir

As I have just come acrost one of your letter I thought I would write you a few Lines just to let you know that I have not for goting you. I am enjoying good health as well as my Family. Cince I last saw you I was married. I have been married two years to day. I have got a little boy ten months old on the 18 of this month and I named him after you so you see I have not for goting you. How is the times in Washington   it has been hard times here but I have got through the winter allright. We have had very cold weather here it has been the coldest winter I ever experance. Work is very dull here now I am not doing much at preasant   how do you get alon out there. I have been away from Brooklyn Two Years next fowl   I was throwed out of work in the New York with about two Hundred others ten days before the Panic from the American Bank Note Co and did not do any thing till January 20th. I came to New Britian Conn and I have been here cince   I do not Like it here   I had rather be in the City some whare   how is Business there if you come on this way I should like to have you come and see me if you can not stay more than one day but *I would like to have you make me a good visit.* I have got a fine boy I can tell you he is as prety as a picture   we all send Love I hope you will forgive me for not writing before this   from your Affectinate Friend,   John M. Rogers

John M. Rogers to WW, New Britain, Connecticut, April 25, 1875

Dear Father & Friend

Your letter came to hand the first of this week and I was glad to hear from you but very sorry to hear of your loss of health & bereavement this liaves me and family all well, my little Boy is growing very fast and is getting as fat as he can be. Worke is very dul here. I have only about two days work in a week and the wages are small   I do not everage two dollars a day when I work   I am working on locks. I do not like the place here and shall get away from here as soon as I can. How is work there I can work at most any thing that comes along I should like very much to see you and if every thing goes well I may come on to see you this summer I got a little behind through the winter and have not quite caught up yet I have got a little Business out side of my work which I do Evenings. I am connected with Sovererns of Industry I Sell Butter & Sigars and that helps me a great deal so that I manadge to get along. And I think by the First of June I shall be all square here. We deal with a firm in Philadelfia Clothers Bennett & Co Tower Hall. I think it is in Market St. there is a Mr Watters with them and he is coming on here soon to take Orders and Measament for the Soverns Do you remember meeting a young Lady with me at the corner of Fulton and Court Sts. once that is my wife she remembers you well so good by for this time I will try to write oftener in future we all send love from your affecinate son &c.

J.M. Rogers

John M. Rogers to WW, New Britain, June 14, 1875

Dear Friend & Father your letter came to hand last week and I was glad to hear from you. This leaves me all well hopeing it may find you the same My Wife & Boy are well as can be Expected. You spoke about your Picture I received one with a paper that I received from there some time ago You want me to write all the particulars about my self I am not doing much at preasant work is very dull here and the waiges is small it is imposable to everage a liveing here from the pay that I receive for work last month I earned a bout ($15) Dollars in the shop and this month I shall not have above ten Dollars. If it were not for what I make out side I should come out short. And I expect to lose that chance for this reason they are a going to open a cooperative Store and keep it open through the day and unless I get a position in the store I shall look for someing else to do. It is a socity call the Soverigns of Inustry. If you see any chanc for me to get any thing to do, let me know as I have given you all the news I will close.

I remain Yours, J.M. Rogers

John M. Rogers to WW, New Britain, July 24, 1875

Dear Friend & Father,

I received your letter Sat. Eve and I was glad to hear from you but I am Sory to hear that you have [been] sick so long. I have been sick with the Chills & Fever I have had one to day my wife and Child have

gone home on a visit to her house at Norwalk Conn. have been gone cince the 20th of June, so I am alone I am at the same employment yet I have plenty of work but the pay is small. My boy was not very well before he went away he has been better cince they have been there they are near the Salt water my wife is well do you remember the young Lady you met with me at the Cor of Fulton and Cort Sts that is my wife. Last wensday I went to Hartford to the reunion of the Conn Vetrans and spent two days I met a good many of my old comrads we had a good time there wa[s] asembled about Four thousands at Charter Oak Park near Hartford. I have grown thin cince you last saw me. I do not weigh so much, [about] 125 lbs. I have worked very hard this sumer and I do not think it agrees so well with me here as it does near the salt[water] and I shall not stay here any longer than I can help, so good by for this time, I remain yours &c,
    John M. Rogers

John M. Rogers to WW, New Britain, March 28, 1876

Dear Friend,
    I is some time cince I heard from you. why do you not write I should like to here from you very much This leaves me well thank God, but I have been sick most all winter my wife is sick at pres-ant But the Lord has been good to me in past and I know if I put my trust in him I shall come of more than conker. I feel that Christ is very prescious to me. I feel that peace and contentment of mind that I never had before. I have learnd to trust him for all things both Spiritual and temperal and I can truly say that he never leaves nor forsakes those that put trust in him and I know that he is able to save to the uttermost all that will come to him and he gives us joy and peace in this life and the life to come. O that all might fell the love of Jesus in their souls. We have had revival here this past winter and about six Hundred have given their hearts to the Saviour and still there is more to follow.
    I suppose they are makeing great prepreratun fo the exabishtion in Philadelphia. I should like to come on there this summer very much to spend a few days and I shall if I can *We all send Love* I remain yours, write soon. John M. Rogers, write soon

John M. Rogers to WW, Arredondo, Florida, February 21, 1878

Dear Friend,
    I receive a postal from you this date address to me at New Britain Conn. I am well and so is my Family. My health is better than it has

been in some time   I have a little place here and are triing hard to get along. I am raising vedgeables for the New York market   it is the busy season here now   I was glad to hear from you and that you are better   I have thought of you a good many times   I should like to see you and if God spairs our lives I hope to see you once more but God know what is best, if we but look to him he will take care of us and make our griefs and pains easy to bear   I have often thought of what you have had to go through and suffer in your sickness. I wish that you whare that I could see you and comfort you. I have got a find little boy   I have named him after you he is now most four years old will be in June next. I should be happy to hear from you as soon as you get this write soon, From your affecinate Friend and well wisher, John M. Rogers.

Jo Baldwin Letters

Joseph C. Baldwin to WW, Elliottstown, Illinois, May 13, 1877

Dear Walt,

I recived yours of fourth to day and was agreeable surprised to here of your improved Health. I had almost come to the conclugen that you had given me up for the lost *child*   many a time   I have wonderd what kind of a fellow you thought I was. I dont suppose there Has a day past over my Head without me thinking of you.

I am also very glad to learn of Mrs. *Siter*s. I suppose she Has a Hard time of it. I recived one letter from her and Johnnys Wife they wrote me rather a lamentable letter. Poor Jo Adams Im sorry he is a fine fellow tell him I send him my pies regards and hope he will get well soon. Johnny Cahall I cant altogether place him did he visit to live in Camden   I guss so.

So they have got the dummies running on Market St. [(]I here they reduced the wages to two dollars) The perment Exhibition I suppose will create almost as big a time this summer as last. Im sorry times is so Hard in Philadelphia and so many famlys are in distress. I am glad Mrs. Siter is going to Have a small famley and perhaps John Pickens will assist her. I suppose Goorge is pretty smart I cant help but think about poor old Granmother Gouth.

Well Walt my dear old friend you say you feel wicked enough at times wich you consider a good sign [(]I hope it is) you say you have been traveling a good [de]al. I hope you will be home to get this any way I will direct to your old Headquarters.

Well Walt I will endevor to give you a rugh scetch of my wander-
ings since I seen you. You know I could not content my self in Phila. —
I was in Hot water all the time   to come and see you before I left I
Had not the corage to do that   so I drawed my money from the
Centennial went down to my sister's   she was not at home but Annie,
Johnny's Wife was thir   I tould her my intentions   I was very sorry I
did not see Mrs *Siter*   Went direct from thir to the Depo and in less
than half an Hour I was behind the iron *Horse* stearing twards Sunsit
came strate through to St. *Louis*. Had a little row with some *Pickpockets*
on the Road — staid in St. Louis three Weeks then came out to Pleasant
Rige whare I wrote you a letter but got no answer   staided thir about
one month then moved East about seven miles to Grays and I think I
wrote you a letter from thir but never received an answer (began to
think you had gone back on me) staid thir until the twentyfourth
March when I Emegrated here to Effingham Co. *Ill*. And am farming
on my own Hack) Thir is two Hundred and sixty acres in the farm and
the way I spraind my Rist was Plowing a stumppy pece of Ground [(]I
Have got about ten acres of corn planted about thirty acres plowed) this
is a very Backward Spring Hear as *you* say it is thir. The times Here is
pretty Hard asposuly with me as I Have got all my captal invested in
starting Farming   But if my crops prospers and the European War
continues I will com out all right and I guess make a big thing.

Walt I have got a big lot of work to do about three mens work; But
I think Compent to the Emergence if I keep my Helth   You asked me
about the women kinder a sticken it at me oh well I can get all the
woman I want out Hear But I havent topt any of them yet. I got to be
afraid of them they are treachers dont you think so   right around
within a gun shot thir is a dozen Widows   this is not a very healthy
part of the world. Walt I still retain the ring you gave me and of course
when I look at that I must think of you. You sent me a peaper which is
very exceptable indeed as news Hear is very scarce   I would like very
much to have a Phila. peaper.

Walt I would like you to go up to no 722 north 36 st. to see my
sisters they are thir keeping a Boarding House do go to see them and
give them some advice thir is so many dambd sharpers now a days im a
little fraid to trust them all by them selves Please go and see them tell
them I sent you to see how they ware gitting along I am alarmed about
them some.

Well Walt I have write a good bit but havent said much you know
my capabilities is limited

do write soon and tell me all the Public and Privit news tell Mrs

Siter to write to me   And Emmie Pickens and Sallie   Be carfull and dont let my adress be known or less I will be trubled to death.

Walt I hope you will get well and be all right when I come home that wont be for some time if I prosper Here But not more than two or three years.

you tould me to write you a long and carful letter. I cant I havent got the potations But I will write again soon as I Hear from you, yours until death   Jos: C. Baldwin

[P.S.] you did not say any thing about Sam Hadford. please tell about him

Joseph C. Baldwin to WW, Elliottstown, Illinois, August 11, 1877

Dear Walt

Thinking you would like to Here from me I would write you a few lines in as much as Im well and Hope this will find you the same

Business is very dull Here now and crops is ruined for the want of rain   all of my worment of mind and toil of body is of no avil   Im feafuly in want now and when my crops is geatherd it wont be much better as I see O I musent say Im in want Because I Have got plenty to eat and some close

But not much money now I dont nead very much

But the fuather looks dark   But may come out Better than I amagn

I will Buy some Hogs on a credit and feed my unsailable corn to them and may come out all right in due time   I received those papers

Many thanks, yours truly, writ soon

Joseph C. Baldwin to WW, Elliottstown, Illinois, September 11, 1877

Dear Walt

I am well now But I Have just got out of a bed of sickness. I Have Had the Intermiten fever and pretty Bad.

Walt a friend in need is a friend indeed. I will ask you wanst[once] more to Help me a little if you could lend me ten Dollars for a short time say six weeks or two months until I can sell som corn. I will Have about 2000 Buishels But it wont be ripe for six weeks or two months and then I will send it Back to you with may thanks after I get things fixt up   then I think I will pay you a visit and we will enjoy ourslves as of old

write just as soon as you get this, yours truly, Joseph C. Baldwin

Joseph C. Baldwin to WW, Elliottstown, Illinois, September 21, 1877

Dear Walt

I just re[ceived] the money all right. many thanks until you are better paid

I am very weak yet but I Have [got] out to sow some Wheat

I Had a very Hot fever last night Im in Hopes I will come all right soon. I cant write much this time.

I will return your money just as soon as I can, yours, Jos C. Baldwin

Harry Stafford, c. 1876. Courtesy of the Library of Congress

CHAPTER EIGHT

Timber Creek

Harry Stafford

HOMOSEXUALS HAVE ALWAYS dreamed of another world, a land somewhere over the rainbow, free of heterosexist presumptions and persecutions. Walt Whitman often proposed going away somewhere with his lovers. He wrote Tom Sawyer in 1863 that after the war, "we should come together again in some place, where we could make our living, and be true comrades and never be separated while life lasts—and take Lew Brown too, and never separate from him" (April 21, 1863). When Peter Doyle was troubled, Whitman promised to find some hideaway where they could escape together: "My darling, if you are not well when I come back I will get a good room or two in some quiet place, (or out of Washington, perhaps in Baltimore,) and we will live together..." (August 21, 1869). While Baltimore may not be everyone's promised land, the dream of escaping persists. In *Culture Clash: The Making of Gay Sensibility* (1984), Michael Bronski identified "the creation of edenic situations free from the world's hostility" as one of "the most common themes in gay writing."

Henry David Thoreau went to Walden to get away from the heterosexual world and be free to greet handsome young men without nosy interference. In *Walden* (1854) he described receiving Alek Therien, who loved to hear him read from Homer about the love between Achilles and Patroclus. Thoreau was turned on by watching Alek chopping wood and sauntering along. "When I approached him," Thoreau wrote, "he would suspend his work, and with half-suppressed mirth lie along the trunk of a pine which he had felled, and, peeling off the inner bark, roll it up into a ball and chew it while he laughed and talked. Such an exuberance of animal spirits had he that he sometimes tumbled down and rolled on the ground with laughter at anything which made him think and tickled him." The Calamus was special to Thoreau, who used its more common, more sexual nickname, "critchi-crotch." He noted in his journal May 27, 1852 : "The fruit of the sweet flag is now just fit to eat, and reminds me of childhood, — the critchi-crotches."

In 1856, Thoreau visited Whitman in Brooklyn, and in 1860 Whit-man came to Boston to supervise the third edition of *Leaves of Grass,* which first included the Calamus cluster. Thoreau must have read these homoerotic poems before publication since he wrote several pages about them the Calamus in his journal, May 23, 1860. That very day Whit-man took the train from Boston for Manhattan. Thoreau praised the erotic Calamus : "How agreeable and surprising the peculiar fragrance of the sweet flag when bruised! That this plant alone should have extracted this odor surely for so many ages each summer from the moist earth!"

To find his own sexual paradise, Charles Warren Stoddard went to the Pacific. He sent Whitman erotic stories of finding a native who gave him "bountiful and unconstrained love. I go to his grass house, eat with him his simple food. Sleep with him upon his mats, and at night sometimes waken to find him watching me with earnest, patient looks, his arm over my breast and around me" (March 2, 1869). And a year later, "In the name of Calamus listen to me! . . . I think of sailing toward Tahiti. . . . I must get in amongst people who are are not afraid of instincts and who scorn hypocrisy" (April 2, 1870). Whitman "warmly" approved Stoddard's "emotional and adhesive nature, & the outlet thereof" and gladly received his *South-Sea Idyls* (1873). Today the tradition has been carried on by Richard Amory's *Song of the Loon* (1966) as well as RFD, *A Country Journal for Gay Men Everywhere.*

Whitman escaped from Washington in 1873 after his stroke, but he ended somewhat stranded in Camden, New Jersey, living with his brother. He rejected the bigger second-floor room in his brother's house for a more private but smaller and hotter in summer, colder in winter, third-floor room. The poet had to bring his tricks cautiously into the drab, domestic life of his brother, who was more interested in pipes than poems.

Whitman soon found an escape with a boy from the country. The *Notebook* entry reads : "Harry Stafford New Rep. printing office March '76 visit Kirkwood (White Horse) April 1, '76." Harry Stafford was a teenager who worked in the Camden *New Republic* office. Whitman was then nearly sixty years old. The two fell in love instantaneously ; Hank invited Walt home to meet the folks. On April 4th, Whitman wrote a letter to Harry's supervisor:

> I take an interest in the boy in the office, Harry Stafford—I know his father & mother—There is a large family, very respectable American people—farmers, but only a hired farm—Mr. Stafford in weak health—
> I am anxious Harry should *learn the printer's trade thoroughly—I want him to learn to set type as fast as possible*—want you to give him a chance (less of the mere errands &c)—There is a good deal really in the boy, if he has a chance.
> Don't say any thing about this note to him—or in fact to any one—just tear it up, & *keep the matter to yourself private.*

Walt Whitman and Harry Stafford spent the next few years together almost all the time. Whitman slept in the same bed with Harry at the farm and Harry shared Whitman's bed when he was in Camden. And when Whitman went on trips, Harry went along. In a letter to a New York friend, Whitman wrote, December 13, 1876, ". . . if perfectly convenient, & if you have plenty of room—My (adopted) son, a young man of 18, is with me now, sees to me, & occasionally transacts my business affairs, & I feel somewhat at sea without him—Could I bring him with me, to share my room, & your hospitality & be with me?" Less than a week later, the kinship had shifted as Whitman added a further request for a common bed: "My nephew & I when traveling always share the same room together & the same bed. . . ." And the following March, Whitman wrote another friend and admirer, John Burroughs, "Should like to fetch my boy Harry Stafford with me, as he is in my convoy like—We occupy the same room & bed—"

The Staffords worked a farm adjacent to Timber Creek, which became Whitman's Walden and Tahiti combined. The place is called Laurel Springs today and the old farmhouse has been restored. Located on the White Horse Highway, the village was then called Kirkwood; in 1879, the Staffords moved to nearby Glendale and the farm went to Montgomery Stafford. To avoid confusion I refer to the place as Timber Creek; on today's maps, look for "Laurel Springs."

The Stafford farm was quite rural in 1876 and is hardly a metropolis now. The railroad had just opened so that Whitman and Harry could move between Camden and Timber Creek with ease. The Philadelphia & Atlantic City Railroad began running in 1877 and was soon joined by the Camden & Atlantic. When Whitman arrived exploitation by tourists and speculators hadn't begun. In 1889 real-estate developers moved in, bought up all the farms around the creek, and built the Walt Whitman House, which could hold up to sixty guests. By 1900 as

Elaine A. Bockorich

Timber Creek, The Pond (1904). In J. Johnston and J. W. Wallace, *Visits to Walt Whitman in 1890-1891* (1918)

many as fifty trains a day went through the town with more on week-
ends. But in the 1920s, tourists moved on to Atlantic City and Cape
May. Timber Creek sank into disrepair and oblivion. In 1977 the
borough of Laurel Springs acquired and has restored what is now called
"The Whitman-Stafford House." The section of Timber Creek where
Whitman dallied is called "Crystal Spring Park."

Whitman recovered from his stroke by walking from the farm house
to the creek (with the help of young Harry or another boy). Where
Whitman entered Timber Creek there was a spring, whose waters were
reputed to be beneficial. Whitman took his clothes off (with a boy's
help) and then rolled around in the nearby marl bed. (Marl was used as
fertilizer and was formed by Delawares who had fished and left piles of
bones and shells.) After covering himself with the pungent mud, he
then washed in the spring water. To stimulate his skin, either his
partner or he himself flagellated his body with switches from the trees.
Gay Wilson Allen explains that "No houses were in sight and tres-
passers were rare, though apparently some of the neighbors did hear of
this solitary nudity and were scandalized — perhaps thereby uninten-
tionally giving him an even more exclusive possession of the creek"
(*The Solitary Singer,* 475). Whitman went there both day and night;
he much exaggerated his solitariness, since he often played with the
boys. Since farmers tend to retire early, nighttime provided even more
privacy.

Whitman's relationship to Harry Stafford is relatively well documented. A majority of the letters back and forth between the two have
survived along with Whitman's *Daybooks,* which give a day-by-day
catalogue of their comings and goings. Edwin Miller in his introduction to Volume III of *The Correspondence of Walt Whitman* (1964) provides
a succinct summary of their interaction. And Justin Kaplan's recent
biography (1980) presents most of the details. While recognizing Harry
as a Calamus lover, both suggest that the relationship was not physical
(perhaps not even homosexual). Had they had one-tenth as much
evidence for a young woman, their Lolita imaginations would have run
wild. Walt and Harry's relationship was not only homosexual but was
peculiarly stormy. Miller and Kaplan suggest that the storm was created by the two males fighting against their homosexuality. Their
homosexuality provided the context for their passionate interaction,
but the storms came less from their pleasures than from their acute
jealousies.

After their affair had cooled, Whitman set aside (but still remembered) the many squabbles: "Of the occasional ridiculous little storms

& squalls of the past I have quite discarded them from my memory—
& I hope you will too . . ." Such continuous perturbations were either
absent or unrecorded with earlier lovers; Fred Vaughan, Peter Doyle,
Tom Sawyer, Lewy Brown and Jack Rogers left no record of fights with
the poet. Doyle may have had the legendary Irish temper; if so, any
hint of it has been lost.

Whitman's famous "Epictetus" entry in 1870 calling for calmness
and detachment on his part suggests that he had a bad temper needing
control. His use of the word "perturbation" (which one critic rhymes
with masturbation!) was used in a *Daybook* entry to describe his feelings
toward Harry after one of their many angry separations: "sitting in
room, had serious inward rev[elatio]n & conv[ictio]n about [blank]—
very profound meditation on all—saw clearly what it really meant—
happy & satisfied at last about it—singularly so. . . . (that this may
last now without any more perturbation)" (evening December 19,
1876). After New Year's they were back in bed together. Whitman and
Harry had many scenes; their fights indicate love and more than
anything else show how intense their feelings for each other must have
been. While Harry was a troublesome lad, Whitman was no less excit-
able. English admirers heard from Harry's mother that "she had seen
him more angry than anyone she knew." "He would suddenly erupt
like a volcano, after which he would be very quiet" (*Visits to Walt
Whitman 1890–1891*).

A dramatic story surrounds the ring he gave Harry. A recently
discovered photograph (*Walt Whitman Quarterly Review,* Spring 1986)
shows Whitman and Harry together in something of a wedding picture. Harry is wearing Walt Whitman's ring on his wedding finger as
he rests his other hand on the poet's shoulder. Episodes around the ring
went on for several years. Whitman would put the ring on Harry's
finger only to demand it back. ". . talk with H S & gave him r[ing] Sept
26 '76—(took r back)." November 1: "Talk with H S in front room
S[tevens] Street [Camden]—game him r again." But by the end of the
month: "Memorable talk with H S—settles the matter." But July 20,
1877, "in the room at White Horse, 'good bye' " had to be said again.
Whitman was down at Timber Creek, November 14 through 17, 1877,
and took the ring back to Camden with him. Harry wrote from the
farm, the day Whitman left, "I wish you would put the ring on my
finger again, it seems to me there is something that is wanting to
compleete our friendship when I am with you. I have tride to studdy
it out but cannot find out what it is. You know when you put it on
there was but one thing to part it from me and that was death." Stafford

went through many little deaths each time Whitman took the ring off his finger, only to face the great joy of getting the ring back again. Whitman should have underlined the word "again" when he wrote in his *Daybook,* February 11, 1878, "Harry here—put r on his hand again." Torturing each other with delightful and exciting pain, they thus transformed their lovelife into an exquisite form of S & M.

The quarrels arose from Harry's jealousy and Walt's promiscuity. Whitman certainly loved the boy and the boy loved him, but the poet didn't want to preclude other lovers. Harry felt less secure. He tried to tease Whitman with other boyfriends such as Edward Carpenter or with a girlfriend Lizzie (who may also have given him a ring and which he offered to return if Whitman asked). Whitman even encouraged him to loosen up by sending friends such as John Lucas to the pond. When Lucas offered Harry a job with perhaps an undertone of solicitation, Harry turned him down and wrote Whitman, "I will explain the matter more particularly to you when I see you."

Whitman managed to see many other boys during his affair with Harry. Sixteen-year-old Elmer Stafford, a younger brother, called on Whitman October 28 and stayed until November 5, 1877. Elmer wrote from Timber Creek on November 9: "I will be down next wendesday night and stay until thursday night . . . I would like to be with you all the time if i could . . ." In the meantime, Harry put in an appearance on November 10, while Elmer arrived three days later. Whitman sent Elmer a Bible as a Christmas present in 1877. I can't tell whether Whitman was using Elmer to make Harry jealous and to secure Harry's love or whether Whitman just wanted to spread his grace around.

A Timber Creek farmhand, Edward Cattell, presents a more explicit case. That they were having sex is clear from what Whitman records in his *Daybooks:* "The hour (night, June 19, '76, Ed & I,) at the front gate by the road saw E.C. . . . Sept meetings with Ed C by the pond moonlit nights." Whitman's letter to Cattell (January 24, 1877) stresses that he didn't want anyone (particularly Harry) to find out about these meetings: "Do not call to see me any more at the Stafford family, & do not call there at all any more—Dont ask me why—I will explain to you when we meet. . . . There is nothing in it that I think I do wrong, nor am ashamed of, but I wish it kept entirely between you and me . . . keep the whole thing & the present letter entirely to yourself." With a masterful stroke of lover diplomacy, Whitman concluded, "as to Harry you know how I love him. Ed, you too have my unalterable love, & always shall have. I want you to come up here & see me." On those

Walt Whitman and Harry Stafford, c. 1876. A previously unknown photograph found among the Edward Carpenter papers, Sheffield (England) Library,
and printed in *Walt Whitman Quarterly Review,* Spring 1986

rather adulterous terms, Ed gladly met Whitman whenever convenient. He wrote Whitman, November 26, 1877, "Would love to see you
once moor for it seems an age Since i last met With you down at the
pond. . . . i Would like to Com up Som[e] Saterday afernoon and Stay
all night With you and Com home on the Sunday morning train. i love
you Walt and Know that my love is returned." In March, Whitman had
Harry up on March 4 and Ed on March 18.

This ring of boys was joined by an international corps. Edward
Carpenter arrived from England on May 2, 1877. Carpenter had been
ordained in 1870 and was a curate at Cambridge before he embarked on
his journey of economic, sexual and artistic liberation. This visit must
have been the one in which Walt Whitman showed him how to give a
good blow job. Carpenter took up right away with the Timber Creek
boys; like Whitman he found sexual joy in working-class boys. Underlining and capitalizing *"Several,"* Harry wrote on May 21, "Mr. Carpenter has been to see me *Several* times since I was away . . ." After
Carpenter had returned to England, Whitman mentioned news of
Harry Stafford in the dozen or so letters he wrote before Harry's wedding to Eva Wescott in 1884. Inspired by Whitman, Carpenter in
Love's Coming of Age (1895) challenged "the arbitrary notion that the
function of love is limited to child-bearing, and that any love not
concerned with the propagation of the race must necessarily be of a
dubious character." The love of comrades he argued could include more
people and need not be so singular and exclusive as traditional heterosexual marriages. Harry's jealousy must have challenged Carpenter's
noble dream of the generosity of homosexual lovers.

Harry got on well enough with Carpenter, but another Englishman
Whitman brought to Timber Creek aroused his intense loathing. Herbert Gilchrist was the well-educated, handsome and sophisticated
young son of Anne Gilchrist, who had come to the United States in
1876 in hopes of being impregnated by Whitman. When that scheme
failed, she used her son to retain the poet's interest. Herbert enthusi-
astically took up the task. He remained a life-long friend of Whitman
and Carpenter, but he aroused the ire of Harry Stafford. Herbert went
out of his way to court Harry, but the country boy was unyielding.

Harry's mother, however, was easily won over by the English boy;
Susan Stafford seems to have been especially fond of gay men. In the
beginning of 1876, she had encouraged Walt to take an interest in her
son. Complaining about Gilchrist, Harry wrote Whitman (October
24, 1877): "Mother thinks him tip top, and it makes her mad if I say
any thing against him. she toled me the other day if I did not want to

sleep with him I could go somewhere else for she was not going to keep a bed for me by myselfe."

Whether or when Whitman and Stafford broke up isn't entirely clear. There were times they did not see each other, but they always patched things up. Whitman noted in his *Daybooks* a visit from Harry, February 5, 1883; how long the boy stayed isn't clear, but the next *Daybook* entry reads: "April 2, 83—John L. Sloan, boy 15, Jackson Prestwitch's friend." During the winter of 1883-84, Harry went to work for Dr. Richard Bucke, who presided over an asylum near Toronto. Did Harry want to get away from Walt, or did Walt arrange for him to get out of town? Harry wrote two pathetic letters, and had big plans for going on to Detroit, but was back in New Jersey in the spring and married Eva Wescott, June 25, 1884.

In 1881, Whitman had written Harry in a reminiscent mode, "Dear Hank, I realize plainly that *if I had not known you* — if it hadn't been for you & our friendship & my going down there summers to the creek with you—... I believe *I should not be a living man to-day* — I think & remember deeply these things & they comfort me — *& you, my darling boy, are the central figure of them all."* There is certainly an element of a lover's exaggeration here; Harry may have received too much credit. "Of them all," he was, of course, the central figure from 1876 to 1884, but not for the poet's entire life. And even during that period, Whitman gained as much from his recovered finances when *Leaves of Grass* began to sell and brought him the income needed to buy gifts and to pay room and board with the Staffords. As the depression of 1873 receded, Whitman's prosperity increased. In 1884 he bought his own house and took up with a new lover, Bill Duckett (see Chapter 9).

While Harry continued to see Walt both at Timber Creek and in Camden, their visits were inevitably fewer after the marriage. Harry Stafford wrote Whitman a letter, November 20, 1888. which is now lost, but to which Whitman quickly replied that Harry's letter was "quite a surprise to me, & a little *not understandable* — But you will tell me plainer when you come up & see me Saturday — Don't do anything too hastily, & from great excitement — I shall look for you Saturday — If anything prevents your coming, write me & write fully." I suspect Harry wanted to leave his wife and come live with Whitman, but whatever the difficulties, the boy was still able to unsettle the poet. In February, 1889, he wrote Harry's mother that the young man's last visit had not improved Whitman's failing health: "I think quite often of Harry, & wish you would send this letter over to him without fail the first chance you get — it is written largely to him — I have what I

call *sinking spells* in my sickness, & I had one the day he last visited me."
The record of contacts continues until Whitman's final days; Harry
visited January 5 and February 3, 1891 and wrote Whitman a note,
January 29, 1892, asking for Whitman's poem on Lincoln. Whitman
died March 26, and according to his will Horace Traubel received his
gold watch and Harry the silver one.

Whitman had little literary rapport with Harry; they were together
five years before the younger man got to read *Leaves of Grass*. Harry
resented Whitman's literary success and threatened sarcastically in
1881 to go on tour and leave the older man at home as he had been left
behind. Certainly Whitman recovered his spirits frolicking in Timber
Creek with Harry. His last major literary effort, *Specimen Days* (1882),
contained his Civil War notes and his meditations on Timber Creek.
New Jersey was not Walden nor was it Tahiti; Whitman celebrated
the bumblebee and the mullein, common and numerous like the people
and like his tricks. In the section "A Sun-Bath—Nakedness," August
27, 1877, he exclaimed, "Somehow I seem'd to get identity with each
and every thing around me, in its condition. Nature was naked and I
was also."

The Timber Creek section in *Specimen Days* mentions few people and
says nothing about Harry and the boys, but like exuberant water
spirits they inhabited the space. Edwin Miller has provided a convinc-
ing reading of a letter from Whitman to Anne Gilchrist (February 22,
1878). The poet wrote (the italics are his) that he spent "At least two
hours forenoon, & two afternoon, down by the *creek*—Passed between
sauntering—the *hickory saplings*—& '*Honor* is the *subject* of my story'—
(for explanation of the last three lines, ask Herby—)." Miller suggests
that Hickory Saplings and Honor Subject stand for "H.S." or "Harry
Stafford." ("Herby," of course, was Anne Gilchrist's son; "creek" might
be Ed Cattell.)

If "Hickory Saplings" stands for "Harry Stafford," Whitman's published account in *Specimen Days,* September 5, 1877, "The Oaks and I,"
becomes one of the most homoerotic passages in literature:

> ... daily and simple exercise I am fond of—to pull on that young
> hickory sapling out there—to sway and yield to its tough-limber up-
> right stem—haply to get into my old sinews some of its elastic fibre
> and clear sap. I stand on the turf and take these health-pulls moder-
> ately and at intervals for nearly an hour, inhaling great draughts of
> fresh air. .... At other spots convenient I have selected, besides the
> hickory just named, strong and limber boughs of beech or holly, in
> easy-reaching distance, for my natural gymnasia, for arms, chest,

can soon feel the sap and sinew rising through me, like mercury to heat. I hold on boughs or slender trees caressingly there in the sun and shade, wrestle with their innocent stalwartness—and *know* the virtue thereof passes from them into me. (Or may-be we interchange—may-be the trees are more aware of it all than I ever thought.)

... How it is I know not, but I often realize a presence here—in clear moods I am certain of it, and neither chemistry nor reasoning nor esthetics will give the least explanation. All the past two summers it has been strengthening and nourishing my sick body and soul, as never before. Thanks, invisible physician, for thy silent delicious medicine, thy day and night, thy waters and thy airs, the banks, the grass, the trees, and e'en the weeds!"

Although it has had to wait a hundred years for publication, a *Notebook* entry, July 14, 1878, uses less code to carry the same message about Whitman's "H.S."—

A delightful day, warm but breezy. Had much comfort with H.S., we two all day together, lazily lounging around, shady recesses, banks by the brook where the slight but coolish west wind set in— having long talks, interchanges, cheery and loving confidences, with vacant intervals.

Soothing, human, emotionally-nourishing, most precious hours, costing nothing simple and cheap and near as air. Why should they be such rare oases? Why will we run off, frantic, at vast outlay, for that spirit of blessedness (and don't get it) which hovers invisibly at hand?

Stafford Letters

WW to Daniel Whittaker, Camden, April 4, 1876

Dear Dan:

I take an interest in the boy in the office, Harry Stafford—I know his father & mother—There is a large family, very respectable American people—farmers, but only a hired farm—Mr. Stafford in weak health—

I am anxious Harry should *learn the printer's trade thoroughly—I want him to learn to set type as fast as possible*—want you to give him a chance (less of the mere errands &c)—There is a good deal really in the boy, if he has a chance.

Don't say any thing about this note to him—or in fact to anyone—just tear it up, & *keep the matter to yourself private.*

WW to Edwin Stafford, Camden, April 19, 1876

. . . I want Harry to come up Friday, & stay over till Sunday with me — I will not be down Saturday with you this week.

Susan Stafford to WW, Kirkwood, New Jersey, May 1, 1876

Mr. Whitman, Dear Sir,

I intended to send you A few lines this morning by Harry but he went off in such A hurry I did not get time. It is of him that I wish to speak & I hardely know what to say. I am A Little bothered About him I fear he is giveing you to much trouble I am rather sorry that he left the New Republic office in such A hurry at least untill he had another place as he does not like to work on A farm. he spoke of getting A situation in the park I do not think he can his age & size will Be against him there. I will feel better satisfied about him if he can get in an office or better still fore him to be with you but I fear he is to much trouble to you all ready I do not think it right to impose on the good nature of our friends

I hope Harry will ever be Greatfull to you fore your kindness to him I think you will understand me we hope to see you out with us soon respectfully, S[usan] M. Stafford

WW to Edward Cattell, Camden, January 24, 1877

Dear Ed

I want to write you a few lines in particular. Do not call to see me any more at the Stafford family, & do not call there at all any more — Dont ask me why — I will explain to you when we meet. . . . There is nothing in it that I think I do wrong, nor am ashamed of, but I wish it kept entirely between you and me . . . keep the whole thing & the present letter entirely to yourself. . . . as to Harry you know how I love him. Ed, you too have my unalterable love, & always shall have. I want you to come up here & see me. Write when will you come.

Harry Stafford to WW, Camden, April 21, 1877

Spring has at last commenced. The buds are out on the trees, the early flowers are in bloom, the days have grown to a much greater length, the fields of rye and wheat show their beautiful carpet of emerald, the farmers are busy planting their corn and potatoes and all Nature exhibits the plainest evidences that the delightful season for flowers, vegetables, fruits, grains, and the foliage of Summer is again commencing.

Common as it is in the experience of everyone of us, nothing is more wonderful than the annual return of spring. The dead ground awakening by some mysterious process to all the miracles of life is a spectacle, common as it is, not surpassed in all the infinite processes of the Universe.

Amid these wonders and glories the passions and ambitions of mankind and the objects of their pride and eagerness seem artificial and petty. There is a healthy and elevating lesson in studying the spring.

Saturday evening, end of the week.

We have had a couple of rainy Apriel [days.] It is now a fine evening, partially clear, with an occasional gust of wind, and the moon at times shining out brightly. Mr. Whitman and I are sitting in the room togeather; he is reading the New York Herald, and I am writing these lines for exercise. Today we received a newspaper from our friend the artist George Waters of Elmira, N.Y. It contained an article on W.W. portrait painted by Mr. Waters during our late visit to New York; also an interesting extract from the last letter writen by our lamented hostess, the very day before her sudden death. Of corse we were glad to here from our friend, though the newspaper and letter brought up some very sad recollections.

On Monday next, I expect to commence work again at the printing of the West Jersey Press. Yours, Harry Stafford.

Sunday April 22, 1877.

It is a beautiful morning and you are feeling well and hearty. My friend and I, he says, have had a happy night and morning. I am bound for Kirkwood in the next train.

Harry Stafford to WW, Kirkwood, May 1, 1877

Dear Friend—You know how I left you at the station today. I have thought of it and can not get if off my mind, so I have come up to ask your forgiveness. I know how I have served you on many occasions before. I know that it is my falt and not yours. Can you forgive me and take me back and love me the same I will try by the grace of God to do better. I cannot give you up, and it makes me feel so bad to think how we have spent the last day or two, and all for my temper. I will have to *controol* it or it will send me to the States Prison or some other bad place. Cant you take me back and love me the same. Your lovin, but bad-tempered, Harry.

Harry Stafford to WW, Kirkwood, May 21, 1877

Dear friend—You cannot imagine how bad I was disappointed in not seeing you to night. I went down to the depot to meet you, and not finding you, I thought perhaps you came on the 1 O'Clock train, so I went down to the house but did not find you. I have been over in the *City* today, but did not get any thing to do. I went around untill I got sick and then I came over here. I have been to see *several* over here but none could give me any encouragement. You may say that I don't care for you, but I do. I think of you all the time. I want you to come up to-morrow night if you can. I have been to bed to night, but could not sleep fore thinking of you, so I got up and scri*bbl*ed a few lines to you, to go in the *morning* mail. I hope you will not disappoint me. I want you to look over the past and I will do my best to ward you in the future. You are all the true friend I have and when I cannot have you I will go away some ware, I don't know where. Mr. Carpenter has been to see me *Several* times since I was away and he lef me a book and a letter, the letter was to inform me of his intention of going back to England, I will show it to you when I see you. Good Bye. *Believe* me to be your true and loving friend, Harry Stafford
[P.S.] I shall be at the station to meet you. Yours. H.C.S.

WW to Harry Stafford, Camden, June 18, 1877

. . . Dear son, how I wish you could come in now, even if but for an hour & take off your coat, & sit down on my lap—

Harry Stafford to WW, Kirkwood, July 9, 1877

Dear Walt. I thought I would write a line or so to you and let you know that we are all well. Mother got a letter from you stating that you would not be down tomorrow. We ar[e] all most roasted in this place, the sun is so warm and yet we cannot have the window up for if we do the wind blows all of our papers out doors. Walt there is a couple of letters down at our house for you, one from England and one, from New York, the one from N.Y. is from a bank. I forget the name of the bank it is on the outside of the *envalope*. I wish that I coul[d] get a situation in a good printing office. Try the Democrat of Camden for me, will you? I should like to see you but I suppose I cannot untill you come down. As the paper is runnning out I will have to stop. Ever your loving, Harry Stafford.
Write soon and come down, this is a piece of paper I found in the desk so excuse the appearance of it.

Harry Stafford to WW, Kirkwood, July 21, 1877

Dear Friend — I thought I would write a few lines to you and let you know how I am. I cannot get you off my mind somehow. I heard something that made me feel bad, and I saw that you did not want to bid me good bye when you went away yesterday. I will tell you what it was. I heard that you was going to Washington and stay and be gone fore some time, is it so? I thought it was very strange in you, in not saying anything to me or about it. I think of it all the time, I cannot get my mind on my work the best I can do. I should like to come up to Camden next week, and stay all night with you if I could but I suppose I can not do it. I wish you would write to me soon and let me know how you are. Things are very dull down *here* to day there isn't any excursion to day and it is *quiet* and I don't like it very well. There was an excursion here yesterday, it was given by a *rich* man of Philadelphia to the poor children of the ward in which he lived, there was over 200 in it. They appeared to enjoy it very well. I was up there in the afternoon a little while. Mother got home all safe last night, she was home when I got there. Perhaps I will be up Wednesday night in the 6 train, I will if I can   if I do I will have to come back on the Earley train in the morning so I will be in time to help Mr. Sharp wash the cars. I am sitting by the window and the flys are almost eating us up. We have been trying to kill them, but seems to me the more we kill of them, the more we have. Mr. Sharp got out of patience in trying so he took the *poison* out this morning, I have got to scrub the ofice out *this afternoon,* so you can immagine me down on the floor. Good bye, write if it pleases you. Ever your Harry Stafford

Harry Stafford to WW, Kirkwood, August 6, 1877

Dear friend: as I sit here thinking of you and the plesant time we had Saturday I thought I would drop you a line and let you know I got home all safe yesterday morning, had a good lot of woork to do before I went home, waite for the fast line and reported it to Camden   shut up the station and went home, got there about 11 O'clock, had a cup of coffee and then went to bed and slept untill dinner time, got up and went to Sunday school, came home and got supper, went to the pond. I had a headache, did not sleep very well last night, but feel first-rait to day. Herbret cut me prety hard last night at the supper table. You must not let on if I tell you, he called me a "dam fool," I wasn't talking to him anyway! we was all talking of telegraphing, and father said he was reading of a man who was trying to overdo it and I said that I did not think he could do it and then Herbret stuck in that it did not fit very well, and if I had been near enough to smacked him in the "Jaw" I would of done it you must not say anything about it to him or anyone. he thinks he can do as he wants to with me but he will find out sometime that he is fooling with the wrong one. I think that his oldest sister is splendid, but I don't like the other one so well. I will be up to see you on Thursday to stay all night with you, don't want to go any wares then, want to stay in and talk with you, did not get time to say anything to you when I saw you, did not have time to say scarcely anything. The folkes are all well as usual, and things go on the same as wen you was here with us. I ballieve that I have toled you all of the news and I think I will stop. This is the 3rd letter I have written without an answer, I remain your true and loving friend, Harry Stafford

Harry Stafford to WW, Woodbury, New Jersey, August 14, 1877

Dear Walt, I have wrote to father and now I think that I will write to you and let you know how it goes with me. I like the place very well, but it is dry here & not knowing anyone and have no one to put me through the *mill* (as the saying is) it is hard to get along. The folkes are very nice but most too particular, but it is the way of some to be that way you know. When you get up to Camden it will be better for me for I then will have some place to go. I want to get up to see you once a week at least and have a good time for I dont let myself here they are too mild for that. The old Gent asked me if I was a member of Church, and I toled him I was not and he seemed disappointed but gathering that I was not, he then asked me if I went to church and I toled him that I did sometimes[; he asked] w[h]at church I went to and I said I was not of any denomination and he then asked me if father was a church member and I did not know what to tell him, but I got through with it and he said that he would set me at work after dinner, so that was the way I spent the first day. Yours truly, Harry Stafford
Write soon

Harry Stafford to WW, Kirkwood, September 25, 1877

Dear Walt, will be at your place on Saturday, if you are at home, drop a line and let me know. Yours, Harry Stafford

Harry Stafford to WW, Kirkwood, October 4, 1877

Dear Walt, I don't think I will get to get to come to Camden this week but will be down on Saturday a week if nothing happens more than I know of at present. Ed has gone to the city today and I have to tend for him and Ben wishes to go to the city on Saturday so I will have to be at the Station and will not get off until the train will be gone so I will have to stay home. I want to come bad don't know how I will stay away. I want you to have some place to go when I come down some place where there is plenty of girls. I want to have some fun when I come down this time.

All well at home, father went away with Ed today. Debbie is away to her Aunt's. Ever yours, H. Stafford

Harry Stafford to WW, Kirkwood, October 17, 1877

Dear Friend Walt:

I don't know as I have anything to say that will interest you, but I feal as if I would like to write something and so I will begin by telling you about the fun I had last night, it was with a fellow that has been thinking for a long time he could throw me, so last night him and I came together for, the first; he said he could throw me and I said if he thought so he was welcome to try his hand, so we bucked in, he his first holt and mine second, his holt we *puled* around for a short time and then I let loose on him and down he went, then come my holt (he did not want me to hav it but I got him in to it) and I asked him if he was ready and he said he was so I stood him on his head, he got up and said he would go home, but he did not have much to say all the way home, I guess that I hurt his neck by the way he went, but he did not say anything. There is one more fellow who I want to take the conceat out of and that is B. K. Sharp, he thinks he could do what he pleased with me but I want to show him he cannot do it. I was out Sunday night had a good time, went to church and then come home. Cousin Lizzie was over to our house Sunday and went to Sunday school, then came home & ate our suppers and then went out for a ride. I will be down to see you Saturday if nothing happens more than I know of now will be down on the (5 1/2) train, perhaps on the (2). I don't know yet for certain.

The folks are all well, and myself the same. I think of you when ever I have a moment to think. I don't get much time to think about anyone for when I am not thinking of my business I am thinking of what I am shielding, I want to try and make a man of myself, and do what is right if I can do it, I havent heard from Jo Allen yet. I will have to stop writing now for my sheat is giving out and I must go to work, so good bye, & write and let me know how you are, Ever your true and loving friend, Harry Stafford

Edward P. Cattell to WW, Kirkwood, October 21, 1877

[*Does "to G.B." in this letter mean "to Get Blown"?*]

Old man,

i got your Kind and Welcom letter last week and was glad to hear from you my loving old friend i love to hear from you and to Know that you are well and i would Com up To see you But i Cant get of a day now for we are so Bisse now husking Corn! i Went with Some Boys up the Pond to day and i seen your old Ch[a]ir floting down the Strem. Then went up to the house to Gorge Stafford, then seen hurburt Gillcrust and all of Georges folks. i Would like to Com up to town. i think of you old man   think of the times down on the Creek. i did Want to Com up to Camden on Wensday to G.B. But i Cant get of i hop next Summer we Will Be togearter more than we was this.

May this find you well as i am so good   dear Walt I Want Com up to town next Satday or Satday Week and i would like to See you and have a talk. i love you Walt and all ways will So May God Bless You is my prayer, from a young frand, Edward P. Cattell

Harry Stafford to WW, Kirkwood, October 24, 1877

Dear Walt — thought perhaps you would like to get a note from me so I have come down to the Store to write to you. Father has been to the city today and came home sick with the headache, so sick he had to go to bead, the rest of the family are all well. I ballieve I am getting fat myself. You won't know me hardly when you see me, every one who sees me tells me that I look so much better and what is more I feel better than I have since I left the farm. Walt I want to see you badly, I don't know weather I will get to come down Saturday or no, but if I don't get down Saturday, I will come down Saturday week for certain. I was down to see H. Stafford today, he wants to get in Seca's office for the winter if he can and if he does it will be good for me, he is well and at present working on the farm. H[erbert] G[ilchrist] is down yet. he will be down for several days by the way he talks. him and our folks get along well, Mother thinks him tip top, and it makes her mad if I say any thing against him. she toled me the other day if I did not want to sleep with him I could go somewhere else for she was not going to keep a bed for me by myselfe. You will, please excuse bad writing and other mistakes for the store is full of men blowing and looking at me and I have to get along the best way I can. I will have to stop writing now so good bye for here is Hackman and I now have to stop. Ever your true and loving friend, H. Stafford

Harry Stafford to WW, Kirkwood, October 29, 1877. Western Union Telegraph Company letterhead.

Dear Walt: I received your letter this morning and was very glad to get it, and as I have nothing to [do] now I will write to you, and let you know how we are down at the farm. The folks are all well and hard at work. Father is going to the City today and Brother is away, so the house is almost deserted of inhabitants, George & Ruth to are at school and there is no one home but Debbie. I have wrote to you more for to thank you for the dollar than anything else as I don't have any money but what you give me, I don't know but what it is as well for me not to have any for if I haven't any, I don't smoke any and it is best for me not to, I guess, I have not smoked any for nearly a week, so you se I am all alone now for when I have no company I can get a Cigar and pass the time away by myselfe, I did not se Lizzie last night and I think that I will give up going with her if she will be willing for I have so much to think of just at present that it will be best for me, although I love her as well as ever, but I must get in some business before I think of the girls. I am doing well at the Telegraph business they all tell me and like it first rait but don't like the country. I will stay here untill I am fit for an office though I think that I will be by the time spring opens if I have good luck. I was very lowly Saturday night. I wanted to come up to see you but did not get to. Cousin Hosmer was over to se me yesterday and staid all night and came over with me this morning and went from here to Philadelphia, he is looking for a situation at Telegraphing, him and Ed went to Haddonfield in Ed's new wagon. I have had one ride in it. Yours truly, write soon, Harry Stafford

Harry Stafford to WW, Kirkwood, November 2, 1877

Dear friend, I received your welcome letter on the 31, was glad to get it. I received one from H. Gilchrist the same day. he wishes me to come up to his house and go out to the theater with him on Saturday, but I will not get to go. if I could go anywhere I would come up to see you, but I will have to put it off until next Saturday week, I think, I want to come up and see you so bad but cannot. I did not get my head of cabbage and perhaps he has not received it. I am still with B. K. Sharp, him and I had a row one day last week, he came in as he always does with some of his fooling and I gave him back as good as he sent and he got on his ear about it and toled me if things did not suit me here I was free to leave at any time, then I cursed him and went out of the ofice and went over to the Narrow Gauge and found a job, but when I came back to tell him, he made up with me, and I scal'd, had to leave them with a commissioner, over in the city, I got all wet and caught cold and have not been well since, have had the head ache all the time. It is raining very hard there, and when I went out to get the paper to write to you I got all wet and got the paper wet also you must excuse the paper I wrote a letter Jo today. I have not heard from him for a long time. I think that I wrote the last letter to him, but perhaps he did not get it, for I put it in a Telegraphic enevelope the same with him so I did not go.

The folkes are all well I ballieve, and I feel better than I have for the past 3 days, but not as well as I did before I went to market. I hear that Elmar was over to see you 2 times and you and him went over to Mrs. Gilchrist's to spend the evening, hope you had a good time. I must close. Ever your true and loving friend, H. Stafford, Ps write soon

Harry Stafford to WW, Kirkwood, November 7, 1877. Western Union Telegraph Company letterhead.

Dear Friend Walt,

I received your letter yesterday P.M., was glad to hear from you. H[erbert] G[ilchrist] was down to see us last Sunday, he walked down and stade all night and came over with me to the depot and the[n] went on the cars from here to Phila[delphia], he wants me to come up Saturday and stay all night with him, but I will not do it, we can go over for a little while and then come back to your house and stay all night. I will have to go over for a few hours any way for if I don't mother will get on her ear   she was very much put out because I did not go and see him the last time I was up in your house. I am feeling well now but have not for some time untill today, sick about half of the time, but I guess I will be over to a party tonight, but I think that I will have to stay home and tend store for Ed, he wishes to go and that will be [an ex]cuse for me. H.G. tells me that you are well and doing fine and sais that you come over to see them every evening. You must enjoy it or you would not do it. I think it will be good for you to keep it up for going out will give you strength and exercise both. I would lik[e] to be down with you. I suppose that you go to Woolston's once in a while, how does Elmar like the folkes there? I think that I would like to come up and board there again if I ever come to Camden again to work. I want to board with them. Hope you are still well, father has been quite sick but is better at present, he will not live long. I am afraid he is sick more this fall than he has been for a long time. Mont & Daniel still at shucking   the[y] have got someone to help them now I believe. Well I have filled up the paper with nothing and I will have to stop, good bye, write soon, true loving friend, H. Stafford [P.S.] Thanks for the dollar.

Elmer Stafford to WW, Glendale, New Jersey, November 9, 1877

Dear Sir,

I am well and hope you the same. I would be very glad to see you as i did expect to come down [to see] you to day or i would of wrote sooner. and if nothing hapins I will be down next wendesday night and stay until thursday night   I would like very much to see you   you must rite right a way and tell me how you are a getting along. I would like to be with you all the time if i could i would like very much to go with you on your trip to washington, we are very busy husking just now and will be fore a few days and we will have nothing to do for a while   I am in a hurry i cant rite any so it is good by i hope you well Elmer E. Stafford

Harry Stafford to WW, Kirkwood, November 13, 1877

Dear friend Walt —

Father has been very sick and wishes to see you very badly, he toled me to stop and tell you Yesterday, but I did not find you in when I was there so I thought that I would write a few lines to you; the first thing that he asked me when I got home was if I had seen you. We thought he was dying Saturday night for a time. I had to go after the doctor about 12 o'clock. You must come down as soon as you get this letter. come down on the 4 train from Phila tomorrow if you can, any how I will have to close for the present. Ever yours   Harry Stafford

Harry Stafford to WW, Kirkwood, November 17, 1877

Dear friend Walt —

As I sit here in the Office with nothing to do, I thought that I would write a few lines to you: I don't know as I have anything to say that will be news to you, but thought I would write more for practice than anything else. Ben has gon away to day but Geo. Fox is here with me, Ben will not be home for a coupel of days or more, he has gon to N.Y. I don't feel very well this afternoon, have got the headache, as usual, worse this A.M. than I have had it for sometime. The folks and I have commenced to miss you aready, they were talking of you as soon as you left. I wish you was down here with us; when you came down Debbie said to me, it seems like home now Mr. Whitman is back.

I wish you would put the ring on my finger again, it seems to me there is something that is wanting to compleete our friendship when I am with you. I have tried to studdy it out but cannot find out what it is. You know when you put it on there was but one thing to part it from me and that was death. Isn't it a fine day out, it does not look like a Fall day, more like a day in April, although there is no birds singing, but still I think that the day has more the appearance of a Spring day than a Fall one. I think I will bring my letter to a close for I have to make out some bills for the Freight-master. Good bye. Ever true your friend, Harry Stafford. P.S. Write soon and come down when you can. Yours.

Harry Stafford to WW, Kirkwood, November 21, 1877

Friend, Walt,

I received your letter this a.m. was glad to hear from you. Father is a gereat deel better today, he is going out a little, he came out yesterday to see me and Homer kill the pig, but he felt so bad he had to go right back to bed again when he got in. I am not feeling very well nor haven't for a week nearly. I have the headache all the time and have had it for a week, I caught cold somehow, I don't know how though. I wish you would bring me down a coppy book, Spencerian if you can find it, No. 8, and about 6 pens of the same kind. I will be much oblidged to you if you will. You write and let me know how you are. Received the box alright Monday eve, Yours Truly, Harry Stafford

Edward P. Cattell to WW, Kirkwood, November 26, 1877

dear Walt

i am Well and i hope you are the Same old man. Would love to see you once moor for it seems an age Since i last met With you down at the pond and a lovely time We had of it to old man. i would like to Com up Som Saterday afternoon and Stay all night With you and Com home on the Sunday morning train. i love you Walt and Know that my love is returned   so i will Close, from your friend, Edward P. Cattell

[P.S.] My love to you Walt, i think of you in my prayers old man Every night and Morning.

Harry Stafford to WW, Kirkwood, November 27, 1877

Dear friend Walt,

I arrived home [last night] at about 7 PM, [and I was feeling] bad
and I [was going slow] but the horses did not like it much they wanted
to troot all the way home, they felt good I guess they have not been
doing much for a couple of weeks or more, so they wanted to show off,
you know how it is your self when you feel like *licking* me; but I held
them down as I do you, when you feel that way. I have a kind of a cold
from coming up yesterday[; am] good other ways. Father is a little
better today than he was yesterday, but he looks very badly yet. Debbie
and Joe got home about 9 O.K. they were over to Philadelphia after
they left our house & Conrad Schwartze's and had a good time from
what I heard them say. Ed and I went over to Glendale to church
Sunday ev, they had *distracteed* meeting (as I call it over there) there was
3 up seeking there souls salvation. It looks as if the rain was not over
with yet, and the "rooster" is crowing (that is a sure sign) they say.

When I saw you on Federal St., yesterday, I thought you did not
look very well, what was the matter with you? did you not feel as well
as usual? Ben is not collecting today and it seems lonely here without
him here. I don't have anyone to talk to unless he is here, everything is
as still as the dead of night not a sound reaches my ear and the ticking
of the clock almost appears to be looking out of the store window over
here. I wonder what his thoughts are about; there the click of the
register has broken the stillness of the place, it seems like the presence
of an old and loving friend, it is telling of the death of a man out in the
St[ate] of Oregon, I don't know to who but here comes a fellow around
now he sais put in a word for him he is blagwarding me, let him crack
away, I will have to close ever yours   write soon, come down when
[you] feel   good bye

Elmer E. Stafford to WW, Glendale, January 11, 1878

Dear Walt. I am very sorry that i aint wrote sooner, but it seems to me
I aint had time. I have received my bible and I think a grate [d]eal of it
I think it is very nice indeed.

I am very well and hope you the same   I would be very glad to see
you. I believe there is no new news   it is now about 10 o'clock. the
weather is cloudy and rainy. I went to haddonfield school a little
wile but i have quit and I do not go any more now I am at home

I wanted to go to the city but pop thinks i had better go to
haddonfield

I think I will come down next week if i can   I must end my letter so
it is   good by my Dear friend. Elmer E. Stafford

Harry Stafford to WW, Kirkwood, January 18, 1878

Dear Walt

You know that I had written to you last, and I cannot tell how it is
that you will not answer my letter, I did not mean to offend you, but if
I did, will you please foregive me, I am here with friend Sharp, and a
lonely time I am haveing of it ; I have not been away from here any time
till Tuesday, since I was up to see you then as father was so sick that he
could not do anything I had to stay home and work for him ; as he was
going to kill hogs Wednesday ; so I had to loose three days right off ; I
was to Camden yesterday and would of stoped to see you until I [was
prevented] you know that I cannot enjoy myselfe any more at home, if
I go up in my room I always come down feeling worse than I do when
I go up, for the first thing I see is your picture, and when I come down
in the sitting room there hangs the same, and whenever I do anything,
or say anything the picture seems to me is always looking at me ; so I
find that I am better satisfied when I am here than when I am home.
When Herbert [Gilchrist] was down he said you was very well and
happy. I talked to him and got out all I could but that was not much.
I have [found a girlfriend] and, that is to say, she is a good and true
friend to me, we have had many good times together, but none that
hangs with me like those you and I have had. I received a letter from
her last night, she said that she was well and thought of coming over
soon. I suppose you know that father has had another hemorrhage, but
he is better now but he will never be able to do any more hard work.
"Ned Rogers" is coming over to help him today . . . They have got
through with the deviding of the place ; they have each taken a part of
it, and now it is *settled.* I hope that you will not keep this letter or tell
anyone what it contains, I don't want our folkes to know that I have
been so foolish as to write to you when you will not answer. There is
one thing that I have foregotten, it is that Mont has been going to
School at the Haddon institute for sometime he likes it fy[r]st rait. I
will have to close my letter as the paper is running on so adieu, if I
never hear from you will think of you as an old friend that is dead and
gone, good bye Harry Stafford

Elmer E. Stafford to WW, Glendale, January 18, 1878

Dear Walt I have received your letter and very glad to hear from you.
I am well and hope this letter will find you the same.

Dear Walt, I would like to see you. there is nothing very new, the W[eather] is clear & the stars is shining very bright, as you stated in your letter you would like to [k]no[w] Wesley Address Wesley Stafford, Dixie, Polk Co, Oregon.

I would like to come down & stay all night with you. I will come down as soon as I can. It is now 4 minutes after 8 oclock I have been hauling wood to day we have bin Clearing off the swamp & now are very near don. we are all well The weather has not been very cold yet but we [expect more snow] now perty soon I will come down and stay with you some day just as soon as I can if it could be so I would like to be with you all the time. I must end my letter now so it is good by Walt, Dear Walt, Elmer E. Stafford

Harry Stafford to WW, Kirkwood, January 24, 1878

[Parts of this letter are water-stained.]

Walt, I am & have been well since I saw you but Father is very sick today, he has been in bed almost all day, he looks very badly; he wanted to know wheather you asked after him or no, he asked me if I asked you to come down, he wants to see you and so do I and [all the rest] of us . . . They all seem put out because you don't come down. You must come down as soon as you can. I will be up to see you soon. You did not give me what you said you was going to was it because I [had accepted] this one if so I will give it back to Lizzie . . . I am in such a hurry I have to write fast but I will show you some of my writing on the envelope. I will have to close now as there is some folks here that are waiting for me now. Good bye, write soon, ever true and loving friend, H. Stafford

Harry Stafford to WW, Kirkwood, March 26, 1878

[Parts of this letter are water-stained.]

Dear Walt —

As I have thought of you almost constantly since I came home I thought I would write a few lines to you to let you know that I am feeling pretty well and sincerely hope that you are the same. Mother [may be going to the] . . . City before [long, if she] did she should [visit] no doubt but that she will stop in to see you on her [way back] Things are about as they were when you was down here, any more than we have had a fearful storm of wind and sand. The wind blew so hard last Sunday night that it almost upset me when I was coming home, "for I was *out* then, as usual," Father and all are well. "John," the 'darkey man' is here yet [Van] and George have their fun . . . about drinking it to [turn] his skin white; it rather gets to him, but he takes it all in good part; he asked Van the other day whether the first man on earth was black or white and Van told him the first man was white and then John asked him where the black man came from, and Van told him that a black man was a monkey with his tail cut off, so he gave up talking to him and went on with George. . . .

I have been thinking of the suit of cloths which I am to have like yours: I have had myself all pictured out with a suit of gray, and a white slouch hat on about fifty times, since you spoke of it; the fellows will call me Walt then. I will have to do something great and good in honor of the name. What will it be? . . . [Well, I] have to close, Yours truly, Harry Stafford

P.S. Write soon and let me know how you are. Yours. H.S.

Harry Stafford to WW, Kirkwood, June 5, 1878

[*Parts of this letter are water-stained.*]

Dear Walt,

I have said that I would not write to you any more until you wrote to me, but I have got some more of my troubles to tell you: . . . it is this, last Monday morning Lucas stoped me as I was coming from the pond with a pail of watter on my way to the Station and asked me how I would like to come over to his office and help the boys with the books and do the letters myself. I said I [would] like to come and he talked [with me and] asked me several questions which I answered to suit him and then he asked me to come over during the day and he would talk farther [about] the subject, so when I got thru he said that he would give me $50 for one year and [I would have to] board myself in the meantime he went away and left me with the boys, so when I came away they asked me if I would come back [I answered] that I would see Mr. Lucas at the [station] in the morning and give him [my answer] and my answer was no, of corse, I told him that I could not work for any less than my board he did not think I could earn that I guess for he left me and went home. The result was this, he refuses to let me practice on his line. What do you think of a rich man . . .

[that's the] rough [of] it. I will explain the mater more particularly to you when I see you. The folks are all well and all wish to see you very much. Excuse writing for I am in a hurry. Your affectionate sir, Harry Stafford

Harry Stafford to WW, Laurel Hills, New Jersey, July 27, 1878

[*Parts of this letter are water-stained.*]

My Dear, Dear Friend,

I received the rubard to-day, it came just in time: I have been sick for some time past, I took a dose of it as soon as I got it. . . .

Mr. Whitman, I want to ask you do you think if I study and write all the spare time I have that in the corse of two or three years I would be able to be an educator? I have been thinking for about two months that I would like to be something. . . .

I see you [think we can] work to-gather [when the] times have become settled, and our love sure (although we have had very many rough times to-gather but we have stuck too each other so far and we will until we die, I know. . . .

Mother is very sick and has been ever since I came home, she was taken sick that day I was up there. Father is well as usual he was to market today with potatoes. We are having a fine rain to-night down here, it hasn't come any too soon things were kneeding [the water and this] will make . . . Well I have to close as the paper is given out. Your loving son. H. L. Stafford

P.S. Write soon and oblige yours.

Harry Stafford to WW, Laurel Hills, August 26, 1878

Dear Walt —

As mother wrote to tell me that you visited us [and asked me] to write to you Thursday, until Friday, of course I could not do it but I was very sorry when I learned that you wer not comming down Saturday as you perdicted when you went away, but we have not been lonely, for we have had the Englishman [Herbert Gilchrist] with us ever since your departure; he has also taken his departure do day, for Egg Harbor. I believe he is a counting on having you with him through the fall monts or at least he said he was he has given us a strong invertation but I rather think that the mosquitoes are too thick for me down there.

Mont and I went to "Darkey" Camp Sunday . . . the devil they wanted and then they would not shout, dont you think they they were awful mean? I do. I saw one of them today, and he asked me if I was coming any more, and I told him that I hat went my last time, and he asked me how it was and pretty damn quick [I] told him he said it worse, rather mean but "de broderin did not get de [Spirit?] on Sunday night," I said no but that [they got] money in dar pocket didn't they? and he said yes. They are all damned humbugs, and ought everyone to be sent to Africa. . . .

Sharp is tyring to crawl back to me now but he can't do it he has "cooked his goose" with me now. I like working at the office very well. It has given me such an awful apetite that Mother says that I will eat her out of house and house, if I keep on, that is a good organ, isn't it? The folks are all well and myself too—[brother?] is in bed isn't asleeping, stirring like a thrashing machine   Mother is downstairs talking like a [hell] fire—dads gone to bed too. [—] isn't come from the store yet   writing to Walt Whitman up in the old room [watching] june bugs   dad's been to town today and bought himself a new suit of clothes.

Well as this is the second letter I have written this evening and I am out of rows, I will have to stop. Your Loving Friend H.L. Stafford   P.S. Write soon and let me know how your are, yours, HLS

Susan Stafford to WW, Kirkwood, December 29, [1878].

[*This letter was marked Sunday, which would fit 1878; however, Whitman sent a kit of fish November 24, 1877, so the date may be 1877.*]

Dear friend, we have looked for you down with us so long & you have not come that we have given up all hope of ever seeing you again with us so I write to say the kit of fish and all the nice presents that you have so kindly sent us have all come safe and we all thank you more than words can tell. I should have written for you last weeks to spend Christmas with us but I had a very severe attact of the heart & was not able to do so   I am better now will you please come this week   we shall look for you   do not disappoint us. We have waited so long please write what day you will come & we will meet you at the Station, ever your friend, S.M. Stafford

Harry Stafford to WW, Laurel Hills, January 13, 1879

Dear Walt: As I have been hard at work ever since I was up to see you I thought I would write a few lines to let you know how I am getting on with it (threshing I mean) we will finish by Saturday, if nothing happens, and I will be very glad of it, for I am very sick of it. Mont is helping me, he is as bad against it as I am. Father went to the city with a load of straw today; perhaps he will be over in time to stop and see you. I believe the work is doing me good in some ways for it is making me eat more than ever. You will not know me when you see me. I am getting so brown and fat.

Mont received your papers today, those giving the account of the execution, it went over to Glendale before he got it. He was much pleased with it.

Dear Walt, I have saved enough out of that dollar you gave me to come up and see you. I have been trying to find a day to come up and see you but cannot until we finish threshing. I have been thinking it all over and will be up on Tuesday next one week from tomorrow if nothing happens. I want to spend the day with you, and have a good talk, have some good cigars for me. (I know you will, won't you?) Debbie and Joe were home yesterday and stayed all day. Capt. Townsend and wife were over too. Lizzie was over Saturday afternoon, stayed until late and of course I went home with her, had a good time with her, I told her about you sending your love to her, she sends you back the same, she says she would like to see you.

I have been home ever since I was up to see you; there is but very little news about here now, everything is the same as when you left here. Father is about the same as when you were down. Mother is well and all the rest of the folks. Mont and all the rest sends their love for you. Will have to close as Ed wishes to close up the store. Will be up Tuesday if nothing happens. Ever your true friend, Harry L. Stafford

WW to Herbert Gilchrist, Camden, February 6, 1879

... Harry Stafford was up to see me ten days ago—They are all going to move from the Creek (as Montgomery S wants the farm)— They are going over to Glendale, to take the store there on the corner, opposite the church—are to move early in March...

WW to Harry Stafford, New York City, May 28, 1879

Dear Son,

Your letter dated 27th [lost] has reached me here, & glad to get it—glad to hear you are having such good health this summer—as to that spell you speak of, no doubt it was the devilish lemonade & cake—I always told you you was too heedless in the eating & drinking, (sometimes going without too long, &)—(I tell you Harry, it is the *stomach, belly* & liver that make the principal foundation of all *feeling well—with one other thing)—...*

WW to Harry Stafford, Camden, April 19, 1880

Harry, I shall come down on Wednesday in the 4 p m train (as I said)—Nothing new—I am well—I had a good day yesterday (Sunday) perfect day—went over to late breakfast to the Steamer *Whillden,* Arch Street wharf—every thing jolly and plentiful & sailor-like—there four hours—then in the evening to Col: Johnston's family—I have got your blue flannel shirts for you—

WW to Harry Stafford, Camden, October 31, 1880

. . . I have just had my dinner & am up here in my third story room finishing this—it is a bright sunny day here, after the three days' storm—I have been alone all day, but busy & contented—my room is just right for all the year except the very hottest months—the sun pours in here so nice, especially afternoons—I wish you was here to-day, Hank (I haven't got any *wine* though) . . . Love to you, dear son—I shall be down Saturday—

WW to Harry Stafford, Camden, February 11, 1881

Dear Hank—

Yours of 9th rec'd [lost]—am a little surprised you take to L of G so quickly—I guess it is becasue the last five years had been *preparing & fixing the ground,* more & more & more—& now that the seed is dropt in it sprouts quickly—my own feeling ab't my book is that it makes (tries to make) every fellow *see himself,* & see that *he has got to work out his salvation himself*—has got to pull the oars & hold the plow, or swing the axe *himself*—& that the real blessings of life are not the fictions generally supposed, but are real, & are mostly within reach of all—you chew on this—. . .

WW to Harry Stafford, Camden, February 28, 1881

. . . Of the past I think only of the comforting soothing things of it all—I go back to the times at Timber Creek beginning most five years ago, & the banks & spring, & my hobbling down the old lane—& how I took a good turn there & commenced to get slowly but surely better, healthier, stronger—Dear Hank, I realize plainly that *if I had not known you*—if it hadn't been for you & our friendship & my going down there summers to the creek with you—and living there with your folks, & the kindness of your mother, & cheering me up—I believe *I should not be a living man to-day*—I think & remember deeply these things & they comfort me—& *you, my darling boy, are the central figure of them all*—

Of the occasional ridiculous little storms & squalls of the past I have quite discarded them from my memory—& I hope you will too—the other recollections overtop them altogether, & occupy the only permanent place in my heart—as a manly loving friendship for you does also, & will while life lasts . . .

Harry Stafford to WW, Glendale, April 4, 1881

Dear Walt:

I have watched and waited for some friendly line from you, for about one month. Yet not a line have you pened. I suppose you have forgotten your rural friend, in the bustle and fashions of Boston life. I don't blame you very much; yet it seems to me that you would occasionally think of the loving times we have had in days gone by. I notice that is the way you always use me, but I will get square with you when I go off on my lecturing trip not a line will I write you, and dont you forget it. Here I have been waiting in this dry and dusty office for some account of you and your happy trip, and this is the way you serve me, is it. Well I have a new *gal* and a mighty nice little thing she is too; Just such a one as you would like, and I now if you were to see these pretty rosy lips you would be charmed beyond measure with them. Yet you shan't see her now that you used me so. She is a wild rose, plucked from the bosom of the forest, pure as a lily and gentle as the summer breezes.

Mother is unwell and has been for some time, she has to work too hard I think; she has tryed to get some one to help her but it seems that she dont succeede very well. Hope she will be able to have some one er'e long. Aunt lizzie has been to see us twice since you were here, and is coming home to stay three or four days next week. Would like you to see her, think you would like her. Father is well as usual, and so we all are with the exception of Mother. Hoping to see or hear from you soon, I am yours as ever, H. Stafford

WW to Harry Stafford, Camden, January 25, 1882

. . . I wish it was so you could all your life come in & see me often for an hour or two—You see I think I understand you better than any one—(& like you more too)—(You may not fancy so, but it *is* so)—& I believe, Hank, there are many things, confidences, questions, candid *says* you would like to have with me, you have never yet broached—me the same—

Have you read about Oscar Wilde? He has been to see me & spent an afternoon — He is a fine large handsome youngster — had the good sense to take a great fancy *to me!* . . .

Harry Stafford to WW, London, Ontario, Canada, November 28, 1883

My Dear Old Friend;

I arrived here safely Saturday evening 6⁴⁵. Have had quite a good time so far. Came direct to the Asylum. Went on duty as turnkey Monday morning but will not remain here over six weeks or two months as the occupation is not pleaseant. Cannot sleep at night there are so many unearthly noises and besides I want to get a position where I can make better wages. And as you know I am of a nervous tempaerament — and the least scene shocks me.

I want to go to Detroit, Mich., after I leave here; from there to Chicago and want you to give me a letter to any business man you know there. Your recommendation has been the means of making me some good friends and I am shure with your letter, I can get something good in either of the cities. If you are not personally acquainted there give me letters to some of the newspapermen. It will carry lots of weight. You know how I have started. I want to make a lot somewhere. If I could only get in a telegraph office I would be one of the happiest fellows you ever saw.

Don't have any privilage here, not even time to write. I am up in my little room writing this while my patients are sadly pacing up and down the hall. Have 42 men in my charge. Will have to close for the present so good-bye. Please don't forget that your boy is away among strangers and a good long letter from his dear friend will do him good. Ever your Harry.

P.S. Dont forget to write soon and send the letters.

Harry Stafford to WW, London, Ontario, Canada, December 17, 1883

My Dear Old Friend:

Your postals came "OK" and found me pretty well. Was glad to hear from you, even though it was through a postal: as you know I am down on that kind of business and never pay any attention to them only from you but it pleases me now to even get that much from an old friend. As I have told you the position I now have is not a desirable one but better than nothing. Have only saw Dr. Bucke once since he came home, that is privately, and that was the day after he arrived. He then said he would by and [by] get something better for me. Will remain here until we find the prospects and if nothing better promises will go to Detroit and from there to Chicago;. I am *determined* to make a hit somewhere and dont forget it. I haven't had a blue spell yet and think I can get along without any. By the time I receive this month's pay, I will be in *easy circumstances,* financially, and will decide on a turn and let you know. I think I can manage to get pretty well over the N.Y. and Canada by working here and there. I love to travel and see. We have a deep snow here, fell a week ago. Haven't heard from home directly but once since my arrival. With lots of love and a good old time kiss I am ever your boy Harry. Write me a letter soon.

Harry Stafford to WW, London, Ontario, Canada, February 10, 1884

Dear Old Friend,

Am quite well with the exception of the abcess in my neck. It has come again. Dr. B[ucke] lanced it few days ago but it dont appear to get much better. Received the papers and am glad to get them for it is the only way I can get posted. Most of my friends appear to have forgotten me or think me of too little importance to drop a line.

Will leave here the first of next month and start for Detroit, where I will put in a month or so if I can find bread and shelter. Please send me a letter of introduction to someone there if you know anyone it will make it much better for me and I will not feel entirely alone. I think perhaps Dr. B[ucke] can give me a letter to some of his friends there as he is going to give a lecture there Wednesday evening. Don't get the blues worth a damn and dont expect to. Will close for the present. With lots of love, I remain as Ever your distant and devoted son, Harry

Harry Stafford to WW, Kirkwood, January 29, 1892

Dear Walt Whitman,
Dear sir! would you oblige me by bringing me one of your books containing the "Poem on the death of ex-President Lincoln," If so you will oblige your true friend. I wish it for a particular purpose. Yours and etc., H. Stafford

Walt Whitman with Bill Duckett, c. 1886. Courtesy of the New York Public Library

CHAPTER NINE

Man-Boy Lovers

Walt Whitman
and Bill Duckett

B ILL DUCKETT'S relationship to Walt Whitman can be glimpsed in the photograph of the two taken together around 1886. Whitman liked to sit for photographs, but in almost all of his poses he is on stage alone. (Another exceptional photograph shows him in 1865 perched on a love seat with Peter Doyle whose hand touches the poet's thigh.) The sexual aura of the Whitman-Duckett photograph comes through despite the studio trappings of fake shore, flowers and balcony. His elbow wavering near the crotch, Whitman leans one arm against Bill's thigh. Duckett, meantime, has his arm somewhat self-consciously around the old man's neck. Duckett's crotch comes through in the photograph, and, despite scratches, there's just a distinct hint of cock under the formal pinstripes.

Bill Duckett looks awkward and ill at ease in the photograph. His short coatsleeves suggest he was still growing. In the nineteenth century, young men began wearing suit, tie and hat at a very early age in order to bring them more rapidly and directly into the world of adulthood. The age of sexual consent was ten in many states, and there were few child labor or compulsory school attendance laws. All accounts agree that Bill was young. In a letter of reference which Whitman wrote trying to get the boy employment, the poet vouched, "He is used to the city, & to life & people — is in his 18th year — has the first Knack of Literature — & is reliable & honest —" (22 June 1886). Many young people add a few years in order to get a job; when I first went to work I lied and said I was fourteen, even though I was younger. As late as 1889, a press notice brought to Whitman's attention claimed "that a young man of 12 who drives him out, likes and will lecture on him after he is dead, having taken notes of all he has said." This press account distressed Whitman no end and the poet called it a "*lie* in big, big type" (*With Walt Whitman,* VI:167). The boy was probably not twelve in 1889, but neither was he eighteen in 1886. My estimate is that Bill was fourteen when the two began going together in 1884 and was eighteen when they parted in 1888. He was unquestionably a teenager when Whitman knew him.

The two met in 1884 when Whitman was sixty-five years old. In Walt Whitman's handwriting, there is a two-page description of their life together, which purports to be written by Duckett, presumably for the poet's first biographer Richard Bucke. Duckett recalled, "I became acquainted with Mr Whitman in 1884 when he bought and moved in the little house 328 Mickle Street, within three doors of which I lived. We boys had a quoit club, and W. made us a present of a handsome set of quoits for pitching." (Thomas Eakins has a painting of boys pitching quoits, a game resembling horseshoes.) Whitman had a reputation in Camden which must have been known by the boys. Horace Traubel recalled that when he first met Whitman, neighbors "went to my mother and protested against my association with the 'lecherous old man.' They wondered if it was safe to invite him into their houses. . . . I got accustomed to thinking of him as an outlaw."

Bill Duckett was drawn by such a reputation; moreover, his father was dead. When Whitman invited him to move in, the boy readily accepted. After they had broken up, Whitman said that his house-keeper, Mary Oakes Davis, had invited the boy in, but Bill claimed Whitman himself had taken the initiative. Whitman pretended to be outraged: "think of it!—that I invited him here, that he was my guest!—the young scamp that he is! why, that is downright perjury, outrageous lying" (*With Walt Whitman,* IV:64). Despite the later litigation, no one disputed that Duckett lived with Whitman (they disputed only the board charges).

For about five years Whitman kept close track of the boy in his notebooks. The two were nearly inseparable in 1885, particularly after September 15, when Whitman's friends bought him a horse and buggy. The poet wrote in his notebook in November, 1885, "go out in wagon every afternoon—Wm Duckett drives." There is an 1885 picture of Duckett and Whitman in the buggy all hitched up ready to go. Duckett evidently moved into Whitman's house May 1, 1886, and except for some short absences, the two lived together until December,

Walt Whitman in 1885, aged 66, sitting next to Bill Duckett, then about 15–16. Whitman's paralysis had worsened after a sunstroke in July. Many friends contributed to buy this horse and phaeton, since Whitman could walk only with great difficulty. Courtesy of Yale University Library

Walt Whitman's house (with people in doorway), 328 Mickle Street, Camden, New Jersey (1890). In J. Johnston and J. W. Wallace, *Visits to Walt Whitman in 1890–1891* (1918)

1888, when the housekeeper expelled Bill because he wasn't paying
board. The short times Bill was away from Camden were carefully
noted by Whitman. That the relationship was more than casual might
be shown by Whitman's wanting to cover up such a simple matter as
Billy's driving. In the summer of 1887 both the artist Herbert Gilchrist and the sculptor Sidney Morse moved into the house. Not only
was Bill shunted aside, but Whitman wrote a sketch in Morse's notebook, describing himself: "He wrote generally two or three hours a
day, and often went out for a drive in a phaeton that his friends had
presented him with. He drove himself" (*In Re Walt Whitman*, 382). The
last sentence cannot be true — at least in 1887 — because Whitman was
rather feeble for driving alone.

Duckett's own writing suggests he and Whitman both recognized
their tie. On November 29, 1886, Duckett recorded among the visitors "a handsome young Englishman who came to this country with
Wilson Barrett the actor, with whom he is now acting. He Bore a
letter of introduction from Oscar Wilde, one of Mr Whitmans best
friends and comrade." As Barrett's boyfriend was to the actor so Duckett
was to the poet; the actor's lover was both "handsome" and "young."
In his recollections, Bill wrote that Whitman "was entirely free from
indelicacy or any unchastity ['in any form' is cancelled] whatever."
Again, there seems to be a note of apology and cover-up in even
mentioning the question of chastity. Why would there be a need to
even argue the issue?

Whatever might have been the sexual relations between Duckett
and Whitman, they were certainly lovers even if they never had sexual
intercourse. After their unharmonious separation, Whitman still recalled that "we were quite thick then: thick: when I had money it was
as freely Bill's as my own: I paid him well for all he did for me" (*With
Walt Whitman*, IV:65). Not only did Bill go everywhere with Whitman — perhaps a necessity because of the older man's weaknesses — but
many of their expeditions were more dates or outings than anything
else. Thus they went to Billy Thompson's in Gloucester, New Jersey,
for what Whitman called "a rousing dinner of shad & champagne"
(*Correspondence*, III:27). Another time they went to Sea Isle City and
"stayed there at the hotel two or three days." In the summer of 1887,
Whitman told the sculptor Sidney H. Morse, "I detest lemonade. . . .
If one is going to drink anything — champagne, abstemiously taken,
goes to the spot and don't make a fool of a fellow. A copious draught,
also, not from habit, but, for instance, as the boys say" (*In Re Walt
Whitman*, 388). Mary Oakes Davis claimed that after the poet died in

1892, the boys broke into the basement and drank all the champagne. Might Bill have been among their number?

Their most public performance together was in New York City, where Whitman delivered his lecture on Abraham Lincoln, April 14, 1887, at the well-filled Madison Square Theater. "He was accompanied," recalls Elizabeth Leavitt Keller in *Walt Whitman in Mickle Street,* "by William Duckett, a young friend who acted as valet and nurse, and it was on his arm the old man leaned as he came forward on the stage and stood a few minutes to acknowledge the applause of the audience." The house was packed and the author received $250 from gate receipts; Andrew Carnegie threw in an extra $350 for his box seat. Whitman wrote a friend that afterwards he "had a stunning *reception* — I think 300 people, many ladies — that evn'g Westminster Hotel — newspapers friendly, everybody friendly even the authors" (*Correspondence,* IV:87). Bill not only shared hotel facilities with his mentor but he served as hostess at the reception. The New York *Evening Sun* reported, "A young man who bore the double burden of receiving the cards of the callers and having the toothache had come over from Camden with Mr. Whitman as his attendant. He is William Duckett. In an hour Mr. Duckett had a very full hand of the cards of distinguished men and the crowd became so great that he gave up trying to announce each newcomer" (*Daybooks,* 417–8). For a Camden orphan this event at the elegant Westminster Hotel must have been astonishing in its elegance: the *Evening Sun* leader began, "Poets, Artists, Men with Horse Sense, and Lovely Women in Line," and went on for thirty-eight column inches.

At a time when a first-class blast-furnace laborer in Carnegie's mills received only one dollar for a twelve-hour day, the steelmaster's contribution of $350 represented an enormous amount of money. Possessions were at the heart of the falling out between Whitman and Duckett. In April 1889, Whitman was looking for some printed photos of himself; there had only been 250 to begin with; Whitman thought there had been 305. A rival suggested Bill might have taken them, and Whitman went off on a tirade, "I must not say who — only that they are probably stolen. I have had many things purloined, stolen, from the rooms here — books, pamphlets, papers, clothing, pictures. I had fully six or seven pairs of gloves — choice gloves given to me — gloves of some value; attractive, too, evidently to others. I had also half a dozen handkerchiefs, presents, some of them silk; choice, fine, beautiful; they are gone, too. Some of these things were souvenirs, some not." But he had to admit, "I am a great forgetter, mislayer: I hesitate to explain the missing things this way till all other explanations are exhausted" (*With Walt Whitman,* v:82). Bill lived with Walt Whitman until forced to leave. When he gathered his belongings, they had necessarily fallen together with his mentor's. Whose handkerchief was whose; Whitman himself had said that they shared everything.

Even if Bill had confused his own and his lover's belongings, this was presumably not a new development in 1888-9. Why did the falling out come then? People are always changing — something of a shock both to the self and to others. Sometimes these changes weld the couple further together; other times pull them apart. If one of the lovers is a teenager, the difficulties are compounded by the stresses of growth in these years. Likewise with an elder partner — particularly in his sixties and seventies — physical changes can be rapid. When Whitman ended his stay with Peter Doyle in Washington, he had a stroke. So now as his ardor cooled with Duckett, his body collapsed. In June, 1888, the poet suffered another stroke, which essentially left him bed-ridden the rest of his life.

Whitman had hopes for Duckett which were not realized. He wanted the young man not only as as companion, but also as a Boswell. Duckett's letters and notes to Bucke attempting to record details of life with the poet were carefully supervised by Whitman. Some have suggested that Duckett was only interested in wheedling money out of Dr. Bucke, but I think a more likely explanation was that Duckett failed to become the amanuensis Whitman was looking for. Between men and boy lovers tension can develop if the more experienced man tries too hard to shape a boy into an unwanted mold. Whether Duckett tried and failed to please Whitman or whether Duckett simply resented the pressure being laid upon him is unclear now.

Whitman gave up the relationship so readily because he found another young man more suitable to his needs. He had first tried to get Sidney Morse to keep a journal of the home life of the poet; he had given him a blank book and dedicated it in May, 1887. Whitman even wrote a sample for Morse as he had for Duckett, but the artist was no more cut out for such work than the quoit player. The great amanuensis was found a year later in Horace Traubel. Unlike Duckett, Traubel was not working-class: he was a newspaper man, highly literate. Born in Camden in 1858, Traubel, when he meshed with Whitman in 1888, was nearly twice as old as Bill. Whether Traubel ever had sex with Whitman or whether they were lovers is less important than the way in which Traubel immediately supplanted Bill. Traubel began his daily journal *With Walt Whitman in Camden* March 28, 1888, and kept it

until the poet's death in 1892. The book has been published in six
volumes to date and has only reached July, 1890 (Volume I appeared in
1906, VI, 1982). Traubel hardly disguises his loathing for Bill Duckett. In getting rid of Bill, the housekeeper was a ready ally. Some have
suggested that Mary Oakes Davis was in love with the sage, "gladly
sacrificing her life for one whom she doggedly, though secretly loved."
She also seems to have specialized in older, dying men. Before coming
to keep house for Whitman, she had got half the estate of a sea captain
whom she cared for; she married another seaman, who died at sea. And
after Whitman died, she sued his estate, claiming that the thousand
dollars left her was insufficient for all the expenses she had been out in
caring for the famous bard. She succeeded in her suit and essentially
got all the money left by the estate in 1894.

In 1889, the litigious Mary Oakes Davis took William Duckett into
court, claiming he owed her for board. First she retained a Camden
lawyer, who discouraged her; Traubel claimed the lawyer was associ-
ated with Duckett. Then, she retained a Philadelphia lawyer, who
charged her a hefty forty dollars' fee. Bill had some funds held by the
Philadelphia Fidelity Trust from his dead father. Since he was a minor,
the lawyer brought a claim against the estate — a case which could be
handled in Philadelphia, Pennsylvania, where the money was being
held — rather than in Camden, New Jersey, where the debt had been
incurred. On February 1, 1889, Bill Duckett took the stand and said
he had been invited in by Walt Whitman and had always been a guest.
Accepting Davis's word over the boy's, the judge rendered a decision
against the Duckett estate, granting Mrs. Davis $190.

Whitman's role in this eviction is somewhat curious. He was now
quite bed-ridden and dependent on his housekeeper. In fact, she even
threatened to quit after Whitman had his stroke. "Mary has lived with
me now for some years," the poet told Traubel, "three or four years: we
have never even had any misunderstanding: no words: yet the nearest
we ever came to quarrel was just about Bill: this young rascal who's
now trying to evade his obligations." While calling the boy a liar,
Whitman indicated that he still had a soft spot for the "poor boy! poor
boy! I pity him: I would receive him today if he needed me: would
help him: I am sure I would be the first to help him. I liked Bill: he
had good points: is bright — very bright." Whitman claimed that he
himself had asked the boy to leave many times, "told him he must not
stay. Bill would swear by all that was holy that he would by and by
make all this right: would almost literally get down on his knees: then
I would weaken" (*With Walt Whitman*, IV:64).

Both Traubel and Davis kept Duckett from seeing Whitman. When the boy came to call at Mickle Street, he was not allowed to get to the poet's bedroom on the second floor. But in June of 1889, when Whitman was out by the front stoop, Bill was able to melt the older man's heart again with a story of his deceased sister. Whitman gave him ten dollars from some recently collected birthday money. However, when Bill wrote in December requesting a loan of ten or fifteen dollars, the letter seems to have been left unanswered. That letter of December 20, 1889—just at Christmas time—is the last surviving connection between the two men.

For Whitman, Bill was his wild-driving horseman; the poet tried to get the boy a job on the railroad—twice he got jobs with the railroad, but Duckett lasted only a short time. Recording the episode, Traubel was mistaken when he thought Whitman had "got on a new track," when the poet switched from talking about Duckett to transport men. "Do you know much about the transportation men?—the railroad men, the boatmen?" Whitman mused, "It seems to me that of all modern men the transportation men most nearly parallel the ancients in ease, poise, simplicity, average nature, robust instinct, firsthandedness: are the next the very a b c of real life. . . . I am *au fait* always with wharfmen, deckhands, train workers" (*With Walt Whitman,* IV:66). Bill doesn't seem to have been cut out for the transport any more than for the writing business—perhaps like Whitman, he enjoyed more watching than being a deckhand—perhaps he was more suited to be a counter jumper (i.e., sales clerk) at a notion store on Market Street in Philadelphia, where he worked for a while.

Whitman's word on Duckett is confused and inconsistent; Duckett's on the older man may be equally disingenuous, but it's a happy note to conclude on: Bill said of Walt: "He always gave me good advice and help, and was the best friend I ever had."

Bill Duckett Letters

Bill Duckett to R. M. Bucke, Camden, December 27, 1886

Sir—
Knowing that you are collecting all you can about Mr. Whitman, I write to ask whether you would like my collection of notes about him. I have been with him for nearly a year and have taken many notes.

November 28, 1886
After dinner about 2 clk Walt Whitman said Billy go and get my rig
and we'll go and take a ride   accordingly I had the horse and wagon at
the door in a few min.   and the poet well bundled up for it was a cold
bright day was soon in his seat with the wolf-skin robe over his lap and
we were trotting over the road   the weather was fine   cool and sunny.
We drove out our habitual road 3 miles and Entered the Cemetery of
the Evergreens, where the poets beloved mother and little nephew are
buried. It was his costume to visit these graves every few days. He
generally leaned against the railing or seated himself near in meditation.

On this occasion we drove over the country roads for several miles,
and returning went on the Ferry boat at Federal Street, as he wished a
half hour on the river. he enjoyed this very much for it was a beautiful
afternoon   he talked awhile with the ferry man his friends, and others
he met; and we then drove home.

7:35 pm Monday, November 29, 1886
To day has been a very bright and quite cool. missed our usual drive, on
account of the horse having to be shod. Unusual flow of visitors,
among them a handsome young Englishman who came to this country
with Wilson Barrett the actor, with whom he is now acting. He Bore a
letter of Introduction from Oscar Wilde, one of Mr Whitmans best
friends and comrade. He talked much about England, the people their
ways &c, he very much wanted Mr Whitman to see Hamlet as played
by Mr Barrett, and offered to have a private box reserved any Evening
w w would care to go,
Mr Whitman has been feeling very well to day Extra well I may say
convering in a pleasing manner

7.02 p m Tuesday Evening November 30, 1886
To-day has been rather damp and cloudy raing in the afternoon
Took the horse to the blacksmiths and had her shod in the morning
At the Dinner table Mr Whitman said Billy I think we will take a drive
in the Park this afternoon   So few minutes past one I had the horse and
buggy at the door, and we started, stopped at the Post Office to see
about a Mislaid package sent to Dr. R. M. Bucke Canada
   Went to the Bank from there to Fairmount Park Phila. We had a
splendid ride considering the hard rain   drove through the Park as far
as Geroge Hill stopped a few minutes to take a view of the surrounding
after spending about 10 min this rain we return home abou half past
four, have tea about 6 oclock   after receiving a few callers   retire about
9 oclock

Wednesday Eve. December 1, 1886
To day has been rather damp and foggy. Mr Whitman arose about 9
oclock something unusual for him, for he generally rises about 8 or
before. had breakfast about 9:30 after which he enteres the sitting
room, reads the usual morning mail, papers &c. Miss our usual ride on
account of the damp, misty day. Mr Whitman was of bright spirits,
Remarking that he felt exceptionally well, in the afternoon, Mr.
Hunter, "A, Jolly scotchman who Mr Whitman very much likes to
converse with called spent the best part of the Afternoon talking
together   have supper 6pm retire about 9 pm.

December [1886]
This morning Mr Whitman rose about 8:30 had breakfast 9. At the
table Mr Whitman said What a curious bundle of goods man is anyhow, let alone woman who is still more curious.
   About 10:30 brought the horse & Buggy To the door   Entered the
house to help Mr Whitman get ready   I had no sooner got in than the
horse wheeled around and went dashing toward the stable, and at
terrific gate and I after him   Luckily no damage was done the horse
stopping when reaching the stable   We had ride in the cold. It was
cold though   We drove over our acc[ustomed] roads [to] the Cemetery
and back
In the afternoon Mr Whitman received several callers, supper 6 pm.
went to bed before nine.

*The following note is in Walt Whitman's handwriting, evidently also written
in 1886 for Dr. Bucke:*

   I have thus given a few brief notes of my year with Mr. Whitman.
Probably few have had a better chance to know him as he is in reality.
   Among his main traits are patience, good nature, and a sunny
disposition. He is not religious in the usual sense. I never knew him to
have prayer or say grace at meals, nor did he go to church at all. He
gave freely to the poor, and helped indigent old persons and widows
constantly, sometimes with food for fuel or money, sometimes paying
the rent. With great frankness and naturalness he was entirely free from
indelicacy or any unchastity ["in any form" cancelled!] whatever.
   He had some spells of sickness, more or less severe, but while I was
with him was well enough to be around the house, or get out with a
little assistance. He employed himself six or seven hours every day
reading or writing. He was pretty tall, close to six feet high, weighing
over 200 pounds, was full-blooded, had generally a good appetite, and

slept pretty soundly. He knew almost everybody, was found of visitors, and was wonderfully popular among men and women, young and old. He always gave me good advice and help, and was the best friend I ever had.

Bill Duckett to WW, Philadelphia, December 20, 1889. On Pennsylvania Railroad Company stationery.

Dear Friend Walt,

Walt, Can you let me have ten or Fifteen Dollars, have been having pretty hard luck of late and find myself Broke. My board is due Monday & have about 5 Dollars to do it with. Now, will you kindly let me have what you can. You can give to bearer & he will bring to me. Will return you both amounts after 1st of year. How is your health, hope as well as your spirits generally used to be. I was over to see you some days since but you was unable to see me. Would like to see you very much, but you understand the circumstances. Well, I will say so long.

Do what you can as I am in a bad way. Affectionately Yours, Wm. H. Duckett

[P.S.] The Bearer is Geo Anderson one of our messenger Boys here. Bill

Note on envelope:

Dec. 20, '89.
Bro't to me by lad George Anderson from Bill Duckett — sent back word I was quite sick & was hard up — (no money),
W W

Bathing My Songs
in Sex

Selected Poems of
Walt Whitman

THIS SELECTION OF Whitman poems is intended for readers interested in gay love and its celebration. Walt Whitman made continuous changes in *Leaves of Grass* during his lifetime (1819–1892).
Before his death there were altogether six editions (a new edition being
indicated by new plates): first, Brooklyn, 1855, self-published with
twelve poems; second, 1856, New York, Fowler & Wells, twenty new
poems; third, Boston, 1860, Thayer & Eldridge, one hundred and
forty-six new poems, including the "Calamus" cluster; fourth, self-
published in 1867, incorporates Civil War poems; fifth, also self-
published in 1871, includes "Passage to India"; sixth, typeset in Boston in 1881, but after being banned there, published in Philadelphia
in 1882. Until 1897 these last plates were used for re-issues which
incorporated different supplements or annexes. Whitman himself encouraged the use of only the 1881 plates, since sales from them were
his only source of regular income. Plates from the 1860 edition fell into
other hands when Thayer & Eldridge went bankrupt; a somewhat
disreputable source was still trying to sell them in Boston during the
1980s! Thus labeling the 1892 re-issue a "Death-Bed" edition was of
more economic than literary importance.

Early editions of *Leaves of Grass* have been praised for their special
merits. Malcolm Cowley introduced the 1855 edition (New York,
1959); and Roy Harvey Pearce the 1860 edition (Ithaca, 1961); both
editions are currently available in paperback and have been constantly

at my side in preparing this selection. I have restored readings from the manuscripts assembled by Fredson Bowers in *Whitman's Manuscripts: Leaves of Grass (1860), A Parallel Text* (University of Chicago Press, 1955). I also found help in *Leaves of Grass: A Textual Variorum of the Printed Poems,* three volumes, edited by Sculley Bradley, Harold W. Blodgett, Arthur Golden, William White (New York University Press, 1980), and Arthur Golden, editor, *Walt Whitman's Blue Book: The 1860–61 Leaves of Grass Containing His Manuscript Additions and Revisions,* two volumes (New York Public Library, 1968).

"Bathing My Songs in Sex" presents an integrated edition of Walt Whitman's gay poems. Quite simply, out of all the versions of a poem, I have opted for the most erotic reading; otherwise I've incorporated the version which reads best. (I have followed the first three editions in using "-ed" not "-'d" to end past tense verbs.) All of the poems in the Calamus cluster of 1860 are homoerotic, but other parts of the *Leaves of Grass* supply happy surprises and are included here. In the 1860 edition, Whitman simply numbered the Calamus poems; in 1867, he gave them the title of the opening line. Even when the first line has been changed by a new reading, I have followed the standard titles as used in *Leaves of Grass: Comprehensive Reader's Edition* (1965) and the 1980 *Textual Variorum.* Titles have been provided for other selections, such as those from "Song of Myself."

To explicate all the changes in the Calamus and other gay poems would require a book in itself, but such an extended study is hardly necessary to follow the drift of Whitman's changes. At every stage he became more impersonal and less sexual. The joy is that he kept as many poems as he did with as few changes as he did. Three very important and clearly gay poems were printed only in the 1860 edition: "Long I Thought That Knowledge Alone Would Suffice," "Hours Continuing Long," and "Who is Now Reading This?" John Addington Symonds specifically asked Whitman why he had excluded the first poem, but the poet never answered that question. You would have to be disingenuous or stupid not to understand a line like, "Is there . . . one other man like me — . . . distracted — his friend, his lover, lost to him?" To Whitman that anguish was too revealing once the heat of his relationship with Fred Vaughan had passed.

There are other important differences between manuscript versions and printed versions. A few poems from the "Children of Adam" have been restored to the "Calamus" sequence because in the manuscript they were clearly man-to-man love but in the published version they were rewritten to suggest heterosexual intercourse. Thus the manuscript of "Once I Passed Through a Populous City" substitutes "woman" for "man" in the line "I remember I say only that woman who passionately clung to me" I have restored a number of similar manuscript readings which are nearly as dramatic as in "Populous City." Thus "Not Heat Flames up and Consumes" contains a manuscript line "Does the tide hurry, seeking something, and never give up?—O I, the same, to seek my life-long lover" becomes in print: "Does the tide hurry, seeking something, and never give up? O I the same . . ." Or the later suppressed "Long I Thought That Knowledge Alone Would Suffice" had already repressed the line "I have found him who loves me, as I him, in perfect love" into "One who loves me is jealous of me, and withdraws me from all but love . . ."

I have also rearranged the poems so that their interconnections become more evident. Perhaps Whitman meant to tuck some of his gay offspring between other, more acceptable poems; or perhaps he just preferred a random arrangement. Whitman himself said, "Some of my friends feel . . . I should bind my pieces in better — make them one book. I suppose every college-bred man must feel my book very deficient in this way. But I have felt to make it a succession of growths, like the rings of a tree. My book is terribly fragmentary. It consists of the ejaculations of one identity . . . in the latter half of the nineteenth century, in presence of the facts and movements around him" (*Visits to Walt Whitman in 1890–91*).

Elaborate schemes explaining the architecture of the *Leaves* have never gained any universal acceptance and are more complicated to understand than the poems themselves. Before the Calamus edition in 1860 appeared, Whitman had projected 365 poems for the *Leaves of Grass,* one for each day. But that arrangement was abandoned as he pursued gay and less linear, less straight themes. Then he resorted to what he called a "cluster" arrangement. My arrangement is in itself a reading of the poems, as is my restoration of suppressed lines and whole poems. "Bathing My Songs in Sex" provides something of a gay guide to *Leaves of Grass.* Such guides can be dangerous in opening up our cruising spots and habits to hostile investigation but they can also be helpful in bringing out an expanded audience.

In most cases, the poet's last word would be enough, but here I think special circumstances have to be taken into account. During Whitman's lifetime, great changes occurred in attitudes toward manly love and sexual discourse. For instance the infamous Comstock Law was passed in 1873, under which Victoria Woodhull and Ezra Heywood were both prosecuted and persecuted. And while the trials of Oscar

Wilde began after Whitman's death, Walt Whitman lived under fear of a similar scandal in his own life. While he enjoyed Wilde's visit and remained in close correspondence with English gay liberationists such as Edward Carpenter and John Addington Symonds, Whitman moved to protect himself against such persecution as awaited Wilde. That some cannot accept that Walt Whitman was both a poet worth reading and a homosexual says more about the lies, fears and hatred still lingering about homosexuality than about his poetry. Even today, many heterosexuals will not willingly read the work of a poet who is known as a homosexual because, they claim, gay poetry lacks any universal appeal. To be identified as a gay poet, they hope, will put nails in the coffin of a poet's career.

This edition may startle scholars, but I am only incidentally writing for them. I want to embolden poets, homosexuals and all readers to come off your old tired ethics. I intend to enliven sadists, sodomites, pederasts, cocksuckers, butt-fuckers and other so-called degenerates — the "venerelee" was Whitman's term. I intend to manifest the hidden vascular connections between our sexuality and our poetry. Exposing Whitman's disguises has been an act of love and identification. I don't think he is or was a god or goddess. And I reject the notion of "great." Let the theologians debate whether *Leaves of Grass* was greater than the Bible; let the critics quibble whether this poet is greater than another. Such categories are totally antithetical to Whitman's message. His rough trade, working-class heroes and street tricks were everything to him. If poetry too often becomes an institution, we must reread Whitman's "I am neither for nor against institutions. . . . Only I want to establish . . . The institution of the dear love of comrades."

For gay liberation, poetry has always been our guiding star, "Venus like blazing silver well up in the west." All other professions may have betrayed us and individual poets may have betrayed their own poly-morphous/sexual cells out of which have come their voice, but the sensuous planet of poetry has long embodied our love. Sappho, Homer, Whitman, yourself, dear reader. If you don't like Whitman's poems or you don't like my editions, do your own. As Whitman wrote,

> Stop this day and night with me and you shall possess the origin of all poems . . .
> You shall no longer take things at second or third hand . . . nor look through the eyes of the dead . . . nor feed on the spectres in books,
> You shall not look through my eyes either, nor take things from me,
> You shall listen to all sides and filter them from yourself.

Frontispiece engraving of Walt Whitman in the first edition of *Leaves of Grass* (1855)

Bathing My Songs in Sex:
Selected Poems of Walt Whitman

Unless otherwise indicated all the poems below are from the Calamus *cluster in* Leaves of Grass.

IN PATHS UNTRODDEN

In paths untrodden,
In the growth by margins of pond-waters,
Escaped from the standards hitherto published, from the usual pleasures,
    profits, eruditions, conformities,
I know now a life, which does not exhibit itself, yet contains all the rest,
And now, separating, I celebrate that concealed but substantial life,
And now I care not to walk the earth unless a friend walk by my side,
And now I dare sing no other songs, only those of lovers.
Was it I who walked the earth disclaiming all except what I had in
    myself?
Was it I boasting how complete I was in myself?
O little I counted the comrade indispensable to me!
O how my soul—How the soul of man feeds, rejoices in its lovers, its
    dear friends!
Here by myself away from the clank of the world,
Tallying and talked to here by tongues aromatic,
No longer abashed—for in this secluded spot I can respond as I would
    not dare elsewhere,
Resolved to sing no songs today but those of manly attachment,
Bequeathing hence types of athletic love,
I proceed for all who are or have been young men,
To tell the secret of my nights and days,
To celebrate the need of the love of athletic comrades.

THROUGH ME FORBIDDEN VOICES

Through me forbidden voices,
Voices of sexes and lusts — voices veiled, and I remove the veil,
Voices indecent by me clarified and transfigured.

I do not press my finger across my mouth,
I keep as delicate around the bowels as around the head and heart,
Copulation is no more rank to me than death is.

I believe in the flesh and the appetites,
Seeing hearing and feeling are miracles, and each part and tag of me is
    a miracle.

Divine am I inside and out, and I make holy whatever I touch or am
    touched from;
The scent of these arm-pits is aroma finer than prayer,
This head is more than churches or bibles or creeds.

If I worship any particular thing it shall be the spread of my body or
    any part of it;
Translucent mould of me it shall be you,
Shaded ledges and rests, firm masculine colter, it shall be you,
Whatever goes to the tilth of me it shall be you,
You my rich blood, your milky stream pale strippings of my life;
Breast that presses against other breasts it shall be you.
My brain it shall be your occult convolutions,
Root of washed sweet-flag, timorous pond-snipe, nest of guarded dupli-
    cate eggs, it shall be you,
Mixed tussled hay of head, beard, brawn it shall be you,
Trickling sap of maple, fibre of manly wheat, it shall be you;
Sun so generous it shall be you,
Vapors lighting and shading my face it shall be you,
You sweaty brooks and dews it shall be you,
Winds whose soft-tickling genitals rub against me it shall be you,
Broad muscular fields, branches of liveoak, loving lounger in my wind-
    ing paths, it shall be you,
Hands I have taken, face I have kissed, mortal I have ever touched, it
    shall be you.

[from "Song of Myself," Section 24]

WELCOME IS EVERY ORGAN

Welcome is every organ and attribute of me, and of any man hearty and
     clean,
Not an inch, nor a particle of an inch, is vile, and none shall be less
     familiar than the rest.

I am satisfied — I see, dance; laugh, sing;
As the hugging and loving Bed-fellow sleeps at my side through the
     night, and withdraws at the peep of the day, with stealthy tread,
Leaving me baskets covered with white towels, swelling the house
     with their plenty,
Shall I postpone my acceptation and realization, and scream at my eyes,
That they turn from gazing after and down the road,
And forthwith cipher and show me to a cent,
Exactly the contents of one, and exactly the contents of two, and which
     is ahead?

[*based on* 1860 Leaves of Grass]

ALLONS! THE ROAD IS BEFORE US

Allons! the road is before us!
It is safe — I have tried it — my own feet have tried it well — be not
     detained!

Let the paper remain on the desk unwritten, and the book on the shelf
     unopened!
Let the tools remain in the workshop! let the money remain unearned!
Let the school stand! mind not the cry of the teacher!
Let the preacher preach in his pulpit! let the lawyer plead in the court,
     and the judge expound the law!

Camerado, I give you my hand!
I give you my love more precious than money,
I give you myself before preaching or law;
Will you give me yourself? will you come travel with me?
Shall we stick by each other as long as we live?

[*from* "Song of the Open Road," *Section* 15; "*Camerado*" *replaced an earlier*
"*Mon enfant!*"]

LOAFE WITH ME ON THE GRASS

Loafe with me on the grass — loose the stop from your throat;
Not words, not music or rhyme I want — not custom or lecture, not
even the best,
Only the lull I like, the hum of your valved voice.

I mind how once we lay, such a transparent summer morning;
How you settled your head athwart my hips, and gently turned over
upon me,
And parted the shirt from my bosom-bone, and plunged your tongue
to my bare-stript heart,
And reached till you felt my beard, and reached till you held my feet.

[*based on 1860* Leaves of Grass]

AND SEXUAL ORGANS AND ACTS!

And sexual organs and acts! do you concentrate in me — for I am
determined to tell you with courageous clear voice, to prove
you illustrious.

I will sing the song of companionship,
I will show what alone must finally compact These States,
I believe the main purport of America is to found a new ideal of manly
love, more ardent, indicating it in me;
I will therefore let appear from me the burning flames of adhesiveness
that were threatening to consume me,
I will lift what has too long kept down those smouldering fires — I will
now expose them and use them.
I will give them complete abandonment, I will make the new evangel-
poem of comrades and lovers.

[*from "Proto-Leaf," Section 21–22, 1860, with restored Ms readings*]

PICKING OUT HERE ONE THAT I LOVE

Picking out here one that I love, and now go with on brotherly terms.

A gigantic beauty of a stallion, fresh and responsive to my caresses,
Head high in the forehead, wide between the ears,
Limbs glossy and supple, tail dusting the ground,
Eyes well apart, full of sparkling wickedness — ears finely cut, flexibly
      moving.

His nostrils dilate, as my heels embrace him,
His well-built limbs tremble with pleasure, as we speed around and
      return.

I but use you a moment, then I resign you stallion,
Why do I need your paces, when I myself out-gallop them?
Even, as I stand or sit, passing faster than you.

[*based on* 1860 Leaves of Grass]

THESE I SINGING IN SPRING

These I singing in spring collect for lovers,
(For who but I should understand lovers and all their sorrow and joy?
And who but I should be the poet of comrades?)
Collecting I traverse the garden, but soon I pass the gates,
Along the pond-side, wading in a little, fearing not the wet,
Along the post-and-rail fences where the old stones, picked from the
      fields, have accumulated,
(Wild-flowers and vines and weeds come up through the stones and
      partly cover them, beyond these I pass,)
Far, far in the forest, or sauntering later in summer, before I think
      where I go,
Solitary, smelling the earthy smell, stopping now and then in the
      silence,
Alone I had thought, yet soon a troop gathers around me,
Some walk by my side and some behind, and some embrace my arms or
      neck,
Spirits of dear friends dead or alive, thicker they come, a great crowd,
      and I in the middle,
Collecting, dispensing, singing, I wander with them,
Plucking something for tokens, tossing toward whoever is near me,

Here, lilac, with a branch of pine,
Here out of my pocket, some moss which I pulled off a live-oak,
Here, some pinks and laurel leaves, and a handful of sage,
And here what I now draw from the water, wading in the pond-side,
(O here I last saw him that tenderly loves me, and returns again never
     to separate from me,
Therefore, this shall be the special token of comrades, this calamus-
     root shall,
Interchange it, youths, with each other! Let none render it back!)
And twigs of maple and a bunch of wild orange and chestnut,
And stems of currants, and plum-blows, and the aromatic cedar,
These I compassed around in dusk by a thick swarm of lovers,
Wandering, point to or touch as I pass, or throw them loosely from me,
Indicating to each one what he shall have, giving something to each;
But what I drew from the water by the pond-side, that I reserve,
I will give of it, but only to them that love as I myself am capable of
     loving.

[*1860 version with Ms lines restored; Whitman also used the second line "For
who but I should understand lovers and all their sorrow and joy?" in "Starting
from Paumanok."*]

NOT HEAT FLAMES UP AND CONSUMES

Not heat flames up and consumes,
Not sea-waves hurry in and out,
Not the air delicious and dry, the air of ripe summer, bears lightly
     along white down-balls of myriads of seeds,
Wafted, sailing gracefully, to drop where they may;
Not these, O none of these more than the flames of me, consuming,
     burning for his love whom I love,
O none more than I hurrying in and out;
Does the tide hurry, seeking something, and never give up?
O I the same, to seek my life-long lover;
O nor down-balls, nor perfumes, nor the high rain-emitting clouds,
     are borne through the open air,
Any more than my soul is borne through the open air,
Wafted in all directions, for friendship, for love, for you.

[*1860 Calamus with restoration from the Ms; "to seek my life-long lover" was
never printed.*]

WHEN I HEARD AT THE CLOSE OF THE DAY

When I heard at the close of the day of the plaudits given my name in
  the capitol, still it was not a happy night for me that followed,
Nor when I caroused, nor when my plans were accomplished, was I
  happy,
But the day when I rose at dawn from the bed of perfect health,
  electric, refreshed, singing, inhaling sweet breath,
When I saw the full moon in the west grow pale and disappear in the
  morning light,
When I wandered alone over the beach, and undressing bathed,
  laughing with the cool waters, and saw the sun rise,
And when I thought how my friend, my lover was coming, O I was
  happy,
Each breath tasted sweeter, and all that day my food nourished me
  more, and the beautiful day passed well,
And the next came with equal joy, and with the next at evening came
  my friend,
And that night while all was still I heard the waters roll slowly
  continually up the shores,
I heard the hissing rustle of the liquid and sands whispering to con-
  gratulate me,
For the one I love lay sleeping by my side, under the same cover in the
  cool night,
And in the stillness his face was inclined toward me, while the moon's
  clear beams shone,
And his arm lay lightly over my breast—and that night I was happy.

SCENTED HERBAGE OF MY BREAST

Scented herbage of my breast,
Leaves from you I glean, I write to be perused best afterwards,
Tomb-leaves, body-leaves growing up above me above death,
Perennial roots, tall leaves, O the winter shall not freeze you delicate
  leaves,
Every year shall you bloom again, out of your roots where you retired
  you shall emerge again;
O I do not know whether many passing by will discover you or inhale
  your faint odor, but I believe a few will;

O slender leaves! O breast blossoms of my blood! Tell in your own way
   of the heart that is under you,
O burning and throbbing, surely one day I will find the dear friend,
   the lover, in whom all will be accomplished;
O I do not know what you mean there underneath yourselves, you are
   not happiness,
You are often more bitter than I can bear, you burn and sting me,
Yet you are beautiful to me you faint tinged roots, you make me think
   of death,
Death is beautiful from you, (what indeed is finally beautiful except
   death and love?)
O I think it is not for life I am chanting here my chant of lovers, I
   think it must be for death,
For how calm, how solemn it grows to ascend to the atmosphere of
   lovers,
Death or life I am then indifferent, my soul declines to prefer,
(I am not sure but the high soul of lovers welcomes death most,)
Indeed death, I think these leaves mean you,
Grow up taller sweet leaves that I may see! grow up out of my breast!
Spring away from the concealed heart there!
Do not fold yourself so in your pink-tinged roots, timid leaves!
Do not remain down there so ashamed, herbage of my breast!
Come I am determined to unbare my breast, I have stifled and choked
   too long;
I will escape from the costume, the play, the sham!
I will say what I have to say by itself,
I will sound myself and love, I will utter the cry of friends,
I will raise new reverberations through the States,
I will give an example to lovers till they take shape and will through
   the States.
Through me shall the words be said to make death exhilarating.

ARE YOU THE NEW PERSON DRAWN TOWARD ME?

Are you the new person drawn toward me?
To begin with take warning, I am surely far different from what you
    suppose;
Do you suppose you will find in me your ideal?
Do you suppose you can easily be my lover, and I yours?
Do you suppose I am trusty and faithful?
Do you trust this pliant and tolerant manner of me?
Do you suppose yourself advancing on real ground toward a real heroic
    person?
Have you thought O dreamer that it is all maya, illusion?
O let some wise serpent hiss in your ears how many have prest the same
    as you are pressing now,
How many have fondly supposed what you suppose now—only to be
    disappointed.

[*Ms version contains the title "To a New Personal Admirer."*]

WHOEVER YOU ARE HOLDING ME NOW IN HAND

Who is he that would become my follower?
Who would sign himself a candidate for my affections?

The way is suspicious, the result uncertain, perhaps destructive,
You would have to give up all else, I alone would expect to be your sole
    and exclusive standard,
Your novitiate would even then be long and exhausting,
The whole past theory of your life and all conformity to the lives
    around you would have to be abandoned,
Therefore release me at once, before troubling yourself any further, let
    go your hand from my shoulders,
Put me down and depart on your way.

By stealth in some wood O my lover,
Or back of a rock in the open air,
(For in any roofed room of a house I emerge not, nor in company,
And in libraries I lie as one dumb, a gawk, or unborn, or dead,)
But just specially with you on a high hill
Watching lest any person for miles around, approach unawares,

Or possibly with you sailing at sea, or on the beach of the sea or some
    quiet island,
Here to put your lips upon mine I permit you,
With the comrade's long-dwelling kiss or the new husband's kiss,
For I am the new husband and I am the comrade.

Or if you will, thrusting me beneath your clothing,
Where I may feel the throbs of your heart or rest on your waist or hip,
Carry me when you go forth over land or sea;
And thus merely touching you is enough, is best,
And thus touching you would I silently sleep and be carried eternally.

But these leaves conning you con at peril,
For these leaves and me you will not understand, O my lover.
They will elude you at first and still more afterward, I will certainly
    elude you,
Even while you should think you had unquestionably caught me,
    behold!
Already you see I have escaped from you, O my lover.

For it is not for what I have put into it that I have written this book,
Not is it by reading it you will acquire it, O my lover,
Nor do those know me best who admire me and vauntingly praise me,
Nor will the candidates for my love (unless at most a very few) prove
    victorious,
Nor will my poems do good only, they will do just as much evil,
    perhaps more;
For all is useless without that which you may guess at many times and
    not hit, that which I hinted at;
Therefore release me at once, take your hands from my shoulders, and
    depart on your way, O my lover.

NOT HEAVING FROM MY RIBBED BREAST ONLY

Not heaving from my ribbed breast only,
Not in sighs at night in rage dissatisfied with myself,
Not in those long-drawn, ill-supprest sighs,
Not in many an oath and promise broken,
Not in my wilful and savage soul's volition,
Not in the subtle nourishment of the air,
Not in this beating and pounding at my temples and wrists,
Not in the curious systole and diastole within which will one day cease,
Not in many a hungry wish told to the skies only
Not in cries, laughter, defiances, thrown from me when alone far in the
    wilds,
Not in husky pantings through clinched teeth,
Not in sounded and resounded words, chattering words, echoes, dead
    words,
Not in the murmurs of my dreams while I sleep,
Nor in the other murmurs of these incredible dreams of every day,
Nor in the limbs and senses of my body that take you and dismiss you
    continually — not there,
Not in any or all of them, O adhesiveness! O pulse of my life!
Need I that you exist and show yourself any more than in these songs.

OF THE TERRIBLE DOUBT OF APPEARANCES

Of the terrible doubt of appearances,
Of the uncertainty after all, that we may be deluded,
That maybe reliance and hope are but speculations after all,
That maybe identity beyond the grave is a beautiful fable only,
Maybe the things I perceive, the animals, plants, men, hills, shining
    and flowing waters,
The skies of day and night, colors, densities, forms, maybe these are (as
    doubtless they are) only apparitions, and the real something has
    yet to be known,
(How often they dart out of themselves as if to confound me and mock
    me!
How often I think neither I know, nor any man knows, aught of them)
To me these and the like of these are curiously answered by my lovers,
    my dear friends

When he whom I love travels with me or sits a long while holding me
    by the hand,
When the subtle air, that words and reason hold not, surrounds us and
    pervades us,
Then I am charged with untold and untellable wisdom, I am silent,
    I require nothing further,
I cannot answer the question of appearances or that of identity byeond
    the grave,
But I walk or sit indifferent, I am satisfied,
He ahold of my hand has completely satisfied me.

O TAN-FACED PRAIRIE-BOY

O tan-faced prairie-boy,
Before you came to camp came many a welcome gift,
Praises and presents came and nourishing food, till at last among the
    recruits,
You came, taciturn, with nothing to give — but we looked on each
    other,
When lo! more than all the gifts of the world you gave me.

[*First printed in* Drum Taps (*1865*)]

LONG I THOUGHT THAT
KNOWLEDGE ALONE WOULD SUFFICE

Long I thought that knowledge alone would suffice me, O if I could
    but obtain knowledge!
Then the Land of the prairies, Ohio's land, the southern savannas,
    engrossed me — For them I would live — I would be their orator;
Then I met the examples of old and new heroes — I heard of warriors,
    sailors, and all dauntless as any — And it seemed to me I too had
    it in me to be as dauntless as any, and would be so;
And then, to enclose all, it came to me to strike up the songs of the
    New World — And then I believed my life must be spent in
    singing;
But now take notice, land of the prairies, land of the south savannas,
    Ohio's land,
Take notice, you Kanuck woods — and you Lake Huron and all that
    with you roll toward Niagara — and you Niagara also,

And you, Californian mountains—That you each and all find somebody
    else to be your singer of songs,
For I can be your singer no longer—I have ceased to enjoy them. I have
    found him who loves me, as I him, in perfect love,
With the rest I dispense—I sever from what I thought would suffice
    me, for it does not—it is now empty and tasteless to me,
I heed knowledge, and the grandeur of The States, and the example of
    heroes, no more.
I am indifferent to my own songs—I am to go with him I love, and he
    is to go with me,
It is to be enough for each of us that we are together—We never
    separate again.

[*This poem appeared only in the 1860* Leaves.]

HOURS CONTINUING LONG

Hours continuing long, sore and heavy-hearted,
Hours of the dusk, when I withdraw to a lonesome and unfrequented
    spot, seating myself, leaning my face in my hands;
Hours sleepless, deep in the night, when I go forth, speeding swiftly
    the country roads, or through the city streets, or pacing miles and
    miles stifling plaintive cries;
Hours discouraged, distracted—for the one I cannot content myself
    without, soon I saw him content himself without me;
Hours when I am forgotten, (O weeks and months are passing, but I
    believe I am never to forget!)
Sullen and suffering hours! (I am ashamed—but it is useless—I am
    what I am;)
Hours of my torment—I wonder if other men ever have the like, out of
    the like feelings?
Is there over the whole earth one other man like me—
Is he as I am now distracted—his friend, his lover, lost to him?
Does he rise in the morning, dejected, thinking who is lost to him? or
    at night, awaking, think who is lost?
Does he too harbor his friendship silent and endless? harbor his anguish
    and passion?
Does some stray reminder, or the casual mention of a name, bring the
    fit back upon him, taciturn and deprest?
Does he see himself reflected in me? In these hours, does he see the face
    of his hours reflected?

[*This poem appeared only in the 1860* Leaves.]

TRICKLE DROPS

O drops of me! trickle, slow drops from my blue veins leaving,
Candid, from me falling, drip, bleeding drops,
From wounds made to free you whence you were prisoned,
From my face, from my forehead and lips,
From my breast, from within, where I was concealed, press forth red
    drops, confession drops,
Stain every page, stain every song I sing, every word I say, bloody drops
Let them know your scarlet heat, let them glisten,
Saturate them with yourself, all ashamed and wet,
Glow upon all I have written or shall write, bleeding drops,
Let it all be seen in your light, blushing drops.

RECORDERS AGES HENCE

Come, recorders ages hence! Mind not so much my poems,
But publish my name and hang up my picture as that of the tenderest
    lover,
The friend, the lover's portrait, of whom his friend, his lover, was
    fondest,
Who often walked lonesome walks thinking of his dearest friends, his
    lovers,
Who pensive, away from one he loved, often lay sleepless and dis-
    satisfied at night,
Who dreading lest the one he loved might after all be indifferent to
    him, felt the sick feeling — O sick! sick! — lest the one he loved
    might secretly be indifferent to him,
Whose happiest days were those far away through fields, in woods, on
    hills,
He and another, wandering hand in hand, they twain, apart from other
    men.
Who ever, as he sauntered the streets, curved with his arm the manly
    shoulder of his friend — while the curving arm of his friend rested
    upon him also.

ROOTS AND LEAVES THEMSELVES ALONE

Mine offered fresh to you, after natural ways, folded, silent,
Roots and leaves unlike any but themselves,
Thoughts, sayings, poems, poemets, put before you and within you to
    be unfolded by you on the old terms,
Scents brought from the wild woods and from the pond-side,
Breast-sorrel and pinks of love — fingers that wind around tighter than
    vines,
Gushes from the throats of birds, hid in the foliage of trees, as the sun
    is risen,
Breezes of land and love — Breezes sent out on the living sea — to you,
    O sailors!
Frost-mellowed berries and Third Month twigs, offered fresh to young
    persons wandering out in the fields when the winter breaks
    love-buds.
If you bring the warmth of the sun to them, they will open, and bring
    form, color, perfume, to you,
They have come slowly up out of the earth and me, and are to come
    slowly up out of you.

[*Readings restored from Ms version, originally titled "Buds."*]

OF HIM I LOVE DAY AND NIGHT

Of him I love day and night, I dreamed I heard he was dead,
And I dreamed I went where they had buried the man I love but he was
    not in that place,
And I dreamed I wandered searching among burial places to find him,
And I found that every place was a burial place;
The houses full of life were equally full of death, (this house is now,)
The streets, the shipping, the places of amusement, the Chicago,
    Boston, Philadelphia, the Mannahatta, were as full of the dead as
    of the living,
And fuller, O vastly fuller, of the dead than of the living;
And what I dreamed I will henceforth tell to every person and age,
And I stand henceforth bound to what I dreamed;
And now I am willing to disregard burial places, and dispense with
    them,

And if the memorials of the dead were put up indifferently everywhere,
    even in the room where I eat or sleep, I should be satisfied,
And if the corpse of any one I love, or if my own corpse, be duly
    rendered to powder and poured into the sea, or distributed to the
    winds, I shall be satisfied.

[*The version titled "Poemet," published in 1860 "Calamus," but moved to
"Whispers of Heavenly Death" cluster in 1871.*]

NATIVE MOMENTS

Native moments! when you come upon me — Ah you are here now!
Give me now libidinous joys only!
Give me the drench of my passions! Give me life coarse and rank!
Today, I go consort with nature's darlings — tonight too,
I am for those who believe in loose delights — I share the midnight
    orgies of young men,
I dance with the dancers, and drink with the drinkers,
The echoes ring with our indecent calls,
I take for my love some prostitute — I pick out some low person for my
    dearest friend,
He shall be lawless, rude, illiterate — he shall be one condemned by
    others for deeds done;
I will play a part no longer — Why should I exile myself from my
    companions?
O you shunned persons! I at least do not shun you,
I come forthwith in your midst — I will be your poet,
I will be more to you than to any of the rest.

[*from 1860 version of "Enfans d'Adam" cluster*]

CITY OF ORGIES

City of orgies, of my walks and joys!
Not the infinite pageants of you, not your shifting tableaux, your
   spectacles, repay me
Not the interminable rows of your houses, nor the ships at the wharves,
Nor the processions in the streets, nor the bright windows with goods
   in them,
Nor to converse with learned persons, or bear my share in the soiree or
   feast;
Not those, but as I pass O Manhattan, your frequent and swift flash of
   eyes offering me robust, athletic love, fresh as nature's air and
   herbage,
Offering full response to my own — these repay me,
Lovers, continual lovers, only repay me.

I DREAMED IN A DREAM

I dreamed in a dream of a city where all the men were like brothers,
O I saw them tenderly love each other, I often saw them, in numbers
   walking hand in hand;
I dreamed that was the city of robust friends — Nothing was greater
   than manly love — it led the rest,
It was seen every hour in the actions of the men of that city, and in all
   their looks and words.

TO WHAT YOU SAID

To what you said, passionately clasping my hand, this is my answer:
Though you have strayed hither, for my sake, you can never belong to
    me, nor I to you,
Behold the customary loves and friendships — the cold guards,
I am that rough and simple person
I am he who kisses his comrade lightly on the lips at parting, and I am
    one who is kissed in return,
I introduce that new American salute
Behold love choked, correct, polite, always suspicious
Behold the received models of the parlors — What are they to me?
What to these young men that travel with me?

[*Ms poem in Library of Congress Feinberg collection*]

WHAT THINK YOU I TAKE MY PEN IN HAND?

What think you I take my pen to record?
Not the battle-ship, perfect-modeled, majestic, that I saw today arrive
    in the offing under full sail
Nor the splendors of the past day, nor the splendors of the night that
    envelops me,
Nor the vaunted glory and growth of the great city spread around me.
But the two simple men I saw today on the pier in the midst of the
    crowd, parting of dear friends,
The one to remain hung on the other's neck and passionately kissed
    him,
While the one to depart tightly prest the one to remain in his arms.

BEHOLD THIS SWARTHY FACE

Mind you the timid models of the rest, the majority?
Long I minded them, but hence I will not, for I have adopted models
    for myself,
Behold this swarthy and unrefined face, these gray eyes,
This beard, the white wool in tufts unclipt upon my neck,
My brown hands and the silent manner of me without charm;
Yet comes one a Manhattanese and at parting kisses me lightly on the
    lips with robust love,
And I, in the public room, or on the crossing of the street or on the
    ship's deck, kiss him in return,
We observe that salute of American comrades, land and sea,
We are those two natural and nonchalant persons.

I SAW IN LOUISIANA A LIVE-OAK GROWING

I saw in Louisiana a live-oak growing,
All alone stood it and the moss hung down from the branches,
Without any companion it grew there glistening out joyous leaves of
    dark green,
And its look, rude, unbending, lusty, made me think of myself,
But I wondered how it could utter joyous leaves standing alone there
    without its friend, its lover, for I knew I could not,
And I plucked a twig with a certain number of leaves upon it, and
    twined around it a little moss,
And brought it away, and I have placed it in sight in my room,
It is not needed to remind me of my friends,
(For I believe lately I think of little else than of them,)
Yet it remains to me a curious token, it makes me think of manly love;
For all that, and though the live-oak glistens there in Louisiana solitary
    in a wide flat space,
Uttering joyous leaves all its life without a friend, a lover, near,
I know very well I could not.

TO YOU

Let us twain walk aside from the rest;
Now we are together privately, do you discard ceremony,
Come! vouchsafe to me what has yet been vouchsafed to none—Tell me
    the whole story,
Tell me what you could not tell your brother, wife, husband, or
    physician.

Stranger! if you, passing, meet me, and desire to speak to me, why
    should you not speak to me?
And why should I not speak to you?

[*based on* 1860 Leaves of Grass]

TO A STRANGER

Passing stranger! you do not know how longingly I look upon you,
You must be he I was seeking, or she I was seeking, (it comes to me as
    of a dream,)—
I have somewhere surely lived a life of joy with you,
All is recalled as we flit by each other, fluid, affectionate, chaste,
    matured,
You grew up with me, were a boy with me or a girl with me,
I ate with you and slept with you, your body has become not yours only
    nor left my body mine only,
You give me the pleasure of your eyes, face, flesh, as we pass, you take
    of my beard, breast, hands, in return,
I am not to speak to you, I am to think of you when I sit alone or wake
    at night alone,
I am to wait, I do not doubt I am to meet you again,
I am to see to it that I do not lose you.

THIS MOMENT YEARNING AND THOUGHTFUL

This moment yearning and pensive sitting alone,
It seems to me there are other men in other lands yearning and pensive,
It seems to me I can look over and behold them in Germany, Italy,
    France, Spain,
Or far away, in China, India or in Russia or Japan, talking other
    dialects,
And it seems to me if I could know those men I should love them as
    I love men in my own lands,
O I know we should be brethren and lovers,
I know I should be happy with them.

I HEAR IT WAS CHARGED AGAINST ME

I hear it was charged against me that I sought to destroy institutions,
But really I am neither for nor against institutions,
(What indeed have I in common with them? or what with the destruc-
    tion of them?)
Only I will establish in the Mannahatta and in every city of these States
    inland and seaboard,
And in the fields and woods, and above every keel little or large that
    dents the water,
Without edifices or rules or trustees or any argument,
The institution of the dear love of comrades.

THE PRAIRIE-GRASS DIVIDING

The prairie-grass accepting its own special odor breathing,
I demand of it the spiritual corresponding,
Demand the most copious and close companionship of men,
Demand the blades to rise of words, acts, beings,
Those of the open atmosphere, coarse, sunlit, fresh, nutritious,
Those that go their own gait, erect, stepping with freedom and com-
     mand, leading, not following,
Those with a never quelled audacity, those with sweet and lusty flesh
     clear of taint, choice and chary of its love-power,
Those that look carelessly in the faces of Presidents and governors, as to
     say, *Who are you?*
Those of earth-born passion, simple, never constrained, never obedient,
Those of inland America.

WE TWO BOYS TOGETHER CLINGING

We two boys together clinging,
One the other never leaving,
Up and down the roads going, North and South excursions making,
Power enjoying, elbows stretching, fingers clutching,
Armed and fearless, eating, drinking, sleeping, loving,
No law less than myself owning, sailing, soldiering, thieving, threat-
     ening,
Misers, menials, priests alarming, air breathing, water drinking, on
     the turf or the sea-beach dancing,
Cities wrenching, ease scorning, statutes mocking, feebleness chasing,
Fulfilling my foray.

WHEN I PERUSE THE CONQUERED FAME

When I peruse the conquered fame of heroes and the victories of mighty
  generals, I do not envy the generals,
Nor the President in his Presidency, nor the rich in his great house,
But when I hear of the brotherhood of lovers, how it was with them,
How together through life, through dangers, odium, unchanging,
  long and long,
Through youth and through a middle and old age, how unfaltering,
  how affectionate and faithful they were,
Then I am pensive — I hastily walk away filled with the bitterest envy.

A GLIMPSE

One flitting glimpse, caught through an interstice,
Of a crowd of workmen and drivers in a bar-room around the stove late
  of a winter night, and I unremarked seated in a corner,
Of a youth who loves me and whom I love, silently approaching and
  seating himself near, that he may hold me by the hand,
A long while amid the noises of coming and going, of drinking and
  oath and smutty jest,
There we two, content, happy in just being together, speaking little,
  perhaps not a word.

I AM HE THAT ACHES WITH LOVE

I am he that aches with love;
Does the earth gravitate? does not all matter, aching attract all matter?
So the body of me to all I meet or know.

[*from 1860 version of "Enfans d'Adam" cluster*]

ONCE I PASSED THROUGH A POPULOUS CITY

Once I passed through a populous city, imprinting my brain, for future
use, with its shows, architecture, customs and traditions,
But now of all that city I remember only the man who wandered with
me, there for love of me,
Day by day and night by night, we were together—all else has been
long forgotten by me,
I remember, I say, only one rude and ignorant man who, when I
departed, long and long held me by the hand, with silent lips,
sad and tremulous.

[from 1860 version of "Enfans d'Adam" cluster]

AS ADAM EARLY IN THE MORNING

Early in the morning,
Walking forth from the bower refreshed with sleep,
Behold me where I pass—hear my voice—approach,
Touch me—touch the palm of your hand to my body as I pass,
Be not afraid of my body.

[from 1860 version of "Enfans d'Adam" cluster]

AGES AND AGES RETURNING AT INTERVALS

Ages and ages returning at invervals,
Undestroyed, wandering immortal
Lusty, phallic, with the potent original loins, perfectly sweet,
I canter of Adamic songs,
Through the new garden the West, the great cities calling,
Deliriate, thus prelude what is generated, offering these, offering my-
self,
Bathing myself, bathing my songs in sex,
Offspring of my loins.

[from 1860 version of "Enfans d'Adam" cluster]

A PROMISE TO CALIFORNIA

A promise to Indiana, Nebraska, Kansas, Iowa, Minnesota and Cali-
fornia,
Inland to the great Pastoral Plains, and on to Puget Sound and Oregon;
Sojourning east a while longer, soon I travel toward you, to remain, to
teach robust American love,
For I know very well that I and robust love belong among you, to the
East and to the West,
To the man of the Seaside State and of Pennsylvania,
To the Kanadian of the north, to the Southerner I love,
These with perfect trust to depict you as myself, the germs are in all
men,
I believe the main purport of these States is to found a superb friend-
ship, exaltè, previously unknown,
Because I perceive it waits, and has been always waiting, latent in
all men.

[*lines restored from Ms*]

WHAT SHIP PUZZLED AT SEA

What ship puzzled at sea, cons for the true reckoning?
Or coming in, to avoid the bars and follow the channel a perfect pilot
needs?
Here, sailor! take aboard the most perfect pilot,
Whom, in a little boat, putting off and rowing, I hailing you offer.

SPAN OF YOUTH! EVER-PUSHED ELASTICITY!

Span of youth! Ever-pushed elasticity!
Manhood balanced and florid and full!

My lovers suffocate me!
Crowding my lips, and thick in the pores of my skin,
Justling me through streets and public halls — coming naked to me at
    night,
Crying by day Ahoy from the rocks of the river — swinging and chirping
    over my head
Calling my name from flowerbeds or vines or tangled underbrush,
Or while I swim in the bath — or drink from the pump at the corner —
    or the curtain is down at the opera — or I glimpse a man's face in
    the railroad car;
Lighting on every moment of my life,
Bussing my body with soft and balsamic busses,
Noiselessly passing handfuls out of their hearts and giving them to be
    mine.

[*from "Song of Myself," Section 45*]

NO LABOR-SAVING MACHINE

No labor-saving machine
Nor discovery have I made
Nor will I be able to leave behind any wealthy bequest to found a
    hospital or library,
Nor reminiscence of any deed of courage for America,
Nor literary success nor intellect, nor book for the book-shelf,
But a few carols vibrating through the air I leave,
For comrades and lovers.

EARTH, MY LIKENESS

Earth! my likeness!
Though you look so impassive, ample and spheric there,
I now suspect there is something terrible in you, ready to break forth,
For an athlete loves me, and I him,
But toward him there is something fierce and terrible in me, ready to
     break forth,
I dare not tell in words — not even in these songs.

A LEAF FOR HAND IN HAND

A leaf for hand in hand;
You natural persons old and young!
You on the Mississippi and on all the branches and bayous of the
     Mississippi!
You friendly boatmen and mechanics! you roughs!
You twain! and all processions moving along the streets!
I wish to infuse myself among you till I see it common for you to walk
     hand in hand.

SOMETIMES WITH ONE I LOVE

Sometimes with one I love I fill myself with rage for fear I effuse un-
     returned love,
But now I think there is no unreturned love, the pay is certain one way
     or another,
(I loved a certain person ardently and my love was not returned,
Yet out of that I have written these songs.)

THAT SHADOW MY LIKENESS

That shadow my likeness that goes to and fro seeking a livelihood,
     chattering, chaffering,
How often I find myself standing and looking at it where it flits,
How often I question and doubt whether that is really me;
But among my lovers and caroling these songs
O I never doubt whether that is really me.

UNKNOWN OCEANS OF LOVE

O I saw one passing alone, saying hardly a word, yet full of love I
    detected him by certain signs,
O eyes ever wishfully turning! O silent eyes!
For then I thought of you oer the world O latent oceans, fathomless
    oceans of love!
O waiting oceans of love! yearning and fervid! and of you sweet souls
    perhaps for the future, delicious and long:
But Dead, unknown on this earth—ungiven, dark here, unspoken,
    never born:
You fathomleses latent souls of love—you pent and unknown oceans of
    love!

[*from* Notebooks, *p. 523*]

AMONG THE MULTITUDE

Among the multitude,
I perceive that you pick me out by secret and divine signs,
You acknowledge none else, not parent, wife, husband, friend, child,
    any nearer or dearer to you than I am,
Some are baffled, but you are not baffled—you know me.

        Ah lover and perfect equal,
I meant that you should discover me so by faint indirections,
And I when I meet you mean to discover you by the like in you.

TO A WESTERN BOY

Many things to absorb I teach to help you become élève of mine;
But if blood like mine circle not in your veins, if through you speed
    not the blood of friendship, hot and red,
If you be not silently selected by lovers and do not silently select
    lovers,
Of what use is it that you seek to become élève of mine?

O YOU WHOM I OFTEN AND SILENTLY COME

O you whom I often and silently come where you are that I may be
with you,
As I walk by your side or sit near, or remain in the same room with you,
Little you know the subtle electric fire that for your sake is playing
within me.

O CAMERADO CLOSE

O rendezvous at last! O us two only!
O power, liberty, eternity at last! O to be so blithe!
O to be relieved of distinctions! To make as much of vices as of virtues!
To level occupations and the sexes! To bring all to common ground!
O adhesiveness! O the pensive aching to be together — you know not
why and I know not why;
O a word to clear our path ahead endlessly!
O something ecstatic and undemonstrable! O music wild!
O now I triumph — and you shall also,
O hand in hand — O wholesome pleasure — O one more desirer and
lover!
O haste, firm holding — haste, haste on, with me.

[*concluding section of "Starting from Paumanok"; "Proto-Leaf" in 1860 and
Ms versions*]

WHO IS NOW READING THIS?

Maybe one will read this who recollects some wrong-doing of my life,
Or maybe a stranger will read this who has secretly loved me,
Or maybe one will read this who looks back and remembers all my
    grand assumptions and egotisms with derision,
Or maybe one who is puzzled at me.
As if I were not puzzled at myself! Or as if I never deride myself!
    (O conscious-struck! O self-convicted!)
Or as if I do not secretly love strangers! O tenderly, a long time, and
    never exhibit it!
Or as if interior in me were not the stuff of wrong-doing (follies,
    defections, deeds of the night)
Or as if it could cease transpiring from me until it must cease!

[*based on Ms reading and 1860 Calamus 16, which was not later included
in* Leaves of Grass]

NOW LIFT ME CLOSE

Now, dearest comrade, lift me close to your face till I whisper,
We must separate awhile — Here! take from my lips this kiss;
Whoever you are, I give it especially to you;
So long! — And I hope we shall meet again.

[*based on 1860* Leaves of Grass]

HERE THE FRAILEST LEAVES OF ME

Here the frailest leaves of me are yet my strongest lasting,
Here I shade and hide my thoughts, I myself do not expose them,
And yet they expose me more than all my other poems.

CAMERADO, THIS IS NO BOOK

My songs cease—I abandon them,
From behind the screen where I hid, I advance personally.

Camerado, this is no book,
Who touches this, touches a man,
(Is it night? Are we here alone?)
It is I you hold, and who holds you,
I spring from the pages into your arms—decease calls me forth.

O how your fingers drowse me!
Your breath falls around me like dew—your pulse lulls the tympans
    of my ears,
I feel immerged from head to foot,
Delicious—enough.

[*based on* 1860 Leaves of Grass]

FULL OF LIFE NOW

Full of life, sweet-blooded, compact, visible,
I forty years old the eighty-third year of the States,
To one a century hence or any number of centuries hence,
To you yet unborn these, seeking you.

When you read these I that was visible am become invisible,
Now it is you, compact, visible, reading my poems, seeking me,
Fancying how happy you were if I could be with you and become your
    lover;
Be it as if I were with you. (Be not too certain but I am now with you.)

ACKNOWLEDGMENTS

MY FIRST AND OVERWHELMING debt has been to the gay liberation movement; this book grew within the consciousness awakened by the Stonewall Uprising of 1969. Winston Leyland as a movement publisher (Gay Sunshine Press) has shown courage and foresight in finding writers, developing audiences and propagating a gay revolution. Continuous conversations with John Mitzel, Michael Bronski, Mike Riegle, Boyd McDonald and others have sharpened my wit and often corrected my deficiencies. Neither myself nor any of my friends have tried to curb my excesses, which have made this a better book.

I am also a poet and have been nourished by the extraordinary outpouring of the Beat and movement poets. In the 1930s Edmund Wilson declared that poetry was dead, and now he is dead while poetry has exploded. I have learned continuously from fellow poets. John Wieners, Allen Ginsberg, Ron Schreiber, Aaron Shurin, Carl Morse, Robert Duncan, Stephanie Byrd, Salvatore Farinella, Judy Grahn, Gerrit Lansing, David Eberly, Pat Kuras, George Thérèse Dickinson, Freddie Greenfield, Jack Spicer, Frank O'Hara, David Emerson Smith, Walta Borawski, Paul Mariah, Ruth Weiss, Maurice Kenny and others have taught me about being a poet and thus about being Walt Whitman.

My lovers insofar as they have known about this book have resented it. So many men have written books about Whitman dedicated to "Eve as much her book as the author's," "Lillian, who participated from beginning to end," "Betsy," "Jeanne," "Fran," "Irene," "Vikki and Genevieve," "For Eleanore: One of the ways," or "To my wife, my partner as well as my unwearied encourager and sustainer in this and other literary enterprises." What do these dedications mean? Are the authors trying to suggest they are not homosexual? Are they really grateful for their womenfolk? Do they feel guilty about the ways they've benefited by male and heterosexist supremacy? None of my lovers have provided the support suggested in such dedications. Has the pampering of the married scholars, however, prepared them to understand a gay poet? Whitman wrote, "One who loves me is jealous of me, and withdraws me from all but love." How I identify with that!

I suppose I should thank my mother; Walt Whitman would appreciate that. (So far as I can find, not a single Walt Whitman book has been dedicated to the author's mother!) Both my mother and father taught me the meaning of being working-class in a middle-class world. The Chinese Cultural Revolution is now in great disfavor, but I think most academics who have never done any manual labor would benefit from a little fieldwork. And all fieldworkers would benefit by expanded cultural opportunities. *Leaves of Grass* attempted to reach the common people and create a cultural revolution. My mother is now legally blind, my father dead, and my lovers have promised not to read the book; nonetheless, I will be happy if my own Walt Whitman book brings some joy of recognition to a common reader somewhere.

Having said this, I will acknowledge some academic debts. My first study of Whitman was undertaken for my dissertation, "A History of American Conceptions of Death, 1650–1850," under Donald Fleming's direction at Harvard University. In 1980, I attended an NEH summer seminar directed by the late Paul Zweig at CUNY and then began my study of Whitman's gayness. And in 1983, I attended another NEH summer seminar at the Thoreau Lyceum with Walter Harding, who encouraged my Whitman studies. Michael Lynch kindly invited me to Toronto to present the first version of my study to the October, 1980, Walt Whitman in Toronto Conference. Lynch's own writings, poems and encouragements over the years have been most helpful. I have likewise beneited from lectures, conversations and reading the work of Robert K. Martin, Jonathan Katz, Allen Helms and Joseph Cady. Joseph Interrante kindly arranged for me to present a talk on "Love Letters to Walt Whitman" to the Boston Area Lesbian and Gay History Project. Finally, I want to thank Dorr Legg and the One Institute for providing materials and inviting me to speak on Whitman in Los Angeles.

The following friends have assisted and encouraged me along the way: Salvatore Salerno, Peter Gillis, Larry Mitchell, Eugene Weber, Chris Walker, Victor Bloise, Arnie Kantrowitz, Peter Linebaugh, Siang Huat Chua, Jesse Mauvro, Kenneth Dudley, Jim McNeil, Shanon Austin, Dan Tsang, Maria Gonzalez, Rudy Bleys, Jerald Moldenhauer, Ed Hermance, Paul MacPhail, Jean Humez, and many others. Michael Chesson provided essential information about the Doyles in Richmond. I want especially to thank Larry Anderson, Mike Riegle, and Peter Childers, who copied Whitman manuscripts. Mike Riegle and I combined research in the Library of Congress with the 1981 Gay March on Washington. Walta Borawski took precious time out from listening to blues singers and from his own writing to proofread my text.

In slightly different form, earlier versions of Chapters 2 and 9 appeared respectively in *Fag Rag Twelfth Anniversary Issue* (1982) and the *Nambla Bulletin* (May, 1986). An account of some of my field work appeared in *Contact/II: A Poetry Review* #36/37 (Fall, 1985), "Day Tripping with John Wieners, Searching for Mr. Whitman." My thanks again to Betsy Vandrasek of the Walt Whitman Birthplace in Huntington, L.I.; to Eleanor Ray of the Walt Whitman House in Camden, N.J.; and the staff of the Stafford House in Laurel Springs, N.J.

The following repositories have kindly allowed reproduction of the photographs, letters and notebook entries in this book: University of Virginia; Duke University; Pierpont Morgan Library; Feinberg and Harnet Collections, Library of Congress; Berg and Lion Collections, New York Public Library; Bieneke Library, Yale University; and University of Texas.

Both Winston Leyland from editing Allen Ginsberg's and Peter Orlovsky's letters and Mike Riegle from editing prisoners' letters impressed on me from the earliest stages the importance of accurately reproducing letters as they were written. Heartfelt declarations of those without college degrees need no translation into current middleclass English. The letters as written hastily from the field look strange translated into typeset and book format. I am especially grateful to Bill Rock for his sensitive and understanding typesetting of these nonstandard writings. There is a lack of correspondence between spontaneous speech, letter writing and more formal discourse. These boys' letters printed as-is may help destroy the destructive gauges of so-called literacy.

*Published in paperback and limited trade cloth edition of 200 copies.
A special edition of 10 lettered copies has been handbound in boards
and signed by the editor.*